BLOOD FAE

AMBER K. BRYANT

CITY OWL
PRESS

BLOOD FAE
Spirit Seeker, Book 2

CITY OWL PRESS
www.cityowlpress.com

Cover Design by Mibl Art. All stock photos licensed appropriately.

Edited by Tee Tate.

For information on subsidiary rights, please contact the publisher at info@cityowlpress.com.

Print Edition ISBN: 978-1-64898-026-8

Digital Edition ISBN: 978-1-64898-025-1

Printed in the United States of America

To Drew and Silas,
my pandemic survival team.

CHAPTER ONE

SYBILLE

SWEAT DRIPPED FROM THE GIRL'S TINY BODY. WRITHING, SHE SPOKE IN TONGUES like an ancient profit, or so it sounded to Sybille Esmond. She sat on the edge of the bed, hands pressing down on her young charge's shoulders.

"Keep hold of her," Sybille's uncle, Peter, instructed. He lit a match and brought the flame under a bundle of dried juniper until it caught on fire. Blowing out the match, he waved the smudge stick until the flame faded to glowing embers. A steady plume of smoke wafted up, coiling into thick circles as it fought with a draft from a crack in the bedroom window. "Margot," he called to Sybille's mother, "bring me my book please."

The three adults worked in tandem as though their actions were commonplace—heat the kettle for tea, vacuum the carpets, keep the demonic tendencies of a nine year old at bay. The mechanics of what they were doing wasn't unprecedented for them. They made their trade as psychics specializing in releasing the spirits of undead monsters. Harboring a child possessed by an ancient evil, however, was new territory for them. They were working, blind and desperate, to save this girl. Sybille knew going in that they were gearing up for a fight.

The girl gave a sharp cry, her eyes opening wide and her nostrils flaring.

Sybille increased the pressure on her shoulders. Firm but gentle. "It's going to be all right, Charlie." She forced melody into her words, a lullaby meant to soothe both the child and her monster. "I'm here."

"I hate you!" Charlie focused on Sybille's face as she yelled, then closed her eyes again.

"That's good. I don't mind if you do. Just stay with me." The tension in Sybille's jaw eased. A decipherable human language instead of the gibberish she had been spewing meant this little girl still had fight left in her. "Don't let it win."

Charlie struggled beneath Sybille. Her thin arms went rigid as she grasped the sheets between her fingers and pulled.

"Try not to ruin my bedding while your demon is surfacing, dear heart," Margot cooed.

Sybille's throat tightened. "Who cares about your damn sheets, Mother? She's suffering."

"Don't you think I know that? I'm just trying to speak to her as I normally would. She needs to know there are repercussions for becoming a hellion." She handed Peter his book, placed a palm against Charlie's forehead, then turned to Sybille. "Her fever is worse. I'm going to make her some elderflower tea."

"I don't think we'll convince her to drink anything."

"I'll add lots of honey. Charlie, you like sweet things, remember?"

The girl hissed.

"I'm going to take that as a yes." Her voice echoed from the hallway as she hurried away. "Call me if you need me."

Peter waved his smudge stick over Charlie's body while thumbing through the book on his lap. The crisp, woody odor of juniper battled against a meaty smell whose source Sybille couldn't place.

"Ah, here it is. It's a Tibetan chant, used for purification. Since the exorcism prayer had little effect, it can't hurt. Here goes." He cleared his throat and studied the page of his book. *"Ki ki so so ashe lha ghe lo tak seng khung druk di yar kye."*

Charlie kicked and screamed as Sybille did her best to keep the girl under control. If only Elis were here to help. He had yet to answer her frantic text about Charlie having another of what Margot had coined a "Low fit." Sybille shouldn't have been annoyed. Just because they were dating now didn't mean he had to be at her beck and call. He had his undead life to lead, which mainly consisted of overcharging hypnotherapy clients too naïve to realize they were being mesmerized by a bloodthirster rather than a certified mental health professional.

Sybille refused to be a controlling girlfriend—poor Elis had had enough of that, given his ex-wife's desire to own his every move, even one hundred years after she'd shed her mortal coil. She couldn't think about that wretched spirit now, though. Juliana had been dealt with. Charlie, on the other hand, needed saving in a major way, and damned if the person most capable of helping her couldn't be bothered to check his fucking messages.

Peter continued chanting and smudging. Sybille studied Charlie's face. Delicate indigo lines began to spread from her lips outward as though her veins were filling with ink.

Sybille scrunched her forehead. "That's new."

Her uncle continued his chant, the slightest of nods the only indication he'd noticed her transformation. Minutes ticked by and Charlie's ink veins spread and deepened over her face, her neck, her shoulders. As they grew, so did her strength. Sybille's arms shook from the exertion.

With a loud grunt, Charlie freed one of her hands and used it to smack Peter in the face. His glasses flew across the room, hitting the wall before crashing to the floor.

"Stop it!" She grabbed hold of Charlie again, only to be pushed away like she was no heavier than Peter's glasses and just as easy to toss. The force lifted Sybille off the bed and slammed her against a dresser. Charlie stood on top of crumpled sheets in her torn unicorn pajamas and snarled. Sybille flashbacked to Charlie's mother, Raelyn. The resemblance, aside from the dark veins spiraling through Charlie's skin, made her want to vomit.

As she fought off dizziness, the door opened. Margot stepped inside carrying a wooden tray with a china teapot and a matching floral cup. "Look who I brought with me!"

Elis trailed in behind her, carrying an easy smile and a picture book with the image of a girl in a blue and white gingham dress on it. "Sorry I've been out of reach. My phone died, but Margot told me Charlie has another fever. I brought our favorite book to read with her and... Holy Hell!"

His smile disappeared.

The relief she felt at his arrival didn't quite make it to her lips. "Gosh,

Elis, I'm sure story time will make her all better. Or, hey, why don't we take her to the ER? A round of antibiotics is sure to do the trick."

"I was just trying to help." Elis ducked as Charlie ran to the base of her bed and attempted to kick him in the head. "You don't have to be so sarcastic."

"If you want to help, bloodthirster, work your magic. Because Peter's isn't doing jack shit. No offence."

Peter, who had stopped chanting long enough to examine his glasses for signs of damage, hunched his shoulders. "I tried; I failed. Elis, you're up next. And be quick about it, before she hurts herself or kills us all."

"Right." Elis dove to the left again as Charlie attempted another kick. "Stop trying to bash my head in for a minute, okay? Uncle Elis is here to help."

Charlie bounced over to the wall and pounded a fist into it. "You aren't my uncle. My uncle isn't here!"

Sybille winced. No, he wasn't. How different things might be if he were. "Get on with it, thirster."

Elis walked toward where Charlie stood, examining the fist-sized hole she'd put in the wall above her headboard.

"Charlie, you are the strongest girl in the world. You are stronger than the terrible thing you're fighting."

The girl turned to him and raised her knee, but Elis didn't back away. Her breath came in ragged, wet gulps, like she was struggling to keep water out of her lungs.

"If you fight it, you will win, and the monster will go back to sleep."

She sneered again, but lowered her knee.

"You've fought this monster before. You've made it go back to sleep. And you've won." The sheets twisted against the girl as she began to move away from Elis's touch, but his tone was soothing and she took his hand, going still when he grasped her fingers. The blue of her veins faded from deep ocean to Easter egg pastel.

"That's it, Charlie," Elis' deep, centuries-old thirster voice continued to croon. "You're good at this. Fighting monsters is what you've always done. You can always defeat them."

Charlie yelped, a sharp, high-pitched cry that sounded more childlike than anything they'd heard from her in the last hour. As if exhausted by the effort it took to scream so loud, she teetered like a bowling pin after being struck.

Catching her in his arms, Elis eased her down onto her mattress, allowing Margot to scoot him aside. She checked Charlie's pulse, felt her forehead, and with gentle fingertips traced a vein, nearly invisible again, over the outline of her jaw.

Margot's face brightened. "Her temperature is down. Pulse is a bit elevated but that's to be expected. I'd still like her to drink my tea when she wakes up."

Peter clutched his book to his chest. "That may be a while. She's quite spent, I'm afraid."

Pressure built behind Sybille's eyes. This was so unfair. "It's getting worse. The episodes are becoming more frequent and more severe."

No one argued with her. Even had they not been experienced in supernatural events, it would have been obvious to them that she was right.

"Sybille." Elis made his way to her side of the bed and placed a hand on her shoulder. "Charlie only partly responded to my mesmerizing her, and even that took time. It worries me. There will come a point when my skills fail her altogether."

Sybille shook him off. "Don't talk like that, not in front of her at least."

"She can't hear me."

"You don't know that."

Margot sighed. "Whether she can hear you or not, you two squabbling cannot be good for her. Why don't you take it downstairs? Peter and I will stay with her."

Sybille hesitated a moment, then nodded. "Let's go, thirster."

"Must you keep calling me that?"

"Today I must."

They made their way down the stairs and into the living room, where Sybille folded herself into her favorite corner of the couch. As soon as Elis joined her, he picked up where he'd left off.

"I don't want to think about it anymore than you do, but facts are facts. Charlie is a child of the Low. She was born there, lived there her whole life. That place bears a curse we're only beginning to understand, but we do know how unearthly powerful it is and that the more time you spend there, the more the Low becomes a part of you. Bringing her here, smudging her with sage and juniper, hypnotizing the shit out of her every time it tries to take over—none of that changes the facts. The Low is stronger than her, stronger than all of us. Charlie can't win."

"Which means we're all going to lose." Sybille pressed her head into the sofa, wishing she could fold herself all the way inside of it and disappear. "I wish Devin was here to help."

Elis tensed beside her. "Well he's not."

"He could be. We just have to find him."

"He was stolen by a fae who blinked him out of our universe and brought him to…who knows where. There's been no progress in locating him, even though we've been searching for two months."

"So? I'll search for twenty years if I have to." She turned towards him. "We need to get him back."

"*You* need to."

"We. Me. Charlie. All of us."

He fingered the obsidian pendant dangling from a silver chain around her neck. "I don't want to start this argument again."

"Then don't. Agree with everything I say and be done with it."

Elis opened his mouth, but before he could argue further, the doorbell rang.

Sybille groaned. "Can you get that? If it's Jehovah's Witnesses, tell them we've already found Satan. She's upstairs sleeping off a bender. Then tell them to go away before she eats them."

Elis walked towards the alcove, and Sybille was left speculating how they would have gotten Charlie under control had Elis not shown up. They'd found nothing that would work, save for Elis' mesmerizing skills. If those skills failed to work, they were well and truly screwed.

"What the hell are you doing here?"

Sybille bolted upright. Not missionaries or salesman or someone delivering a package then. Someone Elis knew. And from the tone of his voice, someone he didn't care for.

Sprinting towards the front door, she had only a few seconds to wonder who it could be and what danger they might present. Raelyn, maybe, but she was busy running the Low now that they'd removed the Blood King from power. The lavender fae woman? But she'd already gotten what she wanted.

It was too much to hope that it might be Devin.

Coming to a stop next to Elis, she stared at their visitor in surprise. A man in his sixties with deep-set eyes and a frown that looked permanently tattooed onto his face stood holding a brimmed hat.

"Can I help you?"

The man's lips quivered as he attempted to force them into a smile. "If you're Margot's daughter, then yes you can."

Elis postured, fangs out. "I'll ask you again, what are you doing here, Laurence?"

Sybille blinked. "Laurence?"

"He's the man who returned my spirit."

"No kidding? You're not here to take it back, are you?" Sybille had been curious about the man capable of plunking a bloodthirster's disembodied spirit back inside its monstrous body ever since Elis told her about the experience.

The man shook his head. "No, no. What's done is done, in that regard."

"Well, then, what?"

He looked past them, straining to see into the house. Sybille crossed her arms.

"Listen, Laurence, if you're responsible for making Elis a reformed thirster, then I owe you one. But you also teamed with his evil ex in an attempt to murder him, so that's a big strike against you. I'm not sure where I stand, but I know I don't trust you. So if you have some purpose here, make it known or leave."

Laurence scrunched his hat between his hands. He kept his shoulders curved forward and seemed to be having difficulty maintaining eye contact. Either their presence made him nervous or whatever situation he'd found himself in did. "I'm here about my granddaughter. If you help me save her, I'll tell you where Devin Vargas is."

The hour struck and the grandfather clock chimed. One... Sybille breathed. Two... She composed her thoughts. Three... She resisted the urge to sic Elis so they could torture out of him whatever information he supposedly had on Devin. Four...

"Who's your granddaughter? Is she a bloodthirster you need us to kill? Because we're sort of busy with another job right now."

Five.

The man stood a little taller, shoulders back. "Oh no, no. She's not one of *them*." He scowled at Elis, then attempted a neutral expression with Sybille. She didn't blink and neither did he.

"Well, who is she then?"

Six.

The last chime resonated through the alcove as Laurence spoke. "Her name is Charlotte. But everyone calls her Charlie."

CHAPTER TWO

DEVIN

DEVIN HELD FAST TO THE SADDLE HORN AS THUNDERHEART GALLOPED OVER the prairie. He clamped his thighs to the horse's sides to keep from falling off, visions of his head dashed against a rock keeping him alert. Squinting into the harsh afternoon sun, a brown dot on the horizon grew larger as he traveled west.

Readying the lasso with his right hand, he raised it up over his head, set to swing. The brown dot became a blob, and then a blob with four legs and a head.

Almost upon it now, he kicked at Thunderheart to spur him on and circled the lasso. As the horse roared past Devin's errant cow, he swung. The rope reached into the air and then loosed itself over the cow's head. Devin pulled taught, the jerk of the stubborn animal nearly undoing his hold on the saddle.

"That's it. Easy now. Don't whine. It's for your own good."

The cow begged to differ. She threw her neck and flared her nostrils as she continued to fight her capture, but she was no match for Devin and Thunderheart. Twenty minutes later, she was back in the corral with the rest of the herd. Devin hopped off Thunderheart's back, steadying himself on aching legs, and led the gentle beast back to his stable. After feeding and watering him, Devin spent a minute stroking his muzzle. Thunderheart leaned into Devin's touch, breathing warm air onto his arm.

"All in a day's work, right boy?"

Thunderheart gave a low neigh and went back to eating his well-earned hay.

After seeing to the other horses, Devin headed to the farmhouse, fifty paces up the hill from the barn. He studied the house as he strolled towards it, trying to decide if he wanted to leave the clapboard in its natural state or whitewash it. A coat of paint would freshen things up, but there was something to be said about the graying wood planks left to weather naturally in the hot sun. A white house would stand out, but maybe it wasn't meant to do that. Sometimes blending in had its benefits.

Sitting on a bench next to the front door, Devin pried off his boots, flexing and straightening his ankles to work the kinks out. The big toe on his right foot peered at him from a hole in his sock. Hopefully, Froya would know how to darn it for him.

Up off the bench, Devin pushed open the screen door and hung his hat on a hook as he took in a deep breath. His mouth watered. Froya cooked up the best biscuits and gravy this side of the Mississippi.

"Smells like heaven!" Devin plopped down at the kitchen table just as Froya served a plateful for him.

"Eat up while it's good and hot." Tucking a strand of short purple hair behind her ear, Froya sat across from him, watching as he took his first bite. "Long day?"

Devin chewed fast and swallowed. "Not so bad. I think I fixed the fence for good now. When we want the herd secured, they should be. How was your day?"

"The usual. Cooking, cleaning, spell casting. Magic weaving. A bit of blood magic to keep the world in order."

Devin paused mid-chew. Froya pondered him with large eyes the color of the plains when the prairie clover was in bloom. The pause ended and he swallowed, then loaded his fork with another mouthful. "Sounds good."

"Does it?"

He tilted his head from side to side. Funny that she should question him about such mundane things. "I guess. It's what you always do."

"Wash the dishes, cook your biscuits, call up the forces of lifeblood to bless our humble abode. That's all normal to you?"

"Should it not be?"

"No. It should be. I'm just determining if it really is."

Devin cocked his head to the side. "You're a funny lady, Froya. Sometimes I'm not sure why you choose to live with me here on this ranch."

"A ranch is what you need to see, so that's why I chose it."

"Come again?"

"You've finished already. Do you want seconds?" She picked up his plate and headed back to the stove.

He watched her backside as she moved away from him, thinking of a few other things he might want before another helping of biscuits and gravy. "Maybe in a bit."

Froya placed his dish in the sink. "I'll wash it later. What do you want to do now, Damhán?"

He paused again, thoughts of desire muddled. *Damhán, Devin, Damhán, Devin.*

"You haven't called me that since…" He couldn't remember when *since* was, only that she had, at some point.

Her eyes flickered. "Think hard. When did I call you that? Where did I call you that? Are you ready to know?"

He stood from the table, napkin falling to the floor. Walking towards the archway leading from the kitchen to the front room, he ran his hand up and down its cherrywood frame. He'd harvested that wood. He'd built this frame. He'd built this whole clapboard farmhouse for him and Froya to live in.

"No Damhán, I built this house. I built this ranch and this world. Have you ever even seen a cherry tree out here?"

Good thing Devin clung to the beam already or he may have fallen over. "What? Did you just listen to my thoughts? You're a mind reader. Some kind of witch…or a psychic."

Psychic. That word didn't fit in this farmhouse on this ranch on this western prairie. But somehow, it felt familiar, like his tongue had spoken the word many times before. Like he knew that word, like he was intimate with it.

"I've been patient with you, and now I think you're as ready as you can be. Try not to become violent this time."

"This time?"

She stepped over to him and raised her hand. He managed to glimpse the dime-sized crystal embedded in her wrist before her hand met his forehead. He had a matching one. Sometimes the skin around it itched and reddened, like his body wasn't used to it being there, though he couldn't recall ever not having it.

Froya leaned in until their heads would have met had her palm not been in the way. A twinge of longing. She was sexy and so close. He slid a hand to the small of her back and pulled her towards him. She didn't resist the force of his grasp, but when she spoke again, it wasn't her usual invitation to have him tear her clothes off. It was a much more sobering command.

"Remember."

He gasped, still gripping her, this time so that he wouldn't collapse.

A command from Froya needed to be followed.

Memories started as a trickle, no more than a leaky pipe, but they grew to a spring waterfall set high upon a mountainside. Too many, too fast.

A life away from the ranch, away from Froya. A lost and found sister, monsters in dark forests. Serums and stakes, and a woman he cared about. A woman with long, dark hair, not short, not purple.

Something beyond memory stirred as well. Something that had been a part of him always but left unused, dormant.

No, not dormant, suppressed. Not a something either. There was a word for it. Power.

Power and memory raged through him. The farmhouse collapsed under the weight of his screams.

Elis

Elis estimated it would take him less than three seconds from where he sat perched on the arm of Sybille's couch to make it over to Laurence, pin him to his chair and sink his teeth into the old man's neck.

This business with Charlie's supposed grandfather could be over and done within a matter of minutes, and then he and Sybille could go out on the date night he'd planned. Dinner at a small bistro that wouldn't scoff at his unique diet, and a horse-drawn carriage ride along Port Everan's waterfront. Knowing Sybille wouldn't care to see abused horses, he'd called three different companies, asking them detailed questions about the ethical treatment of their animals before choosing the one that had the best rating with the ASPCA. It figured that his careful planning would be unraveled by the crazy life that surrounded the woman he loved.

Still fixated on Laurence, Elis let out a loud sigh. The man started in his seat, glanced at Elis, and then looked away. Lucky for him, Sybille maintained a strict "No Biting" rule in her house.

Sybille leaned against Elis from her spot on the couch, her elbow pressed into his thigh to help keep her propped up. Her posture spoke of weariness, but the rate at which she spewed questions at Laurence indicated a brain churning a mile a minute.

"Why do you think Charlie is your granddaughter? Are you Devin's dad?"

"No, no. I'm related to Charlie through her father."

"We don't know who Charlie's father is."

"He's my son."

"So you say."

"What do you want, a DNA test?"

"Maybe. What I really want is for you to tell me where Devin is."

Elis sighed again. Devin's disappearance created a pleasant reality in which he had Sybille all to himself. Or he would have, except Sybille filled many of her waking hours investigating what had happened to him. Devin hitched a ride to some fae land—that much they knew. And they were ninety-nine percent sure that Devin himself was part fae. Sybille guessed he had a great-great fae grandparent no one in the family remembered. Zareen thought his mom had, in her words, "gotten it on with a sweet piece of fae ass." Whatever the case, beyond broad presumptions, their knowledge of Devin and his whereabouts fell off a ledge. Laurence's proclamation, suspect though it may be, marked the first lead they'd received.

Laurence sipped Margot's bergamot tea, holding the saucer in one hand and lifting the dainty cup to his mouth with the other. Cup and saucer clanked as Laurence, hands shaking, set them down together on an end table.

"I don't mean to aggravate you, Miss Esmond, or you." His eyes slid over to Elis and then quickly away again. "Mr. Tanner, I assure you, I mean you no harm."

"Oh, it's *Mr.* Tanner now, is it?"

Sybille placed a hand on his knee. "Not now, *Mr. Tanner.* Laurence, you're not giving us much to go on here. I'm beginning to think you're a sack of lies all tied up in a lie ribbon with a pretty lie bow on top. You don't know where Devin is or how to retrieve him, or you would have led with that in order to persuade us into helping you. So, my question is, how do you know he's even missing? It's not like we filed a police report or put up posters."

"I'm no liar, Miss Esmond. But it's true... I can't say with exactitude where your friend is, only who he's with. And if you'll let me explain that, you'll understand how I know what I know. You can doubt me, you can hate me, but I'm here because I want help for my granddaughter. I haven't been able to see her for nearly three years, but I understand her condition is dire. I'm offering a fair exchange based on principal."

Sybille's grip on Elis' knee tightened. She wasn't buying Laurence's bullshit any more than he was. Words shot out of her like bullets. "The word 'exchange' offered up when talking about Charlie doesn't sit right."

"No, it does not," Elis said, glad that for once tonight he and Sybille could agree on something. "I'm beginning to think you can't help us at all, Laurence. No deal."

More tightening. She clamped her fingers around his knee until he yelped. So much for a show of solidarity. "Ignore him and get to talking." Her voice retained its sense of restrained violence. She might be attempting to play good cop, but she still meant business. "I want to know what you know, and then we'll talk about Charlie. If you really are her grandfather, there are some things you should know as well."

By now, the small man had mangled his hat, pulling and stretching it like taffy. "You've already guessed that Devin Vargas is fae. Half fae to be precise."

Elis jostled Sybille with his elbow. "You owe Zareen drinks," he said. "She called it."

"God damn it, I hate when she wins a bet. She's a gloater. All right, Laurence, now tell us something we haven't figured out already."

"His mother is human," Laurence said. "His father is Ichor."

Sybille nodded as though she understood what that meant. Elis hadn't a clue, and so he asked, "What's an Ichor?"

Laurence smiled. "Bloodthirsters. So ignorant of their own origin. I've never met one of you who knew."

"Okay, then fill me in, smartass."

"There are two fae peoples. Ichor and Ossian. Blood and Bone. These fae exist in different realms of reality. As long as those realms never intersect, there is peace. But too often, the Ichor and the Ossian have found themselves at odds, battling for control of different spheres of existence. This sphere is one of them."

"You mean Earth."

"Earth, yes. And the universe that accompanies it. The Now World as we perceive of it. All of our reality."

"Our reality. Is that all?" Elis couldn't keep the sarcasm from dripping into the conversation. "This can't be real. I've been alive for centuries and up until two months ago I never even knew fae were anything other than folklore creatures. Now you're telling me there are two kinds, they're mortal enemies, and the Now World is one of their battlegrounds? That's a wee bit hard to swallow."

Sybille snorted. "Says the undead beast that got his spirit returned to him by our Low-afflicted hellion's psychic grandfather." Her expression softened. "To be fair, I've only heard the names Ichor and Ossian. I've never gotten their whole story, only snippets. Them being sworn enemies is news to me."

"There's far more to the story than that, to be sure. It's probably best not to go into too much detail, but one thing you should know is that, while I'm mainly human, I have Ossian ancestry dating back seven generations."

Elis struggled to keep up. If Laurence was part fae that meant...

"Charlie has fae blood." Sybille wrapped her arms around herself and shuddered.

"Yes. Enough to give her some psychic ability."

"Back at the cabin, when Zareen showed up with Juliana, Charlie saw her. Now I understand why. And you." She pointed at Laurence. "That's why you were able to give Elis back his soul."

"Wait." Elis glanced at Sybille. "Are all people with psychic abilities part fae? Is Sybille?"

Laurence shook his head. "I doubt it. I know your mother a little. We moved in the same circle decades ago. But who is your father, Miss Esmond?"

"My father is some guy who made a deposit at a sperm bank. Margot raised me on my own, with my uncle's help. But if bio dad was more than just a random human college guy who needed beer money, Margot would know."

"I see. Well, most psychics are humans, as I assume Sybille is. A certain percentage of humans are gifted and there's no clear explanation as to why. But within my family, it is traced back to a fae lineage. Naturally, given how far back in time, the details are murky, but—"

"Okay, Laurence, you've given us a lot to think over, and now it's time for you to go." Sybille hopped off the couch.

"What?" Laurence gripped the arms of his chair as though he was waiting for Sybille to pry him out of it. "What about my granddaughter?"

"You've yet to prove you mean to help rather than harm her," she said. "Also, you claim to want to assist me in finding Devin, but if what you say is true, he's your enemy."

"He's the Ossian's enemy, not mine!"

"You just told us you're Ossian."

"Only in part. Like I said, their influence lies hundreds of years back in my family tree. They don't represent me. I want peace. That's what I've always wanted."

Elis' slow bloodthirster heart ticked. "Is that what you wanted when you agreed to help Juliana murder me?"

Sybille stomped her foot. "Enough! Laurence, we will consider your request. I need some time to process this information, but we'll be in touch soon. Elis, get the man his jacket."

The man's eyes bulged, reminding Elis of one of those stress balls in the shape of a man with eyes that popped out when you squeezed its neck. Elis could think of a neck he wanted to squeeze right about now.

"But I—"

"But," Sybille continued, "you will leave before you wake up Charlie. She didn't have a fantastic day today and she needs—"

"Grandpa?"

Everyone turned to see the girl with the subpar day, still dressed in her torn pajamas, clinging to the banister midway down the stairs.

"Charlie, sweetheart." Laurence stood and moved towards the staircase.

Charlie remained where she was. Her bottom lip trembled. "You were dead. Did Uncle Devin resurrect you too?"

CHAPTER THREE

SYBILLE

SYBILLE BLOCKED THE STAIRCASE AS ELIS HOISTED LAURENCE AGAINST THE wall next to the living room's bay window. The glass shook at his body's impact, and Sybille caught her breath, wondering if either the window or Laurence's head might shatter. Both held out.

"He's not a bloodthirster." Elis sniffed Laurence's neck, eyes glowing as he examined his quarry from two inches away. "I'd have smelled it on him as soon as I opened the door."

Laurence's face turned the same shade of red as his assailant's eyes. "I'm certainly not a bloodthirster. And I'm still very much alive."

Sybille pushed Charlie up a step should they need to make a break for it. "Then why did Charlie say you died?"

"Because that's what my parents told me." Charlie grabbed Sybille's hand. "Daddy said Grandpa wouldn't be bothering us anymore."

"I don't think he's undead, Sybille." Elis sniffed at Laurence one more time, then pulled back. "Still, if you want me to end him, just say the word. I am feeling a bit peckish."

The nerve of him. "Not in front of the child, thirster."

"I've seen worse," Charlie grumbled.

"What if she was to go upstairs? Could I then, maybe?" He pressed Laurence into the wall again.

"I would prefer if you didn't." Laurence squirmed under Elis' hold. "Honestly, you people, we're all on the same side!"

"That's interesting." Sybille motioned for Charlie to stay where she stood as she ventured down to join Elis. "Because I didn't even know there were sides until you brought it up, and I'm pretty sure I haven't decided what fae team to hashtag on Instagram yet."

"I'm not talking about the fae, though they do factor in. What I'm referring to is something much more fundamental." The last word was choked out by a coughing fit.

"Elis, ease up on him. Charlie received bad information from her parents—imagine that. Laurence isn't some immortal blood god, so maybe give the man a chance to catch his breath."

Elis growled, hesitated a minute, and then did as he was told. "Let me know if you change your mind."

Laurence remained by the wall, his face gradually returning to its normal shade. "If I could explain myself."

Sybille resisted telling Elis she'd changed her mind and he could have at him. As much as she wanted to keep the peace for Charlie's sake, this grandfather of hers sure liked to talk in circles. There were few things she hated more than when people thought they could keep secrets from her. "We've been waiting on that ever since you got here."

"What I meant when I said we're on the same side is that you have good intentions, the same good intentions I've always had."

Elis snorted. "You could have fooled me."

"My intentions when I aided Juliana were pure. Every bloodthirster does harm to the world, and I thought I was helping by removing you from it. But good intentions in and of themselves are never enough, especially when the results of them create more harm than good."

"Fine then. What are these good intentions that you think you share with us?" Sybille crossed her arms and waited.

"To rid the world of the damage the fae have wrought."

"Wow, you are a dramatic one." She laughed. "Fae elimination isn't exactly in my wheelhouse. My family deals with ridding the world of bloodthirsters."

"As I said, 'damage the fae wrought.'" He stepped away from the wall in the direction of the staircase. Sybille moved aside for him, gesturing for Elis to do the same.

Charlie closed the gap before her grandfather could, running down the steps and throwing herself at him. He lifted her off her feet and twirled her around, hugging her close. "My gosh, you've grown! I've missed you so much."

Charlie sobbed into his neck. "Why didn't they let me see you more?"

"It's a long story." Joy beamed from his wide grin as he brushed a tangle of hair behind each of her cheeks. "Believe me, it's pained me to be away from you. And now I've found you again, so we can be a family. You don't have to be sad anymore, Charlotte Rose."

Sybille wiped at her eyes, hoping Elis hadn't noticed the tears that had formed in them. Laurence might turn out to be a huge prick yet, but right now he gave Charlie back a piece of her broken family, and he gave Sybille hope there might be a way forward for them. Hope was always precarious, though. Anything could separate Charlie and her grandfather again, including Sybille herself, if she had the inclination to do so.

"I'm sorry to interrupt," she said, tapping Laurence's shoulder, "but we really need to know what the hell you're talking about. And Charlie's grandfather or not, I still reserve the right to have Elis drain you should you turn out to be less than trustworthy."

He set Charlie down, who hobbled onto one of the lowest stairs before leaning into him. "Fair enough. Where was I again?"

Elis fumed. "You were talking about fae folk and damage and how it all has something to do with Sybille's family."

"Ah, yes. Not Sybille's family, but what her family does, professionally speaking. Killing bloodthirsters and releasing their souls."

"What about it?" She hadn't experienced this level of frustration with someone since her mother spent a month's worth of grocery money on yarn and a hot glue gun. "Spit it out or leave."

"Do you both really have no clue?" Laurence stared at them slack-jawed. "Mr. Tanner, have you never wondered how your kind came about?"

"I know how I came about. I fell for the wrong woman."

"No, no, not your thirster origin story, I mean, *all* bloodthirsters. Who created you?"

"I'm guessing the answer isn't God."

"Far from it."

Charlie rolled her eyes. "Grandpa, if you don't speak plainly to these people, they'll never understand a word you say. Elis, all of you nasty bloodthirsters exist because the fae created you to do their bidding."

"Are you telling stories again, Charlie?" Elis' face paled, his cheeks sucked inward like he'd been forced to eat a lemon.

Laurence hung his head. "I'm afraid not. My ancestors, the Ossian, created thirsters to be soldiers, meant to wreak havoc and weaken Earth's defenses."

"To what end?" Sybille asked.

"Victory, of course. Total Ossian domination of the universe."

Devin

The sky changed quickly. One moment, it was polished turquoise, the next, a muddy pond. Devin spurred Thunderheart on. They needed to get back to the ranch before that muddy pond let loose onto the prairie. Thunderheart didn't much like the rain, and neither did Devin. Fact was, Devin didn't care for much these days. He couldn't put a finger on why.

The prairie had lost its charm, as had the ranch. Cows smelled. Horses were a lot of work. It was all a lot of work.

Froya worked too hard as well. She snipped at him lately, little things getting to them both, he guessed. The pattern of life, filled with monotonous routines, was enough to challenge anyone's patience. Even Devin's. That's why sometimes, even though he loved his life, pride rising like the morning sun when he thought about being a rancher, he liked to pretend he was something else. Something more exciting.

He shared this with Froya upon returning to the farmhouse. He came in soaking wet, having not quite missed the rain's wrath, and found himself in the path of Froya's darker storm.

"You're dripping all over my floor."

He wiped up the puddles his wet socks had formed with a rag and then leaned against the kitchen counter. "Sometimes I like to think I'm a hunter."

She slid into a chair at the kitchen table. "You can be one if you want." She pointed out the window. "Go kill us dinner."

"No, I don't mean shooting prairie critters. I mean, something larger."

"Bison? Elk."

"Monsters."

Froya's lavender eyes twinkled the way they always did when he said something that amused her. Her pouty lips spread into a wide smile.

"Don't make fun of me, Froya. I know it sounds stupid."

"Not at all." She got up again, walked over, and pressed the middle of her body against him. Heat spread down his back and into his thighs. "A hunter of nightmare creatures. That's exciting. Tell me about these monsters."

"Really?" He placed his hands on her backside and tugged her closer. He'd done this before. This kitchen. Her ass in his hands. "If I'd known you were into monster hunting, I'd have told you this fantasy a while ago."

"Mmm." She nibbled his ear.

Desire welled up like a dried-up creek bed in a flash flood. "Stop it, or pretty soon I won't be talking about anything at all."

She pulled back. "Go ahead."

He stared into her twinkling eyes and swallowed. He could do this. He could tell her these crazy things. "Well, see, these monsters. They're not like you or me. They're dead, but still alive."

"Undead."

"Undead? That's a word? Okay, the undead can't control themselves. They live off blood. They lust for it, in fact. They'll do all sorts of harm to get it."

"Awful."

"They are. And in my imagination, I go around killing them, and the world is better for it."

"Not in your imagination. In your reality."

Devin scrunched his nose. "No. In reality, I'm a cowboy. A rancher. I've never seen a…an undead monster, much less killed one."

"There are many realities. Just because one is true doesn't mean another is false."

"Okay, but in this case, I'm thinking one can't be true because that would mean these blood monsters are real. I can't believe that."

"Many unbelievable things are real." Froya placed one hand behind Devin's head and one on his forehead. "If it doesn't fucking work this time, I swear I'm going to leave you here to play cowboy all on your own, Ichor Coterie be damned."

"You just used a bunch of words I don't understand."

"Shh." She leaned into him. The smell of prairie flowers after a summer rain fanned from her skin. "Remember, Damhán."

A trickle, a stream, roaring rapids. A memory waterfall. Life before this ranch and a power before anything else.

Devin sputtered. His knees gave way but Froya held him up. "Remember who you are, Damhán."

The room spun. Bile filled his mouth. He turned away from Froya and vomited into the kitchen sink. Eyes shut, he tried drowning everything out, but this effort was pointless. He was in the water and the water was in him. Drowning would only give life to the memories.

From outside his mind, crickets chirped. Wood from the hearth crackled as it burned. Devin opened his eyes. He could float now. In his weightlessness, truth took form. Froya stood beside him, waiting as he steadied himself.

He breathed through another bout of nausea. The unbelievable continued to weave its way through his mind.

Remember.

He believed the unbelievable. The truth of his own reality came into focus. He knew what this place was and why he lived here, accepting a mirage as a life. Of all the places for Froya to pick...

"Why, in the name of everything that's holy," he said, his hands shaking at his sides, "did you choose to stick me on this stupid ranch?"

Froya laughed. At his expense, he thought to himself. And that should bother him. Froya kidnapped him. Drugged him, maybe. Messed with his mind, definitely. Took away his memories and fed him ones she'd manufactured. But she'd also lived with him on this ranch for as long as he could remember. Her body fit against his.

He couldn't hate her, as much as he tried.

"The truth is powerful. When I brought you home, I gave you that power by removing a large portion of the block that prevented your fae abilities from surfacing. It was more than you could handle. If you were a full fae, perhaps the shock would have been less debilitating, but you were cursed with a human mother. And so you suffered from the weight of truth. The coterie and I decided you needed to be eased into your new life. Make a world you'd feel comfortable in and after a time spent living in an Ichor realm, you'd be more able to handle who you are."

"Yeah, okay, but why did you think I'd be comfortable herding cattle?"

"We have records from your human life."

"You have records of my whole life? Like, every part of it?"

"Thanks to what was done to you, no. Most of your life is a mystery to us. But we managed to piece a few clues together. For instance, several of your previous girlfriends called you a cowboy."

"That, um, that didn't actually have anything to do with cows. The only horse I've ever ridden was a pony at a town festival when I was five. We went around in a circle and I cried the whole time."

"You seem to have enjoyed yourself here." She inched closer, her sinuous body ready to wrap itself around his.

He backed away. "Because you did your fairy magic juju on me!"

"*Your* fairy magic juju, Damhán. It belongs to you too, this power."

"Devin. My name is Devin."

"I can call you by your human name if you wish," Froya said, "but it doesn't change the fact that you're an Ichor fae."

"I didn't say it should. It's just that every time you call me that, I feel like I should be asking a leprechaun where my pot of gold is."

"I don't suggest you do that. Leprechauns love tricking humans and killing fae. Seeing as you are both, you're bound to be tricked to death."

"I wasn't planning on... Are you saying leprechauns exist?"

"You are amazingly slow." Giving up on her seduction attempt for the moment, she leaned back. "Why Warin saw fit to breed with a human and create an Earthblood, I'll never know. At least he paid for his sins. And you did get his looks, so there's that."

"Who are you talking about?"

"Your father."

"My father's a leprechaun?"

Froya rubbed her temples. "Fucking hell, I'm going to have to start all over again. At least this time you're not trying to kill everyone, including yourself. And you seem to accept more of your past than before. But I swear, ever since I took you from that spirit seeker, you've been worthless to me. It's getting old."

"Spirit seeker. You mean Sybille?" He turned in circles. The farmhouse lay in ruins, as though it had fallen into disrepair long ago, left for the prairie to reclaim. "Sybille. I have to get ahold of her! She'll be worried about me. How much time has passed since you hijacked me and whisked me away to this fairyland?"

Froya tilted her head from side to side. "What is time, really?"

"Cut the crap! How many hours have you held me against my will in this dude ranch fantasy loop? How many Earth hours."

"Hours? One thousand four-hundred and eighteen," she replied. "Give or take."

"Over a thousand? That's..." He performed the calculations in his head. "Almost two months!"

"For Ichor fae, two months is merely a moment."

"But Sybille is a human, not a fae. All of my friends will be worried sick!"

"They'll be fine."

"I want to contact them."

"You have more important things to do."

"So that's it, then. I'm your prisoner." His head throbbed. "I'm expected to herd cows and horseback ride across the plains until the end of time. Why would you do this to me?"

She studied him, eyes bright, lips turned up in an easy smile. How sick did she have to be to so fully embraced her roll in his misery. "This level of anger is acceptable. You have yourself under control, and I'd caution you to keep it that way. If you do, we can work with you."

"Who's this 'we' you keep mentioning? I haven't met a single other person since you brought me here."

"You have, you just don't remember."

"Whose fault is that?" Exasperated, he threw his arms up. "And why is it I can remember a whole lot now, but not some of the things that would be most useful?"

"I'm only trying to keep you from losing yourself. If you think I want to play rancher's wife any longer, you don't know me very well."

"I don't know you at all." He kicked at one of the fallen beams of his former fake home. "All you've shown me so far are a series of deceptions."

For once, Froya's expression lost its confidence. "Fair enough. Maybe it's time you meet the coterie. Re-meet, I should say." She raised her hand, fingers about to twist around each other. The crystal in her wrist glowed.

Devin shot his hand out to still hers. He remembered the moment he'd left Sybille's world. It had happened so quickly, with no time for goodbyes. "Wait! What about Thunderheart?"

Froya squinted. "What about him?"

"If we leave here, will he disappear, or just...cease to be?"

"You've developed an attachment to the animal."

"Naw, I wouldn't say that."

"I would. You are an Ichor fae, Devin. If you want to bring him with, why don't you?"

"I don't know how."

"You do."

"No, you don't get it. I've never had powers. I don't know any magic."

"You've always had power. You've always held magic."

"You're wrong."

"I'm right. These things were blocked. You couldn't wield them, no one could detect them, and this was all intentional. But they were always with you."

"But if they're blocked, how am I supposed to do any magic?"

He knew as soon as he'd asked the question what that answer was.

Devin was this power. He was magical. He always had been. The block, whatever that was, had shielded him from these things. But no longer.

"I removed the block at the same time I restored your memories," she told him. "I didn't eliminate it entirely, however. You aren't ready for that. But enough has been removed that you can now ease into your power."

"Well, let's ease the fuck out of here then."

"All right, I have an idea. Here." She handed him a pocketknife. "Slice open your finger."

He took the knife but didn't open the blade. "Why in the hell would I do that?"

"Because, I'm going to give you a world-building lesson before we head to our anchor reality, where the coterie members reside. Ichor fae use their own blood to germinate new worlds. I used mine to create this one. Now it's your turn." She tapped the knife. "Just a small incision is all that's necessary. Let's see what you can do."

Frowning, he opened the blade and pressed its tip into his index finger. Blood bubbled out of the cut like tiny ruby-red beads.

"That's enough," she told him. "Blood is life."

"Blood is life," he repeated, then raised the arm with its crystal implant and bleeding finger, thought about Froya, about Thunderheart, about everything she wanted to introduce him to. He twisted his fingers just as he'd seen her do and willed a new world into existence.

CHAPTER FOUR

DEVIN

STEAM AS THICK AS FOG BILLOWED UP FROM GRATES LINING A DANK ALLEYWAY. Devin's body tingled as he ran his bloody index finger over the brick surface of a building lining the narrow lane. A matching wall ran on its opposite side. If he stretched his arms out wide, he could touch both surfaces at the same time. With claustrophobic walls and steam permeating the path ahead, he struggled to get his bearings.

"Froya?" He walked a few paces. The alley closed in until it was only a few feet wide. "Froya, are you here?"

"Unfortunately, I am." She whistled. "Look up!"

Devin craned his neck back as he scanned the upper floors. Froya's purple-framed face could just be made out through the fog about five or six stories above, peeking down at him over the lip of the building's roof.

He brought his hands to form a circle around his mouth and shouted up to her. "I can't find Thunderheart!"

"He's with me. You better get up here too, Earthblood."

Devin's crystal embedded wrist throbbed. Thunderheart must be frightened. One minute he was enjoying his hay in the stable while peering out at the familiar stretch of plains, a panorama of snowcapped mountains in the distance beyond it. The next, he was on the top of a building, nothing but concrete under his feet and dingy buildings and fog in his periphery.

Devin shifted along the wall until he came to a rickety ladder. He hoisted himself onto it and climbed the fire escape as quickly as he could. He'd never forgive himself if Thunderheart, panicked by the noises of the city, galloped his way off the edge of the roof.

When he reached the top, heart pounding, Froya danced in circles around him.

"Congratulations, Devin. You made a world!" She stopped in front of him. "It's a decent effort, but we should probably get out of it before it collapses."

"Why would it collapse?" He gazed upon his masterpiece, expecting to see a glistening skyline, lights from a bustling city center penetrating the steam. But there was nothing but steam, or fog or, for lack of a better word, void. "Oh."

"Like I said, it was a decent first effort. A young child might accomplish something similar."

"A child. I'm at an average fae preschooler level."

"Honestly, it's not so bad." She took his hand. "But we'll die if we stay, so let's not do that."

"What about Thunderheart? You said he was here. I'm not leaving without him."

A flash of grey and black fur shone in Devin's peripheral vision. The creature gave a chirping cry as he jumped into Devin's arms.

"Holy shit, a raccoon!" He tried prying the rodent's claws off his shirt, but the tiny beast wasn't having it. "It's going to give me rabies. Get it off me!"

"Aww, he likes you too!" Froya scratched the raccoon on the top of his head. The critter chirped again.

Devin stared at the creature. The creature stared back, eyes glossy under a forehead where a patch of black fur formed into the shape of a heart. A crystal like his own was implanted in the inside of its foreleg. He couldn't remember Thunderheart the horse having a crystal. But that familiar, fond gaze—that he recognized.

"I'll be damned. But you're supposed to be a horse."

"He's supposed to be whatever he is. Time to go."

Devin leaned his head in towards Thunderheart. A last bit of uncertainty struck him, and he imagined the raccoon taking out a chunk of his handsome cowboy face.

Thunderheart cooed instead. Devin gave his chin a scratch. "You're a good boy. I'm glad I found you."

Froya raised her hand, fingers set to twist. This time, he made no attempt to stop her.

The world didn't fall apart. Instead, it morphed, brick becoming glass, steam evaporating like dew on a warm spring morning, leaving a clear view in every direction. They still stood on a roof, but this one was closed in by a glass barrier. Two stately palms planted in large ceramic pots sat on either side of a couch. Beyond the couch, a small rooftop swimming pool reflected the cerulean blue of a cloudless sky.

"Whoa! Where are we?"

Froya stepped up next to him, her face beaming. "Welcome to the Ichor home realm."

"But it's a city."

"The capital city, yes. You seem surprised."

"I don't want to sound ignorant."

"You don't need to sound ignorant. You just are."

"Right, thanks for that. What I mean is, you're all—we're all fae. Shouldn't we have landed in a meadow surrounded by an enchanted forest?"

"I see. You thought we'd be living inside of flowers hitching rides on hummingbirds."

"Mushroom homes and crows, actually."

"Crows are unsuited toward that sort of thing."

"So, you do ride birds?"

"That was a joke, Earthblood. Speaking of animals, have you noticed?" She gestured toward Devin's chest. Thunderheart had fallen asleep, his little head resting against Devin's shirt—his white feathery head attached to a long beak the color of a ripe banana.

"When the hell did this happen?"

Froya ran her hand along Thunderheart's beak. "I'm not surprised to see him in this form. The Ichor have an affinity for pelicans. When a woman gives birth, she leaves an offering at the cliff temple, where the pelicans congregate."

"Why?"

"Pelicans rend open their flesh and feed their babies with their own blood if no other food can be found."

"Gross. Really?"

She fiddled with the leather strap of her shell necklace. "So the legends say. Ichor mothers live by blood oaths and the first one they take after giving birth is to be willing to sacrifice as pelicans do." She turned towards a set of doors leading into the building. "We should go inside. There's a perch by the entrance. Leave Thunderheart on it before you enter."

Devin followed her. She pointed out a wooden perch mounted on the wall.

Devin shook Thunderheart awake and placed him on the pole. He ran his thumb over the smooth surface of Thunderheart's crystal, now situated on his leg just above a deadly looking talon. "When did he get this crystal?"

"I graced him with it while you were becoming orientated to your cute little doomed brick and cloud world. As soon as you chose to bring him with you out of the ranch realm, he became your familiar. These crystals make it easier for us to jump worlds together, as well as communicate, should we become separated."

Thunderheart bobbed his head as he situated himself on his new perch.

"See you later, Thunderheart." He held out his hand, uncertain how to best show the bird his affection. Thunderheart cooed as he leaned in to have his head patted.

Inside, a set of stairs led down to a wide, open chamber. Light from the room's glass ceiling glistened off a brightly colored stone mosaic inlaid into the floor. Before descending the stairs, Devin took in the intricate pattern, a tree with a red trunk and roots spiraling out in every direction so that no corner of the room was without a crimson vein. Once he'd stepped to the bottom, he looked more closely. The tree roots weren't stone at all. Red liquid flowed like blood. He followed one of the veins back to the trunk of the tree. It stood in the room's center, trunk wide enough that when Devin put his arms around it, his fingertips barely touched. Cheek pressed to bark, the tree let out a slow pulse as it pumped its sap through its veins.

Froya approached him. "I thought the term 'tree hugger' on your world was not to be taken literally."

He unlatched himself from the tree. "I remember. You showed me this the first time I was here. Before you zapped my brain. Inside that trunk, there's an actual heart, isn't there?"

"You could say that. Don't press on its base where the roots stick up. It doesn't like to be stepped on." She tugged on his arm and brought him over to one side of the circular room where a bar was set up. Soon she had made several selections from a shelf lined with bottles of what he assumed where the fae equivalent of hard liquor. Or so he hoped.

"I'll mix you a drink." She poured a green liquid into a tumbler, mixed in a shot of something dark, then added ice and the juice from what looked like a pyramid-shaped lime. She slid the glass over to him.

Despite his desire to mellow the rate his mind was spinning at, he hesitated. "I don't know about this. I always thought eating or drinking anything in a fairyland led to trouble."

"You ate plenty at the ranch and guess what kind of land that was."

"Uh-huh, so, if I drink this, it won't make it possible to keep me here forever?"

"No, I'm saying I can already do that. I don't need to get you drunk first."

"What if I don't want to stay?"

"I'm beginning to regret being assigned to you."

"You were assigned to me? I'm an assignment to you? Like, I'm homework?"

"Yes. See? Every now and then just when I think you understand nothing, you show a smidgen of insight."

"What about all of the touching and kissing and…the sex? We had a lot of that. Were you trying for overtime pay?"

A floral aroma reminding him of the tiny garden supply shop across from his childhood home wafted towards him as she leaned in. "Sometimes work can be fun. If my assignment was to have a lot of sex with you and nothing more, it would be my dream job. Unfortunately, I'm also supposed to help you adjust to fae life. And you've been terrible at that."

"Maybe if you'd focused more on telling me things, actually instructing me, instead of spending half your time on the fun part of your job, I'd be adjusted by now."

"No. That's your fault. And Warin's. He put that ridiculous block in your head. I can't believe you didn't know it was there."

"How would I have known? Wasn't that the point?"

She placed a hand on her hip. "You should have felt like something was missing. No psychic powers. None—that's unusual. Most humans have a drop or two, but not you."

"That's what Peter said. The man I work for."

"Sybille's father?"

"Her uncle. He said I was devoid of all psychic aptitude. Never met someone as lacking as me in that department. That should've been a clue, shouldn't it?"

"What's done is done, unless the coterie sanctions a bend in time so we can go back and unblock you at a younger age. I doubt they will. Time bending is rarely authorized."

"I don't think I'm up for time travel anyways, because that really shouldn't be a thing that people can do. You'll destroy the whole timeline."

"So? There's always more timelines if you need to borrow one."

Before he could ask what she was talking about, three fae, a woman and two men, materialized next to the heart tree.

They paraded over, scrutinizing Devin with deeply grooved foreheads and equally disapproving scowls as they did so.

Froya dropped the flirtation, instead taking on a rigid, soldier-like countenance. "Devin Damhán Vargas, this is part of our coterie."

They each bowed their heads in acknowledgment but didn't extend their arms for a handshake.

Froya looked around. "Where's Ayan?"

"She'll be here soon," the woman said. "You prefer we call you Devin?"

"It's my name. My whole life and everything I thought I knew has changed. I'd prefer my name didn't."

"I understand."

The men receded a few steps and let their colleague continue speaking to him. "And you are no longer homicidal?"

"Not unless there's a bloodthirster around."

Her orange eyes sparkled. "We'd like to talk to you more about that. Specifically, your affliction."

"Which one? I have a number of them, so if you could narrow it down, that'd be great."

"You can turn bloodthirsters immortal to the extent that no matter how they die, they always resurrect." She staggered back, like she'd been struck. "I'm sorry. I'm trying to be open minded, for Ayan's sake. But I find you repulsive."

"Repulsive? Hey, now, that's a little harsh." He sniffed his armpit, noting nothing that would cause someone to lose their ability to stand. "I bathed regularly back at the ranch."

"This isn't about your hygiene. It's about your existence. First, Warin creates an Earthblood, then that Earthblood, unable to perform even the simplest magic, is able to make the undead soldiers of our enemies invincible." She looked to her male counterparts. "My vote is to kill him."

"What? Hell no." The staircase leading to the rooftop terrace wasn't too far away. Devin began his retreat. "Froya, I'm going to conjure my home world back into existence and then will away my memory of this place. See ya around sometime."

He lost the ability to move before he'd made the first step. *Damn these fae and their ability to freeze people.*

"Sorry, Devin, but Leader Yanna is entitled to her opinion. You must stay until everyone in the coterie has voted."

"You didn't tell me there was going to be a vote or that that vote would be on whether to execute me. Seriously?"

"Don't people decide things like this where you're from?"

"Only if you're part of the Mob. Usually they skip the voting part and move right on to the murdering."

Froya flipped her palm over and bent her fingers up towards her face. Devin stumbled in her direction, his feet shuffling back and forth against his will. "Stop that, dammit!"

"Don't worry. Yanna always votes for execution. It's her thing. Grayel will vote to spare you, Norrin is a tossup. And Ayan obviously will want you to remain alive."

"Why is that obvious?"

Froya, her attention shifting from him to something behind him, took a step away. She released her hold on him, but Devin was far from free. A hand reached around his waist, another around his neck. He caught the glint of a knife blade as he struggled.

Trying to twist out of her grasp proved futile. His unknown assailant appeared strong and well trained. She used his momentum against him, spinning him towards a pillar, where she pressed her knife under his chin while her other hand pressed against his torso.

"It's good to see you again, Damhán."

"It doesn't seem so good from where I'm standing." Now facing her, he searched his mind for something familiar. Like Froya, her eyes were lavender, but her hair was a cascade of orange and black ringlets. She seemed too young to be on an important council, or whatever the hell this Ichor Coterie was.

And also, way too sexy. "Do you wear skin-tight cat suits to all of your death penalty court sessions?"

She cocked her head to the side. "Froya warned me males on Earth fear female power."

"Okay, that's not entirely an unreasonable conclusion for her to draw, but hear me out. I'm not like that. The most powerful person I know is a woman. And I lo—never mind. I'm not a misogynist."

"Yet you mentioned what I wear as though it has a bearing on my intellect and my ability to make weighted decisions." She tightened her hold on him.

"Ayan, he's scared. When he's scared, he becomes particularly dimwitted and says things that unintentionally annoy us. Maybe you could lower you knife. We talked about this. As fun as he is to play with, and believe me, I know—this isn't the way to meet your grandson."

Ayan sighed and dropped the knife, but Devin didn't move, and not because he was being held in place by fae juju.

"Hold on now. Did you just say... You're my grandma?"

CHAPTER FIVE

SYBILLE

Sybille placed six tourmaline crystals on her dining room table, one for each person attending tonight's session, minus Nate, who would be present only in spirit form. Margot, Peter, and Laurence sat pressed together on one side of the table. Nate hovered behind her, and Elis, true to form, paced a groove into her floor.

"How is Charlie?" Sybille lit a stick of incense and placed it in a burner in the center of the table. Within seconds, the musky aroma of frankincense had permeated the room. She would have lit candles, but after the episode with the Blood King's possession, resulting in a ruined seventy-year-old tablecloth and second degree burns on Sybille's back, her mother had outlawed open flames during any psychic activities.

"She's sleeping," Margot answered. "Peacefully, or so it seems. Laurence, you have a magnificent calming effect on her."

Laurence cleared his throat as he fanned the top of his shirt collar away from his chest. His cheeks were flushed, and no wonder. Even with only a tank top, Sybille's brow had begun to perspire in the stifling temperature Margot insisted the room be kept at for today's event.

"Thank you, Margot," Laurence said. "I hope between all of us, we can keep the Low from taking control within her."

"One thing at a time." Sybille glanced toward the front room. "Peter, did you hear from Zareen?"

"She'll be here after the kids are in bed." He glanced at his phone. "She texted five minutes ago to say she was reading one last story. The Patron, on the other hand, is running behind. Car trouble. He's asked us to wait."

"Hell no. I don't want him here for this. It's bad enough having to put up with him at possessions, especially with what happened with Nate's. I can't believe he didn't pay us for that."

"He's more than made up for that." Margot touched her gemstone, then put it back towards the table's center. Margot insisted they each needed a tourmaline to keep them from losing themselves during the risky travel they were about to undertake. Sybille, ever the cynic when it came to crystal magic, doubted this, but it also wasn't worth arguing over.

"I don't care, we're not waiting for him." Her chair creaked as she shifted her weight. "Laurence says it's unwise to reveal time magic to a Patron and I wholeheartedly agree. Who knows how those rich fucks might want to exploit it for their own purpose?"

A whoosh of cold air entered the house as the front door opened. "Hey, you guys, sorry I'm late. Simon did not want to go to bed."

Zareen threw her jacket and hat on the back of the couch on her way to the dining room, then took a seat to Sybille's left. Sybille leaned over and gave her a quick side hug. Hearing snippets about Zareen's normal family life felt more grounding to her than what any rock would be capable of doing. "You haven't missed anything. We're just ready to get started. Elis, you're making the humans in the room dizzy, watching you walk in a never ending circle. Take a seat."

"Sorry. It's just that every time you've done psychic magic, things have gotten ugly. Like when Nate was supposed to die but didn't."

"It wasn't too nice for me either." Nate reached out to pat Elis on the shoulder. His hand passed through and, frowning, he brought it back to his side.

"Or," Elis went on, "when Juliana possessed you, then attacked the Blood King, then you attacked them both…with your mind."

"That wasn't ugly, it was glorious." She cringed as soon as those words had left her mouth, remembering the very un-glorious parts of that experience—being trapped in her own head, for instance, or fearing everyone she loved would be murdered by her own hand. "Well, it ended up glorious, at least. Let's not think about that. It's party time."

Elis plunked down on her right and Nate floated behind her. The six corporeal people joined hands.

"We're here today to seek answers." Sybille looked one by one at the faces around the table. "These answers can't be told to us. We must be shown them. With the combined efforts of everyone present, we ask for time to reveal its truths to us. Laurence, you will lead us because you know the path we need to take. But please note, you are dealing with the Esmonds. You know our reputation."

Laurence's expression remained solemn. "I do."

"If you deceive us..." She squeezed Elis' hand and he showed his fangs. "There will be consequences."

"I only want to help you and my granddaughter. I won't lie to you."

She weighed his words. He may be sincere, but that didn't mean he wasn't deluding himself.

"Sybie," Margot said in her sing-song voice. "It's not polite when you threaten to unleash your bloodthirsty boyfriend on our guest before a clairvoyance session in which he plays a key role. Did I teach you nothing?"

"Of course you did, Mom. I'm being cautious. You taught me that too, remember? Like how I can't even have a votive candle floating in a bowl of water anymore."

"So cheeky." She nudged Laurence with her shoulder. "Don't mind her, dear heart. Go ahead and get started. I've always been anxious to learn more about the fae folk."

"All right." Laurence took a deep breath. "I have limited experience in projecting timelines to a shared audience, but I believe that between all of us, we have enough knowledge and ability to make it happen. You'll know I'm not deceiving you because you'll be following history just as I am. My only added piece will be directing us towards those moments."

A surge of energy began in the hand Sybille had clasped in Zareen's and rode her body like a wave until it flowed from her right hand into Elis. He gasped, and she held on so he wouldn't pull away from the shock of it. The energy wave came around again, and then again. Each loop traveled faster than the one before it, and with greater intensity, until the pulse was constant. It reminded her of the driving beat of the music at Elis' hypnotism show at the county fair last fall.

Peter began chanting, more to steady his own nerves, Sybille believed, than to aid them in what was happening. The evenness of his voice helped keep her grounded, so much so that it wasn't until Nate gave a long whistle that she realized what was happening.

The room became an interactive three-dimensional theater. All around them, flickers of their timeline came in and out of focus. Laurence mumbled to himself, "Not that. No, that won't be helpful. Further back. Further still. Time, time, time. Ah, yes. That's the moment."

And that moment became now. Two groups of people, one brightly clothed, with hair and skin a rainbow of brilliant colors, the other barely recognizable as people, a human-like shape, the grey of the cremated. Bone and ash. They stood facing each other and there was no doubt, even had she not known it already, that these people, the Ichor and the Ossian, were at odds.

The "moment" Laurence had captured for them was not a length of time in a linear sense, but a set of intersecting times that together created a picture they could process. Sybille, the hierophant in the group with the most experience at dissecting timelines, steadied the moment for the rest of them.

Elis rocked back and forth in his seat next to her. Poor thing, he'd never had such an experience before, which made this harder for him than for the rest of the group. His usually resonant voice came out husky. "What is this? What in the hell is this?"

All around them, fae folk breathed life into universes and played in realms that had already come into being generations before. The Ichor prided themselves as artists, conjuring worlds out of dreams and blood from their fingertips, living in those created lands for a time until the dream got old or they envisioned something new and went off to actualize it. They returned to their central home realm when they wished it, and there they built a vital society.

The Ossian realm challenged Sybille's concept of reality. Firm foundation, they built towers resembling vertebrae and worlds that seemed more like meteors than planets. Their needs were structural and collective, each person functioning as though connected on either end to someone else.

The leg bone's connected to the knee bone.

Laurence's moment lasted centuries, eons. The fae lived peacefully when their paths didn't cross, but when they did, blood was shed, bone was crushed. Each saw the other as a threat and, to keep each other out, they drew up territories and borders made from the fabric of reality.

Sybille's skin tingled. Her forehead throbbed. If this moment of Laurence's lasted much longer, the strain of keeping all the pieces organized for everyone was going to cause an aneurysm. She moaned, expecting Elis to respond to her pain but he was too immersed in the fae war, brutal battles playing out for dominion over disputed realms.

Zareen's shoulder became a weighted blanket as she leaned against Sybille. "Keep it together, girl. This can't go on forever."

Most of the realities the fae fought and played in bore little resemblance to anything recognizable. Then the moment shifted. Laurence flipped away worlds, bringing the group back to Earth, but not to the Earth of the Esmond's dining room, rather to the Earth of the past—the far distant past. Here too, a battle raged, but unlike previous battles, this one took place in a world populated with sentient beings. The Ichor and the Ossian had no part in this reality's creation but each strove to claim it.

When blood met bone, the world shook. Earthquakes, tsunamis, tempests, floods. The world might break, but it was of little consequence to the fae if they could claim its shattered pieces as their own.

In the end, there would be no winner. During one of a countless stretch of battles, the leaders from both the Ichor and the Ossian fell victim to the other side's magic and were captured.

Even fae had their limits. Sybille and her group watched as the fae met to discuss a truce in which this reality would be left alone should the leaders be returned to their families unharmed. They signed, blood upon bone, bone upon blood, and the fae left earth for many years.

Laurence shifted time again. Sybille struggled to keep everyone in her circle on the same continuum.

Earth again. A dark forest and a long-held treaty broken. A world left without fae influence was a temptation, and over time both the Ossian and Ichor breached the universe. Sybille shook as she realized what this implied, that the fae always meant to come back to this world, that they always meant to take it over, and that if one fae family couldn't have it to themselves without a fight, then a fight they would have.

And humans would pay the price.

"What's happening? I keep asking that and no one answers." Elis shook so hard, the connection between them threatened to break. Sybille peered out into a dark forest, where Ossian fae stood in a circle. In its center huddled a half dozen humans, bound together with twine. A fae dragged one of them forward, and there the young man died by the edge of an Ossian knife to be reborn a monster. The creature howled piteously, then turned on the band of quaking humans. The Ossian let the creature charge. They let him attack his own kind. They watched as he clenched a screaming woman and tore open her throat with his mouth, her cries fading as she did.

"It can't be true." Elis pulled his hand from Sybille's and from Margot's on the other side of him.

The forest faded and the dining room replaced it along with a sense of dread that settled into the pit of Sybille's stomach.

"Bloodthirsters," Elis said in a hollow voice that seemed as ancient as a crumbling castle. "We were created by a sorry bunch of power-hungry magical bones."

Elis

"I had more to show you. Mr. Tanner, I understand your shock, but you shouldn't have broken the circle."

"Like hell I shouldn't have. Seeing it like that... We're just your pawns!"

"Not my pawns. Ossian fae pawns. Meant to spread terror and weaken Earth for an eventual Ossian takeover. Perhaps now you'll understand why I helped Juliana. Bloodthirsters are essentially terrorist sleeper cells. They are harmful already but could become absolutely devastating if unchecked. Their existence doesn't bode well for the planet."

"No, it doesn't. It really doesn't!" Nate flew around the room, his body blurred by movement. "I knew we were bad, but not this bad. No!"

Nate's brief stint possessing Sybille had connected him with his bloodthirster self, however fleetingly. He knew, just as Elis did, the guilt that came with this connection. To know you were meant to help annihilate all humans as part of a fae takeover was hard enough for Elis, let alone a good-natured spirit like Nate.

Elis put his years of studied self-control to use. "It's not your fault, mate."

Peter stood. "I'm going to go check on Charlie. I can't imagine her sleeping through this. Nate, why don't you join me. If she's woken, you can help me by singing her a lullaby. You have a beautiful baritone."

Nate pondered his offer, then followed him to the stairs. "Does she like sea chanties?"

"I learned long ago Ichor fae hated bloodthirsters. Now I know why." Sybille slumped over the table. The time traveling session had left her skin sallow. She kept pressing her fingers into her temples like she hoped they'd break right through her skull. "The Low is an Ossian territory, then. That explains...so much. What about the Ichor? Don't tell me they've been benign little Tinker Bells who have kept their word and stayed out of our universe?"

Laurence remained pensive, but a corner of his mouth turned up. "Your friend Devin wouldn't exist if that were the case."

"Devin, no wonder I hate the guy." Elis felt like spitting. "I'm genetically predisposed to hate anything Ichor."

Margot, uncharacteristically quiet during their time-hopping session, gave his hand a motherly pat. "I think it has more to do with Sybie and the fact that you're jealous of her connection to him, dear heart."

"She doesn't have a connection and I have nothing to be jealous of when it comes to that man!"

"No?" Maternal comfort expended, she turned away from him to pour herself a glass of wine from the side table. "Your outburst feels rather telling, but I suppose I could have read you wrong this time and every other time Devin's name has been mentioned."

Laurence let out a long sigh. "There may be some truth to what Mr. Tanner is saying, and probably some truth to what Margot says as well, though I'd rather stay out of that one. To further answer your question, the Ichor are thought to have an energetic presence here, but it's unknown to me."

"Would it be like Low Hollow?" Elis asked. "Some kind of remote region or an island maybe?"

"It's possible but unlikely. You saw for yourselves what sort of territories the Ichor set up here in the past, before the truce."

"Energy channels." Sybille traced her finger along the patterns in the wood tabletop. "Not places, but lines. Veins."

"Like I said, this is all speculation. The Ichor certainly aren't going to give this information up to me, even if I had a way to ask them for it. For obvious reasons, I am hated by them, and by default, my granddaughter is as well."

Elis remembered his first encounter with the purple Ichor woman. She hadn't cared for him, and Sybille had warned him if he showed his fangs, things wouldn't end well. Plus, she had snarled at Charlie, calling her the "cursed one." It all made sense now.

Elis paced the room, realized that he was doing it, then retreated to the couch.

Zareen remained near Sybille, who seemed on the verge of passing out. "So how is it that Devin was an Ichor fae all along and we never knew?"

"I don't have all the answers," Laurence said. "My guess is that a psychic block was put in place within his mind when he was a child. I doubt he knew himself, and certainly there'd be no way for anyone else to detect his identity."

"How do you know about him then?" Elis wondered for the hundredth time if Laurence's blood, being part fae, would taste as good as Raelyn's had. "That seems a bit suspicious."

"I am sensitive to the presence of all fae, Ichor or Ossian. When I felt Froya's presence, I channeled in and watched the moment when she spirited Devin away."

"Froya. The lavender woman's name is Froya," Sybille said. "What does she want from him?"

"I don't know much about her other than that she's made several trips to our universe. The Ichor are less cautious than the Ossian."

Elis narrowed his eyes. "Creating an army of the undead is being cautious?"

Laurence glanced towards the staircase. "Look, I've shown you what you need to see. I've been completely transparent with you. And I've done so because my granddaughter must be saved."

"Right, we all want to save Charlie," Elis said, "but considering what you've just shown us, it seems Earth may fall victim to an ancient fae war. We're beyond the scope of one little girl now."

"That's where you're wrong! You people have been ignorant. I've tried to explain, tried to enlighten you and you still don't get it."

"Calm down, old man."

"You're older than me, bloodthirster. And I won't calm down. Charlie must be saved. If she isn't, it's not about one girl dying. Charlie is how the Ossian plan on spreading themselves over the whole world."

"Like she's the chosen one?" Elis could accept that he was meant as a soldier for evil fae before he'd accept that tired trope. "It's her destiny to destroy Earth—do you know how crazy that sounds?"

"She's a means to their end. That's all," Laurence responded. "But isn't that enough?"

"That was their game plan all along, wasn't it? I knew there'd be fallout for removing her from the Low—knew it ever since Devin first told me she existed. And now here we are, harboring our very own mini-Death Star." Sybille swore. "If we can't help her, we're all screwed."

The silence that fell over the Esmond house broke when the front door opened and a familiar hooded figure with a crooked nose entered. "Hast thou begun thy magic of space and time? I pray I've missed naught."

As he spoke, Sybille attempted to stand, and then failed to do so in the most dramatic of ways. "Oh my God, I can't handle this now, tell him to shut the fuck up and go away."

Back of her hand pressed to her forehead like a nineteen forties film actress, she exclaimed, "Bless your heart," and then fainted to the floor.

CHAPTER SIX

JULIANA

No matter how hard she scrubbed, Juliana couldn't get the oil stain out of her favorite apron.

"Fiddlesticks!" She held the cloth close to examine the way the brown stain adhered itself to the weave in the fabric, then lowered it and squeezed another nickel-sized circle of stain remover onto it. She resumed her scrubbing.

Juliana prided herself on maintaining a spotless kitchen, toiling day and night to keep everything tidy. Or rather, she toiled day in and day out since it always seemed to be daytime here. She filled her immaculate kitchen with delicious goodies: breads and scones and pies and cookies. Her time was spent mixing batters, baking, and placing fresh from the oven treats on racks to cool. She never tasted them. They were for Elis, who was due to return at any moment.

She waited for him by baking and cleaning and baking some more. When the cookies hardened and the bread molded, she tossed them in the garbage and started over. She scrubbed at grease stains on her eggshell white apron with its teal ruffles because a stain was a blemish and she had to be perfect, just like her kitchen.

Juliana did all these things because she was in Hell. In Hell, you didn't do as you pleased, you did what you hated most. You waited around for a man who never arrived, and you breathed in the intoxicating aroma of food you were never going to eat. You became compliant.

Never in all her years did Juliana think she'd end up resigned to this. If she thought killing herself would have any affect at all, she would have stuck her head in the oven or slit her throat with a bread knife. Whenever she had these dark thoughts, she whipped up a batch of cherry joy cupcakes and frosted the tops to look like unicorn heads. Unicorns always brightened up a room, especially a room from which there was to be no escape for all of eternity.

After removing as much of the stain as possible, Juliana placed her apron on its peg to dry and put on her second favorite apron. This one was pink and had "Cupcake Queen" written on it in big swirly gold letters.

She'd earned that title. By her count, she'd baked and decorated three hundred and twelve unicorn cherry joy cupcakes.

Juliana opened her cupboard and took down a bag of sugar and a canister of flour. From the fridge, she grabbed a carton of eggs. She'd left the butter out by the stove to soften. Placing everything on the counter, she turned the dial of her radio until it clicked on. Much to her chagrin, when she'd first arrived in Hell, country music and only country music blared from it. Changing the channels accomplished nothing. Country music reigned supreme up and down the dial.

At first, she hated it but preferred it to silence. After a while, she hated it a little less, and now she couldn't imagine baking without it.

She listened as she creamed the butter and sugar together. A song she recognized from yesterday and the day before that and the day before that came on. The lyrics spilled off her tongue.

Another layer of hell: singing along to a song you loathed on principal and then discovering that, despite yourself, you loved it.

She whisked an egg into the butter and sugar, then mixed the dry ingredients together in a separate bowl.

The radio crackled. She paused at what she was doing long enough to whack the radio on its side and adjust the knob. The song faded out. In its place, came voices, distant and hard to understand.

She played with the dial as she strained to listen.

"They failed to keep the truce."

"Earth was never safe."

"We were created by a sorry bunch…"

Juliana froze at that last sentence, its cadence unmistakable. Her body surged with electricity as excitement filled her. She'd have to whip up some cookies after finishing the unicorn cupcakes. Maybe he'd like those too, though.

"Calm down, old man."

Yes, it was him. Her beloved Elis was nearby!

"If we can't help her, we're all screwed."

Juliana recoiled. She knew that voice too.

"Tell him to shut the fuck up and go away."

What? No! Who did she think she was, ordering Juliana to dismiss Elis through a kitchen radio?

"I will not, you horrible woman. Do you think you can come here to my own personal Hell and say whatever you want to me? Well..." She dumped the flour mixture into the wet ingredients and started beating them together, probably harder than she should. The texture of these cupcakes was going to come out all wrong, but she was too angry to care. She'd been listening to a lot of country music and so she knew exactly how to respond.

"Bless your heart!" she yelled into the speaker of her radio.

The radio clicked in response and then Sybille's voice came on again. "Bless your heart."

The lights flickered. Not just the bulbs in the ceiling fixture, but the light coming through the window over the sink, as though whatever devil running this nightmare had hiccupped and accidentally shut off her world for a second.

When light returned, Juliana knew without turning around that she was no longer alone.

She sniffed the air—cinnamon—and then wrinkled her nose. Disgusting. Cinnamon belonged in snickerdoodles, not in people. Especially not in this person.

Juliana sighed. Seeing as though she was in Hell, it stood to reason that the woman she hated most would be here too. Anything to up the torture element. Fine then, if that was how it needed to be, she wasn't going to give Sybille any satisfaction. Composing herself, she plastered on her smirkiest grin and slowly turned around. "Hello, Sybille."

To her great delight, Sybille looked as shocked as Juliana could have hoped for. The human shook her head as though that's all it would take to free her from this place.

"Juliana?" She approached the counter where Juliana stood and pressed her fingers into Juliana's arm, recoiling as skin met skin. "Oh, holiest of shits. What the hell am I doing here?"

Devin

Now that Ayan's knife was no longer pressed against his throat, Devin should have felt more relaxed. Instead, the nerves in his fingertips stung like needles were poking into them. He kept himself upright and rigid against the column Ayan had tossed him against just moments before. The hair on the back of his neck stood up.

Ayan slid her knife into a leather holster, her eyes never leaving Devin's body. "He resembles Warin, especially around the nose and jawline. Those are not Warin's eyes, though."

"His human mother must have had blue eyes. Quite dull compared to Warin's but still pretty." Froya stood at Ayan's side, describing Devin as though she was convincing Ayan she'd made a good purchase.

"So, I think I've misunderstood something." He laughed, trying to sound lighthearted, but it came out heavy and forced. The tingling in his fingertips increased. "Froya, you implied that I'm Ayan's grandson, and Ayan, you didn't contradict her."

The women continued to stare and so he continued. "Now, I'm no expert in, well, in most things. But I do know that grandmothers of adult men aren't hot thirty year olds."

"I'm not hot; the temperature is perfectly comfortable here." Ayan's fingers toyed with the handle of her knife as it jutted out of the sheath on her belt. "And I'm not thirty. I'm… Froya, please translate my age into Earth years so he can understand."

"She's one hundred and eight."

"I'll be damned."

"Not unless the coterie wills it."

"What? No, that's not what I meant. It's an expression. It means, I'm surprised."

"What an odd way to express it. Why not just say, 'I'm surprised?'"

"Can we get back to the point?" Devin asked. "I'm struggling to keep up, but so far what I'm gathering is that fae live a long, long time."

"Length of time is relative," Ayan said.

"Relative to my human understanding, then."

"Earthblood. You are an Earthblood. Half-Earth human, half-Ichor fae," Froya reminded him. "Maybe that's why you only seem to half understand anything."

"Okay, fine. Relative to my Earthblood understanding, Fae can pass the hundred-year mark and still look like their college days aren't far behind them. And this means that, until I found out we're related, I was hot for my grandma." He brought his fingers, now burning, to his mouth and covered it. "Oh my God, why did I just say that? I think I might be sick."

"You're not sick," Froya said. "The drink I gave you contained a truth potion. Don't be upset, we give it to everyone going before the coterie. It's important that they hear no lies."

He waved his hands in front of his face. "My fingers feel like lasers are being shot into them."

"A side effect. It will pass."

Ayan turned to go join her fellow coterie members, motioning for them to follow her.

He glanced at the curve of Froya's hip. "You know I think you're hot too, right?"

"I didn't need a truth potion to determine that." She pulled him aside before they reached the others. "You love the human seer—the spirit seeker —don't you?"

"Yes." He blinked. No hesitation.

"And what about me?"

"What about you?"

"Do you love me too? I created a whole world for you."

He didn't have to consider his answer to this for long either. "I don't trust you. I can't love someone I don't trust."

"But you trust this Sybille? Even though she loves someone else. A disgusting Ossian soldier of all things."

"Until the day I die." He wiggled his fingers in the air. Blue color trails swirled around them. "Am I supposed to be high right now? And what's an ocean soldier? I'm pretty sure Elis isn't a merman."

"Let's hope the day you die isn't today." She grasped one of his waving hands, purple swirling with blue, and they made their way towards the awaiting Ichor Coterie.

Four fae stood in a row, Ayan on one end, the other woman, Yanna, on the other. Froya deposited him in front of them and retreated to the bar.

Yanna spoke first. "You are an illegal creation."

"No, ma'am." He swayed to the side, then righted himself up. "I swear to you, I'm done with all of those Low shenanigans. Straight and narrow it is for me from now on. Except for whatever Froya slipped in my drink. Is that legal or illegal?"

"We aren't talking about former drug use. We are talking about you. Ichor are not allowed on Earth. They are especially not allowed to interact with humans and create children. Our laws forbid it."

"Okay, so my fae daddy was a bad boy. Seems my mom has a type, because my Earth daddy is a real son of a bitch."

One of the male counselors—Devin couldn't remember which one he was, spoke next. "It would be better for you if you talked less."

"Why'd you slip me a Mickey then? I can't help myself. It's like I'm at a confessional with three extremely attractive priests."

"There are four of us."

"Fine then, three hot priests and one that could be attractive given the right lighting."

"We're here to inform you of your origins and then decide your fate," said the fae that was not standing in good lighting. "Saying more than you should may not work out in your favor."

"Yeah, but let's be real here. You've all already decided, haven't you? Green hat guy, you don't like me. You'd just as soon pitch me off the side of the terrace now so that this whole thing doesn't affect your dinner plans. Lady, Yanana. Nayana... Yanna. Yanna, sorry. You thought you wanted me dead, but really, you kinda think I should stick around because you find me hilarious. Don't try to hide that smile. There it is! You're not as stoic as you think you are. Ayan, you're my grandma, so I think I'm safe there."

"Don't be so sure."

"No, I'm sure. If you wanted me dead, you had the opportunity to kill me already. You want something from me, though. And it's not to fill out the invites for a family reunion. So, that leaves less attractive guy. No offense. Actually, I don't know about you. But you know about you, don't you? You know what you think of me already. You seem like someone who's sure of himself, but you keep it close to your chest. No letting anyone see your cards. Anyways, can we just go ahead and vote already? Not me. I don't get a vote, obviously. I mean you. And what's with having an even number of you? What do you do if there's a tie?"

"We drain blood, mix it with our blood tree and let it decide."

He hesitated. "You're...you're serious. Jesus. I'd like to avoid that if possible, so..." He gave the less attractive fae a thumbs up. "I'm counting on you, buddy."

"Don't you want to hear about your father and the sacred laws he broke?" Green Hat guy asked.

"I've heard enough. Warin went to Earth, which he wasn't supposed to do. Made it with a human. Also a big no-no. Had a baby. Huge mistake on so many levels, but I'm grateful, nonetheless. Put a block in the baby's head so the baby would grow up like a dumb clod and not realize he was a magical creature from the land of pelicans. Once you all found out, you punished him, and I'm guessing it wasn't with a couple hundred hours of community service. Do I have all of that right? Man, that drink was amazing. I haven't been this wasted since I freebased bloodthirster drugs." He looked towards the bar. "Can I have another one, Froya?"

"Froya, do not give him anymore," Ayan called over. "I'm afraid one has proven more than he can handle."

"Hey, I'm not that much of a lightweight. I can manage..." He reeled to the side like he was on the bridge of the USS Enterprise during a Klingon attack. "Okay, maybe half the amount you gave me last time. Best to cut me off at that point, though." A shock of blinding light shot past outside, its brilliance trailing from one end of the room through the windows to the other. "Holy shit, did you guys see that too or is it just me?"

The whole room filled with the same startling light. Everything became a colorless void. It was all Devin could see before swaying a bit too much to stay upright. Dark replaced light as his head met the floor.

CHAPTER SEVEN

ELIS

She was dead weight in his arms. Her hair covered her eyes, but Elis didn't have a free hand to brush it aside. It wasn't like it mattered anyhow. She was sleeping. Or unconscious. Or in some sort of trance state. Laurence couldn't determine which and neither could anyone else. But everyone suspected it had something to do with their tour of fae history.

He took the stairs two at a time and turned down the hallway, heading for Sybille's room. Margot followed him, babbling about her baby and how she'd thought Sybille could handle it. Elis did his best not to growl.

In her room, Margot turned down the sheets so he could place Sybille under the covers. "She'll be fine," Margot assured him. "She just needs her rest."

"What she needs is a new career."

"Hierophant isn't a major you select in college. You don't choose to have a knack for seeing into different worlds and contacting the spirits of the undead. It's a calling."

"I swear, Margot, this calling is going to kill her one day."

"Am I to assume you think that's a bad thing instead of an opportunity?" She clucked her tongue.

"What an awful thing to say." Unable to maintain eye contact with her, he instead looked down at Sybille. Her head sank into a fluffy pillow, her body barely a lump under the thick comforter, like the bed was about to swallow her. Sitting on its edge, he traced his fingers along the outline of her hand. "I'm trying to be a better person. Sybille's life is her own. I don't want anyone to steal it from her, including me."

Margot patted his shoulder. Not quite motherly this time, her firm touch held a warning. "I hope you're as sincere as you sound."

The bedroom door opened, and Bore entered, rushing around the bed to the opposite side Elis was on. With a dramatic gasp, he took Sybille's other hand in his. "My precious Lady Sybille. How could you to leave us in such a state of misery? I await your return with bated breath."

Elis' eyes glowed. If he couldn't eat Laurence, the Patron might make a tasty snack, if a bit salty.

"Bore, dear, do remember that Sybie needs her rest and your excited state isn't exactly restful."

"She fainted when you showed up." Elis bared his fangs and the Patron seemed to notice his presence for the first time.

"Dost thou thinketh me the cause of fair Sybille's condition?"

Elis leaned in over Sybille's body. "I was born in the same century Shakespeare died in. And I can attest to you that no one—no one—then or since, spoke like you do now. I don't know what the point of it is, but your Middle Earth cosplay is getting on my bloodthirster nerves. Do you know what happens when someone gets on my nerves?"

Bore shook his head and swallowed.

"I get hungry." He glided his tongue over his fangs.

Bore jumped away from the bed. "The Patron position holds great power. You cannot threaten me. I shall report this to them."

"Who is it you report to exactly? I'd like to speak with your manager."

Margot gripped his shoulder. "Elis, maybe you should…"

"Get out of here!" He flung her hand from his shoulder, but his glowing eyes never left Bore. "She needs peace and quiet and you won't give her either."

"Neither will you, it seems." Bore flinched at the reaction he thought his words would illicit, but in truth, they'd taken the wind from Elis' sails.

Thirty seconds later, both Bore and Margot did leave the room, Bore most likely to report Elis' bad behavior to his billionaire boys club, and Margot to consult with Peter and Laurence about Sybille's lack of consciousness.

He welcomed the silence, but after a while, it became oppressive, the weight of nothingness heavier than an elephant. "I wish you'd wake up."

Not knowing what else to do, Elis rearranged her carefully, then lay down at her side, his arm across her belly. He pulled her close. Perhaps if he fell asleep, his spirit self would travel to her, find out where she was and what needed to happen so she could wake up healed and strong again. Just as he drifted, one ghostly leg creeping its way to the dream world, light from the hallway shot into the room and then vanished again.

"Oh great, what did I just walk into?"

Elis rolled towards the door. "Charlie? It's past midnight. What are you doing up?"

She stumbled over to the bed. "I had a bad dream."

Scooting himself into a seated position, he patted the bed next to him. "Sybille didn't happen to be in it, did she?"

She shook her head. "No. Why?"

No sense withholding the truth. This child wasn't easily fooled. "We did some psychic magic time warp thing and Sybille collapsed afterwards. She might be riding out the stress in some dreamland somewhere."

Charlie stared at Sybille. "Is she going to be all right?"

"Margot thinks so."

"Do you?"

"I don't know. But what I do know is that you had a bad dream. Do you want to tell me about it?"

"I dreamed the Low won and I died."

"Oh, Charlie." He wrapped his arms around the girl and squeezed her to him. "That would have woken me up too. But it was just a dream."

"It might happen, though. I know I'm worse."

"But your grandfather is helping us now. We're going to come up with a cure for you."

"Cures take a long time. And uncle Devin is gone and now Sybille is sick too." She sniffled as she buried her face into Elis' chest. "I think we're screwed."

"No." He pulled her away and placed his hands on her shoulders, forcing her to look at him. "It may seem that way, but we aren't going to let that happen. You're going to be okay."

Neither spoke for a moment. Finally, Charlie let out a long sigh. "I was waiting for you to say 'I promise,' but you didn't. That's okay. You should never make promises that can't be kept."

Elis' chest tightened. One of the worst things about having his spirit back was that it meant giving a shit. About the world, about life and death, about people. When they'd brought Charlie out of the Low, Elis had been the first to complain. It was too risky; it would end badly. They were letting their hearts bleed for a girl who could destroy them all.

It hadn't taken long for him to change his mind. Now that he knew he was connected to the Ossian fae and that Charlie was part Ossian, perhaps that explained the depth of his attachment to her. He liked to think it was something more though, something that didn't rely on the supernatural. Something more…human.

"I love you, Charlie, and…I promise you I will do everything I can to destroy the Low and save you." And the world. If Charlie fell, so too fell the world. He wondered if she knew her fate was tied to that of the universe and wished on all the stars in the sky that she didn't. Her burden was heavy enough.

"I'm going to hold you to that." She slumped against him again and let out a long yawn. "You're not like all the other bloodthirsters I know."

"Well firstly, let me say that I'm sorry you know a lot of bloodthirsters. Secondly, I thank you kindly for the compliment. I like to think of myself as special."

"My mom is special too."

"Right. Of course she is." He thought about how Raelyn had tasted when he'd used her to refuel on the day they'd destroyed the Blood King. He cleared his throat. "What about your father?"

"He's not special."

"He must be. He's your dad."

"No, he's really not. Just a Craver my mom keeps around for, you know…"

His eyes grew wide, thinking this poor little girl knew way more than she should but then he realized what she meant. "He's your mom's donor?"

"One of them. Honestly, I told you he's no good and that's just the truth."

"And Laurence? Did he visit you often?"

"A couple times. Mom doesn't like him, and he makes my dad feel bad about himself. Plus, he tried to kidnap me once when I was three. I thought my mom had killed him for doing that but then he showed up a few years later. Then he disappeared again, and she told me he was dead. But before that happened, he bought me a trampoline."

"A trampoline. Those are fun." He didn't know what to say beyond that, but Charlie seemed like she was done talking anyways. She yawned again and before long, her breathing came in deep and even. He shifted her so that she was cradled in his arms, then leaned back against the headboard. Tiny girl, the Low wouldn't get to her tonight. It never would —not if he could help it.

Devin

Half asleep, Devin slapped at his ear to kill the creature buzzing near it. He must have missed, because the noise continued, louder now.

"It's gonna get me." He was sure these were the words he spoke, or meant to speak, but when he thought back a second later, he couldn't remember speaking them at all.

Eyes open, Devin waved his hands around his head. If he couldn't slap it dead, maybe he could whoosh it away. "Goddamn mosquitos."

It only occurred to him then that mosquitos didn't come out in January. "Why am I camping in the middle of winter?"

"You aren't." Froya pressed two fingers into the side of his neck, held them there a few seconds, then released. "You're in the middle of the city inside a building twenty-four stories above the ground. And we don't have winter here. Or mosquitos."

"Do we need to restrain him?" a woman with orange and black hair asked. Grandma. Grandma with the Halloween hair.

Grandma wanted to tie him up.

Froya came to his rescue. "It's not necessary."

"But he just hit himself in the head. Perhaps he wanted us to select death for him."

"I can hear you and no, I don't want you to select death for me." He sat up, but the buzzing only grew louder, and soon he slumped against the floor again. "Does that mean you're going to let me go? Also, how did I end up on the floor and why do buzzing bastard mosquitos live inside my skull now?"

"You're on the floor because you're particularly sensitive to our liquor." Froya lifted his head long enough to slide a pillow under it. "And I told you, there are no mosquitos here, inside or outside of your head. You're simply becoming more in tune with the vibrations of our world and so you're hearing sounds you wouldn't normally."

"Your world vibrates like a bloodsucking disease-carrying bug. That's just perfect."

"You'll learn how to shut it off soon."

"What about my other question. If you've decided against killing me, does that mean you're going to let me go?"

"It means the majority of the coterie has determined the Ichor are better off with you alive." Ayan sat on a low stool near Devin's feet. Her gaze followed Froya as Froya continued to tend to Devin. He wondered who these women were to each other. Were they long-time friends, work colleagues, acquaintances only brought together because of Devin? They seemed like they knew each other well enough not to completely trust the other's motives.

Ayan took out one of her knives and swung it around. "Your peculiarities are worth studying."

"Son of a bitch, I always knew being weird would someday save me from murder at the hand of brightly colored magical beings in a room where trees bleed."

Ayan slapped his foot. "You shouldn't talk about your own mother that way, even if she was just Warin's human vessel."

"Gross, don't say it like that. And I didn't mean—never mind. My mama had her faults but at least she didn't condemn her son to death for breaking some archaic rule."

"Our rules aren't archaic. They have purposes that are applicable to our present society. And I didn't condemn my own son to death. Why would you believe that?"

"Because I was told he'd been punished for his crime, and I see how you people view punishments. They're very…final."

"His punishment was final, but it was banishment, not death."

"Are you saying my sperm donor daddy is still alive?"

"Yes, but not the way you envision."

Ayan paused.

Devin squinted at her. "Aren't you going to elaborate and tell me how I should envision him?"

"No. We need to discuss our next steps."

"I'd like my next steps to be in the direction of home, but I suppose that's not going to happen."

"This is your home." Froya rubbed his temples like she was trying to massage that thought right into his consciousness.

"That's what I figured you'd say. Damn, that feels good." He closed his eyes, letting her touch sooth his aching head. The mosquito's buzz lessoned until he had to strain to hear it. "What if I don't want to stay here, though? Are you going to dose me up or put another happy spell on me so I don't try to leave?"

"If we have to," Ayan said. "We need you, Devin. Here, with us. Ichor don't belong on Earth."

"Bullshit. My father went there. Froya has gone there. And I bet they aren't the only ones."

"Our presence there is one of necessity. You'll see when the time comes."

"When the time comes? What does that mean? My necessity is to be there now. I have someone waiting for me."

Froya let go of his head. "She's too busy with her bloodthirster boyfriend to be waiting for you."

Ayan shivered. "That's another thing. You associated with Ossian soldiers and part-Ossian humans."

"I what now?"

"It's another reason to keep you here. No good can come from that."

"It's true. Quite a lot of bad can, though," Froya said before leaving him on the floor to stand next to where Ayan sat. She picked up a tumbler on a nearby table and swirled the glass. The liquid in it changed from purple to silver to purple again. "There's the matter of your peculiarity. We need to study it, but we can't just let you keep doing it. It's dangerous."

Ayan agreed. "It's the biggest reason Norrin voted to kill you. I can't say I blame him."

With effort, Devin raised himself off the ground enough to prop himself up on his elbows. He looked back and forth between the two of them. "I take it you're not referring to my ability to recite all the lyrics to *Hamilton*? It's only because Sybille and Zareen listened to it constantly for six months straight, by the way."

"Your blood grants immortality to the soldiers you call bloodthirsters," Froya said. "This gives our enemies a grave advantage. Did you think this would be of no interest to us?"

"Grandson." Ayan wrapped her arms around herself. "We just need to make sure we're the ones who get to use you."

"Use me?" He felt winded, like all his energy had been zapped away by these two purple-eyed women. "What am I, a napkin after a lobster dinner?"

"No." Ayan laughed, but the look in her eyes said that this was no joke. "There's a war brewing in your precious Earth world. When the time comes…"

There it was again: *when the time comes.* "Are you saying you'll only let me go home when my home has become a battlefield?"

You understand now," Ayan said. "You are our weapon. And we plan on aiming you at our enemies."

CHAPTER EIGHT

SYBILLE

SYBILLE HAD NEVER SEEN SO MANY GLUTEN-BASED PRODUCTS IN ALL HER LIFE. Cutting through the thick crust of a round artisan loaf of bread released a malty aroma that made her mouth water. She loaded her slice with a generous layer of butter and took a bite.

"Oh my God, this is freaking amazing."

Juliana's face twitched. "It's sourdough, and it is amazing and it's not for you."

She took another bite. "I kinda think it is. You know, it's weird that I'm here and I'm going to have to figure why that is pretty soon, but first I have to say: for an evil spirit who possessed me and tried to use my body for mass murder with the ultimate goal of killing Elis before taking my life, you really know your way around a kitchen. I guess it's true what they say. No one is all bad."

Juliana placed her hand on what remained of the loaf and inched it closer to herself. "You should be more concerned with what you did to end up in Hell with me."

"In Hell?" Sybille laughed. "Is that where you think you are?"

"Where else could this be?"

"Juliana, what do you remember last?"

"I was mixing batter for cupcakes, and then the music on the radio changed and I could hear you and Elis and some other people talking, then the lights went out and when they came on again, you were here."

"Okay, that's interesting. We'll get to that later, but it's not what I meant. What do you remember from before this kitchen?"

"After I was turned, I lived in a nunnery, where I met Elis. He was only a boy, but I knew he'd grow up and become someone very special to me."

"That is beyond disturbing. I don't want to hear about any of that. Jesus, you've lost some of your wit since I plopped you in here." She eyed the loaf, stomach gurgling as it pleaded with her to eat another piece. Juliana pulled it away from her. "What is the last thing you remember before you became trapped in this kitchen?"

The woman paused. Sybille could only speculate at what a being of pure consciousness might experience when finding itself trapped in this tiny world, forced to perform the same tasks repeatedly with no contact from the outside world.

Just as she thought questioning her was a dead end, Juliana spoke up.

"We were at that cabin in the Low. I...helped you. I can't believe I would do such a thing, but it made sense at the time."

"Yes, that's right. What did you help me do?"

"I helped you destroy the Blood King. We melted his brain."

"We did."

"Is his brain still melted?"

"So I'm told," Sybille replied. "I haven't been back to the Low to see for myself, for obvious reasons. Do you remember what happened after we destroyed the Blood King?"

"We...no, you—you became greedy." Juliana's thumb pressed into the loaf as her voice rose in pitch. "You thought that you could have Elis all to yourself and the only way that could happen is if you got me out of the way."

"Wow, that's one way to spin it, I guess."

"It was you!" Juliana shouted. "You sent me to Hell."

"Not exactly."

"So, how did you die?"

"What? I didn't die." She pressed her finger against her wrist, checking for a pulse, just to be sure. "Yep, still alive and kicking in the Now World."

"Are you sure?" Juliana turned her attention to rearranging a tray of petit fours. "Why are you in Hell then? Only dead people go to Hell."

"I'm not dead, and this isn't Hell. It's just an extra special Hell-like area of my mind where you are currently held prisoner—not because I'm afraid you'll reclaim Elis, but because you're a danger to me, and to Elis, and to everyone you encounter."

"Well if that's the case, then why did you eat my bread? How do you know I didn't poison it?"

"How would that work exactly? We're in my mind. You can't hurt me, not as long as you stay in this fake brain kitchen."

"I don't want to stay here. There are things I need to do out in the Now World."

"That's the point, Juliana. I don't want you doing any of those things."

"What if what I want to do aligns with what you want to do?"

"I have a hard time believing that will happen."

"Why?" The spirit's pouty lips and large eyes made her seem genuinely confused. "It happened before, and we accomplished something tremendous together. For the greater good, as I now recall. Why can't that happen again?"

"Teaming up to destroy an immortal monster was a one-off."

"Not in the world you live in." Juliana placed her French pastries on the far end of the counter and then handed the loaf of bread to Sybille. "I've decided you can have this if you want. I'll make another one. And right now, I have to get my batch of cupcakes in the oven or the batter is going to be ruined."

Sybille sliced herself another piece, unable to completely dismiss what Juliana had said. She did have more monsters to fight. It seemed she would never be free of them. Maybe there was a reason she was here in this kitchen with her enemy instead of going on the romantic date Elis had planned for them tonight. Or maybe the effort of helping navigate six people and one lumberjack spirit on a psychic promenade through fae history had been too much. Maybe she was here because it was either this kitchen or death from a brain bleed. If that was the case, she shouldn't be so dismissive.

"What do know about any of it?"

Juliana smirked as she spooned chocolate batter into rainbow colored wax cupcake holders lining a tin. "I heard enough to know you're dealing with fae. Over the many years of my life, I've learned a thing or two about them."

"Enough to admire them or fear them?"

"A bit of both. I heard a voice say they would overrun the world with bloodthirsters." She loaded the oven with her cupcake tin. "You must know me well enough by now to understand I would never want that."

True enough. Juliana hated bloodthirsters, even though she herself had been connected to one once upon a time.

"Dealing with fae is a lot more complicated than my normal gig," Sybille admitted. "What I wouldn't give for a straightforward bloodthirster spirit release job right now."

"See, we do have common ground." Juliana wound a kitchen timer and set it near the oven. "Eighteen to twenty minutes usually does the trick. I set the timer for eighteen and then check them. This oven tends to run hot."

"I think you had another point you wanted to share with me."

"I did?" she glanced up from the stove. "Oh yes. We both enjoy ridding the world of bloodthirsters, and if I'm not mistaken, if we want to stop the fae from taking over, we must also destroy all bloodthirsters."

"Okay, you want to be useful? Tell me how to fix this problem. A friend of mine is at least part Ichor fae. His people came and took him. I don't know where he is other than that he's probably riding unicorns across puffy clouds somewhere."

"I'm making unicorn cupcakes."

"Fabulous. So, what you're saying is, you are still completely worthless to me."

"My worth has nothing to do with you," Juliana said. "Why don't you ask Laurence for help?"

Sybille stood again. "Laurence? How do you know I've been in contact with him?"

"I heard his voice on the radio. At first, I wasn't sure whose it was, but now I am. I do remember things, you know. I just have trouble remembering them all the time."

"He did say he could help me find Devin. But he's been pretty damn vague on the details."

"Devin is fae?" Juliana placed a hand over her heart like she was about to recite The Pledge of Allegiance. "How fascinating! Handsome *and* a magic wielder."

"He didn't know he was a fae. And believe me, he can't even do a card trick let alone bend space and time."

"You seem so sure about things you can't be sure about."

Sybille stepped towards the kitchen door. "I've told you more than I should."

"That door opens to a black chasm. I wouldn't try it if I were you."

"This is your Hell, if that's what you want to call it," Sybille said, turning the knob. "It's not mine." She pushed to door open to reveal a hallway lit by sunlight streaming in from floor to ceiling windows. The hall smelled like freshly ground coffee beans, a sure sign, in Sybille's opinion, that it was the path she should take to wind her way out of her mind and back into the Now World. "Too bad I couldn't stay for those cupcakes."

"You could come back." The earnestness in her voice gave Sybille pause.

"Why would I do that?"

"Like I said, I can help. I can be useful."

"We've been over this. You're stuck for eternity in this room. How could that make you useful?"

"I know things you don't. Plus, I'll have my radio on and I'll be listening closely." She crouched in front of her oven, peering inside at her half-baked goodies. "You never know what I might hear. Things that could be helpful to you, I mean. Although, I'm sure I'll hear other things too. Things that might help your friends, the people you love, or…me. I can't control what the radio plays. Believe me, I've tried."

Sybille cringed at the thought of Juliana overhearing her most intimate conversations. "Remember, Juliana. That's my radio. This is my damn kitchen in my damn head. Those unicorn cupcakes belong to me too. If you want to fuck with me, go for it, but you won't like the consequences."

She stepped through the doorway. A draft from an open window down the hall tickled her bare arms. "Don't try to follow me or I'll let the chasm eat you."

Shutting the door behind her, she proceeded down the hall. The walls morphed with every step taken until it was no longer a dream hallway, but the one leading from the stairs in her house to her bedroom door.

There, an unexpected sentinel stood guard, arms crossed.

"Charlie? Why are you here?"

Charlie uncrossed her arms, but her lips were drawn in a tight line. "You need to find a way out of this."

"That's what I'm doing. I left Juliana and now I'm here."

"No," she spit, her voice shrill. "You need to find a way out."

"I can, Charlie. I will. But you shouldn't be here. This hallway is a bridge between the world we live in and the worlds I've created inside my head to make sense of everything. It's no place for you."

The girl sniffed the air. "I smell something yummy."

Sybille positioned herself in front of Charlie, blocking the hallway leading towards Juliana's kitchen. "No, you do not."

"Something sweet. I love sweet things."

"Charlie, go back wherever you were before you came here. It's not safe."

The girl scowled. "Maybe sometimes I should get to decide what's safe."

"Maybe, but not this time."

Still facing Sybille, Charlie felt for the door's nob and twisted it open. "I'm right there, safe and sound with Elis, see?"

Sybille strained to make out what was happening in the room. Several figures appeared to be lying on the bed, but it was impossible to say who they were.

In this second of distraction, Charlie shoved Sybille over the door's threshold and into her bedroom. The last thing she remembered was the door slamming behind her.

Elis

She woke with a gasp. Elis shuffled so he could free up an arm to calm Sybille while still maintaining his hold on Charlie. "It's okay, Sybille. I'm here. Try not to wake Charlie, she just went back to sleep."

Sybille groaned and then cleared her voice. "How's she doing? Any more fits?"

"No, she's been peaceful. She's been…" He glanced down at the sleeping girl. Strange that this child should elicit such a range of emotions in him. "She's been perfect. What about you?"

"Oh my God, Elis." Sybille wove her fingers through his as he glided his palm over her bare shoulder. "My head feels like I smacked it against a boulder."

"We were all worried about you. Do you remember collapsing right after the Patron arrived? I'm choosing to blame him for your retreat from reality."

"I forgot he was even there."

"Are you all right?" As much as he loved having Charlie with him, he wished she was back in her own bed so that he would be free to turn on his side and pull Sybille close to him. "I thought maybe we should take you to the hospital, but your mother insisted they wouldn't know what they were dealing with."

"It's always a sad state of affairs when my mother's right." She took a deep breath, this one freer and more relaxed than the one she'd woken with. "I feel fine, minus the alcohol-free hangover. I overexerted myself and had to retreat for a bit to recoup. That's all."

"Retreat where?"

"It's a bit hazy, but…I think I was in a kitchen?"

"You mean like the one you said you trapped Juliana in?"

"Damn. No, not *like* that one. *The* one."

"You taxed your brain, you needed a break to heal, and so you ended up vacationing in the same place you trapped Juliana? Sounds like a dream trip. I'm almost afraid to ask, but—"

"Yes, she was there. We had quite the conversation."

His eyes glowed. He'd brought Juliana into Sybille's life. It was his fault Sybille had to act like a prison warden to the demented spirit of his dead wife. "She didn't try to humiliate you or possess you or kill you, or any combination of the two, did she?"

"No, but I think she was about three Swiss cake rolls short of challenging me to a bake-off."

"I used to dream that she dressed up in pearls and baked me cookies."

"Maybe you've got a bit of a hierophant in you because that's what she was doing, Elis. She was baking, not for herself and definitely not for me, but for you. Thinks you'll return home after a long day at the office and she should have a carb-heavy meal ready and waiting. She got very testy with me when I ate some of her bread. And damned if it didn't taste like it came fresh from a bakery."

"That sounds like Dream Juliana, as I recall, but not the Juliana I knew in real life, spirit or bloodthirster. Did she say anything to you aside from giving baking tips?"

"She bragged about her baking. Not exactly free with the tips. Her specialty is cupcakes, by the way, and also yes, but you're not going to like it. She can hear some of the things we say. She has this old radio, and it plays our conversations for her. I'm guessing it works like a spirit box that paranormal researchers use, supposedly letting ghosts make sounds we can decipher. Up until now, I thought those were a scam."

Elis' stomach turned. "Is she listening in right now?"

"There's no way to know."

A hiss escaped him before he could stop it.

"Creepy, right?" Sybille sighed. "She claims she wants to help us with our fae issue."

Elis twisted towards Sybille and leaned in as much as he could without dislodging Charlie. "Juliana, if you can hear me in there," he said, speaking directly to Sybille's forehead. "I'm on to you. You'll say whatever you think will get you out of Sybille's mind prison. You don't have any information we can benefit from."

"I'm not so sure." Sybille bit her lip. "She knows things about fae— possibly things we don't. And she said we should ask Laurence to help us find Devin. There's something to that. She does have a history with him."

Elis groaned. "Don't remind me. Their connection to each other doesn't work in their favor."

"And yet they wanted to banish bloodthirsters, and Laurence knew bloodthirsters were being used as Ossian foot soldiers. His intentions were noble, however horrific they may have been executed."

"Did you have to use the word 'executed'?" Elis wanted to argue, but the more he thought about it, the more he knew it to be true. "You shouldn't visit Juliana's kitchen again."

"I didn't go there voluntarily the first time, but point taken. I need to wrap my head around all of this first. And we need to contact Laurence in the morning to see if he truly can help us find Devin." She gazed at Charlie's sleeping face and tucked a loose strand of the girl's stringy blond hair behind her ear. "The last thing I feel like doing is hanging out with your ex, especially when we have Charlie to worry about."

Her fingers froze on Charlie's cheek.

Elis sensed the tension in her body. "What's wrong?"

"Charlie," she whispered, then she shook the girl and said loudly, "Charlie, wake up!"

Alarmed, Elis propped his charge up, trying to stir life back into her. She remained limp in his arms. "What's wrong with her now? I swear to you, Sybille, she was fine!"

"She was fine, until she figured out how to take a tour of my head." She placed her hands on the sides of Charlie's face. "I remember now. Right before I woke up, Charlie was there."

"Charlie was...in your head? How is that possible?"

"The same way you and fae and magic and the world being taken over by beings from another dimension are all possible—because reality is fucked!"

Elis shook Charlie again, but it was clear the girl wouldn't waken by traditional methods.

"If Charlie is in your head, at least she's safe, right?"

"No, God dammit, she is not safe!" Sybille sat up in the bed and brought Charlie's thin frame towards her. "Not if she's with Juliana. There's so much sugar in that kitchen, all Juliana has to do is feed her cupcakes and she'll want to stay there forever!"

CHAPTER NINE

DEVIN

THE WOOL-COVERED SLAB SCRATCHED HIS BARE TORSO. DEVIN LAY WITH HIS arms relaxed at his side, gazing up at a stained-glass ceiling. He followed the multi-colored beams of light it cast into the space, turning his head to note how they dotted the floor in hexagram shapes of green and red and orange. Gentle lights, not like the blinding flash he'd experienced before passing out. When he'd woken, his first thoughts had been that they must be under some sort of attack, but Froya had assured him that what he saw was a comet passing by without incident. Comets were as common here as high tides were on Earth, seeing as though the Ichor were fond of creating them.

Thunderheart, perched on the back of a nearby chair, bobbed his head in rhythm to a music whose source Devin couldn't determine. A high-pitched reed instrument played discordant notes as a drum beat steadily in the background.

The small room with its high glass ceiling, adjacent to the bleeding tree room, reminded Devin of one of the alcoves at the Catholic church his mom had brought him and Raelyn to on Easter during one of her repentant phases of parenting. Discovering his father hailed from a fairyland shed his mama in new light. He'd thought of her as both victim and perpetrator most of his life, unable to get herself out from under the thumb of her husband and the lowlifes he associated with, but also unable to protect him and his sister from them.

Now that he knew the man he'd thought of as his father was no more than a stand-in, he wondered what had led his mother down the path that had brought him into existence. He couldn't blame her for cheating on her husband, given his inclination to run off on her whenever he grew bored, but he could damn well blame her for staying. Then again, who knew what the circumstances of his conception had been. Most likely, she'd thought Warin just a man who could provide a bit of fun in her unhappy existence. He'd given her that and moved on.

Something stuck in his mind, though. Warin knew he'd fathered a child. That must be the case, or he wouldn't have returned to give Devin the mind block preventing him and the world from discovering his identity. Maybe it was Warin's fae magic, still largely a mystery to Devin, that had made him aware. Or maybe his relationship with Devin's mama was more than a one-night stand.

Devin lay on his slab as the light from the day shifted, the colors in the room shifting with it. There was little point to dwelling on the motivations of his parents nearly three decades ago. He hadn't spoken to his mother in years, and even if he did want to reach out to her, he no longer lived in her universe. As for his father, Froya made it clear that there'd be no contact with him.

Sometimes the past was best left there.

A tiny bell rang next to the room's entryway. He barely heard it over the music, but a second later, Froya's lavender eyes peered down at him. "Have you been meditating on the sunlight like I asked you to?"

"There's not much else to do."

Thunderheart squawked and moved towards Froya so she could scratch his head. "I'm not sure why you insist on keeping this bird in here with you. He belongs outside where he can come and go as he pleases."

"He can leave whenever he chooses. I'll open the door for him. But he wants to stay with me, and I want him to stay with me so that's what we're doing. I've got pretty much zero control here, Froya. At least give me that."

"Did I deny you him? I'm the reason you have him at all. Remember that. I'm not cruel, just driven."

"You're crafty is what you are."

She cocked her head to the side, considering his label. "That sounds better to me. Crafty is creative. The Ichor fae are creatives. We have no real motives beyond being free to express ourselves."

Devin sat up and propped himself against the wall. "You keep telling yourself that."

Froya opened her mouth to say more but stopped when Ayan entered the room carrying a tray containing several gold vials. "Are you ready?"

Devin eyed the vials. "That depends on what's in those."

Ayan placed the tray on a table and then took a needle out of her breast pocket. "Nothing is in them and that's why I'm here. I need a sample of your blood."

"Are you, like, a nurse or a doctor or something?"

"Those are human professions. Do I look human to you?"

"I'm just staring at that needle and wondering if you're qualified to draw blood."

"Would you rather I used one of my knives to collect it instead?"

Froya placed a hand on Devin's shoulder. "Relax. The Ichor are of the blood. We frequently take our own to use in rituals. Ayan knows what she's doing."

"What kind of rituals require your own blood?"

"The kind you'll learn about eventually," Froya told him, "if you show aptitude."

"If, yes. If, if, if." Ayan ran her hand over his upper arm and then jabbed him.

He yelped. "You could have warned me."

"A needle in my hand wasn't warning enough?"

All three watched as blood entered the needle and ran through a short tube leading into one of the vials. When she'd collected what she needed, Ayan removed the needle and handed Devin a swab of cloth to hold against his arm.

"We'll give this to our alchemists, and they'll look for clues."

"Clues on how I make bloodthirsters unkillable?" He laughed. "You could ask me, you know. I do have some pieces to the puzzle."

"Froya told me you're too stupid to know why." Ayan picked up her tray.

Behind her, Froya shrugged unapologetically. "I questioned you about it in several loops back at the ranch and all you'd say is, and I quote, 'When you got it, you got it.'"

"I don't remember saying that."

"Well, you did."

"I don't know how you expected me to give you a fully detailed account of anything when you messed with my memories."

"I expected you to extract the memories I needed when I commanded you to."

"Maybe, Froya, I don't respond well to your commands. Or are we back to you being my goddamn jailor again."

"Stop it, both of you." Ayan raised both her palms, one towards Froya and one towards Devin. Both froze.

Devin narrowed his eyes, which was about all he could do at this point. "I hate it when you use your freeze hands on me."

"I'll let you go if you stop bickering with Froya and tell me what I need to know. Remember, I'm your grandmother and I can still sentence you to any number of unpleasantries if you get on my nerves. And Froya, stop provoking him. You warned me against it, which made me think you knew better."

"It's fun, though."

"Is it really fun when it presents such little challenge?"

Devin sighed. "I have information for you. Can we just get on with it?"

Ayan lowered her palms and Devin wiggled his fingers.

"Okay, so you want to know how I'm capable of creating immortal monsters. It's not like I have it all figured out, but you're right that it's got to do with my blood."

"Yes, that's why we're testing it. I thought you had more information."

"Hold on, I'm getting there. There's this drug called Crave. Popular with humans who donate to bloodthirsters. It gets them high and makes it so they don't care that they're food for the undead."

"Are you saying you take this drug?"

"I've taken it before, yeah. I'm not an addict, but I've used it, including both times I killed and resurrected bloodthirsters."

Ayan and Froya exchanged a look.

"So, you believe Crave, when combined with your blood, is what made this magic?"

"First, it's not magic, and second no."

"No? Why would you mention it then?"

"It's part of the equation, just not all of it. There's this other drug, called Strike."

Ayan slammed her fist into the edge of the slab. Devin's knees shot out like when a doctor struck them with a mallet to check reflexes. "Now you're making things up. It was this drug or that drug. You want to make us think it's drugs, not you, and if so, then we'll give you the freedom you seek. It won't happen."

"Thanks for your honesty, but I'm being honest too. I honestly think you're both nuts. And also, I never said I wasn't part of the equation. As much as I don't want to be, I am the reason there are two bloodthirsters who've been burned and poisoned and staked and who still aren't dead. If you'd just listen to me, you'd realize I'm not trying to play you."

Froya slid herself between Ayan and Devin. "I don't believe you're deceiving us. I'm uncertain how clear you are about yourself, though. Tell me what you know about Crave and Strike."

"All I know about Crave is that one of the ingredients is derived from bloodthirster bone marrow."

Ayan bobbed her head. "Fascinating and repugnant. But that's information we already have. What else?"

"How do you...?" He paused. "Never mind. Look, all I can tell you is that those two drugs coursing through my blood at the same time is the ticket to monster immortality. If you want to know anything more, then you should take that up with the man who made them."

"Are you saying you know who he is?" Ayan asked.

"Sure. He's a psychic witch scientist named Peter Esmond. I work for him. I could go talk to him if you want."

"That won't be necessary." Ayan turned to Froya. They exchanged a knowing glance that made Devin's pulse quicken. Once again, they knew things and they weren't telling him.

"We're aware of these drugs but not how Peter Esmond used them to make you an affliction on our people," Froya said. "Thankfully, we have an informer positioned closely to the Esmond family. He'll get this information from your witch scientist."

"I might be an affliction—thanks for that charming compliment—but I'm also the best person to talk to Peter. He trusts me." He paused as the rest of Froya's words sunk in. "Wait, who the fuck do you have informing on the Esmonds?"

"We have a network of them, one stationed with most of the hierophant families working to destroy the Ossian' soldiers. They make sure the families can operate by funneling money to them. And because they're human, we have broken no treaties."

"Holy fucking shit." Devin flopped against the wall. "That little Shakespeare-talking bastard works for you?"

Juliana

Juliana held her breath. Not knowing how this child would react made her dig her fingernails into her clenched fists. Everything pivoted around this moment, as though her whole life, and after life, had led here. An unfavorable outcome would be her undoing.

The young girl sat at the table, her eyes fixed on the plate Juliana placed in front of her. A plate filled with rainbow sugar goodness. "A unicorn? I love unicorns!"

Juliana remembered to breathe. "Yes, you do. You're wearing unicorn pajamas. But how does it taste?"

She pressed her lips together as her visitor unpeeled the wax wrapper and brought the cupcake to her mouth. "Mmmm!" White and gold frosting dotted the tip of her nose. "Yummy! It's so good!"

"Really?" She released the tension in her hands, her shoulders, her neck. "You're not just saying that to make me happy?"

"Why would I want to make you happy?" She took another bite. "I know who you are. I remember you."

"You do?" Juliana wracked her mind, trying to place this little girl within her jumbled memories. Too old to be one of Zareen's offspring...but she did look familiar. Maybe she was a figment of Sybille's imagination who had managed to wander away from another part of the psychic's consciousness. "Did Sybille make you up?"

The child put down her cupcake. "Excuse me? No, Sybille did not make me up. My name is Charlie and I'm real. I can't believe you don't remember me after you acted inappropriately with my uncle."

"Your uncle?"

"At the cabin!" Charlie scrunched her face. "I knew you were evil, but I didn't think you were stupid."

Recollection flooded back to her. "Yes, yes, you were at the cabin. That attractive, clueless man is your uncle." That attractive clueless *fae* man. "Devin, right?"

"I think that was the worst part, even worse than when you tried to kill Sybille and Elis and everyone. You sexually assaulted Uncle Devin."

"He didn't know I was there."

"Is that supposed to make it better? If he didn't know you were there, he couldn't consent, now could he?" She picked up what remained of the cupcake and shoved it in her mouth. "I'll have another, please."

Juliana couldn't suppress her smile. Charlie liked her baking. She placed the eleven remaining cupcakes onto a serving platter and set it down within arm's reach of the girl. "Have as many as you like. The cake isn't too dry, is it?"

"Maybe a little."

Juliana's smile fell. Charlie laughed. "Nah, I'm just playing. You should see your face right now. Why do you care so much if I like these?"

"I haven't the faintest clue, but I really do want you to."

"Relax, evil cupcake queen. They're way better than anything my mom's chef ever made for me."

Juliana buzzed with happiness again, but something nagged at her at the same time. This girl was Devin's niece, and if she recalled correctly, Raelyn was the common denominator. Such a strange, mixed up family. "Charlie, have you been to the Ichor fae realm?"

"The what?"

There was a limit to what this girl understood, then. Possibly, she hadn't a clue what she was. She came across as confident and all knowing, but adults probably withheld many things from her. Things she deserved to know. Adults were so overprotective these days. When Juliana was a child, she'd been spared nothing. By the time she was Charlie's age, she'd helped birth her mother's stillborn baby and been lashed by her father for serving him lukewarm porridge.

"A fairyland. Have you ever been to a fairyland?"

The girl's eyes grew huge. "Those are real?"

"Believe it or not."

"I've never been anywhere other than the Low and Sybille's neighborhood. What kind of fairy did you say again?"

"Ichor."

"Ichor." She drew out the word like she was slowly pouring it from a bottle. "That sounds sort of familiar."

"Familiar is correct. Your uncle is an Ichor fae."

"Right, that's it. I knew that already. All the adults talk about that. I just didn't know a fae was the same thing as a fairy."

"One and the same."

"I know what you're thinking. If Uncle Devin is an Ichor fae," she said, "then I must be too. You're wrong."

"But you could see me back at the cabin. Normal humans can't see spirits."

"Sybille's a normal human."

"She isn't. She's a hierophant. A psychic with a passible amount of skill."

"Maybe I'm a psychic too, like my grandfather."

"Your grandfather? Who is he?"

"Laurence. You know him, don't you? Elis said you used to work with him."

Laurence. Elis. The room grew hot. Cheeks flushed, Juliana pushed her sleeves up. Those two, together again. What a day of strange revelations it was turning out to be.

"Laurence Torshavn is your grandfather. You're sure about that? He's your blood relation?"

"My dad's dad. Why do you say it like that? You're so weird."

Juliana gazed at the girl, trying to muster up the disgust she knew was her due. "Silly child, don't you know what that makes you?"

"A psychic, like I said."

"No. You have the bones of the Ossian fae in you."

"Excuse me?" She wiggled her arms around. "I don't think so, see? They're just normal bones. Except for spending most of my life in the Low, I'm normal." Charlie looked down when she spoke the last few words, like she was having a hard time believing herself.

Juliana sniffed at the girl's hair trying to make out the repugnant, slightly sour smell of the Ossian, but there were only the sweet scents of vanilla and caramel surrounding her like a halo. "You will never be normal. My God, Sybille is stupid to have brought you into her own home."

Charlie scooted her chair back. Face red, she seemed ready to burst into tears. "She's not stupid. I used to think so, but she's not. She's trying to help me."

"She can't help you! No one can."

Charlie burst up from the table. "That's not true!" She picked up a cupcake and hurled it at Juliana, who screamed as unicorn horn frosting splattered onto her Cupcake Queen apron.

"Your grandfather told me about the Ossian. He knew what they wanted to do, and he knew how they wanted to do it."

"I don't know anything about that!" Charlie aimed another cupcake at her.

"Don't you dare! Think of all that sugar you'll be wasting!"

The girl froze, uncertainty and fear clouding her face. Unable to stop the tears from falling, she let out a pitiful cry.

Another memory surfaced: Zareen with her children and all the care she'd taken to keep her brood safe. She shuddered to think at the careless way Charlie had been handled all her life. There'd been no Zareen to shield her from harm or even tell her what she was so she could be prepared for what was to come. Sybille was no mother either. The hierophant was failing this child, and now the child had come to Juliana for help.

She weighed back and forth, trying to determine what was worse: Charlie as an Ossian weapon who needed to be destroyed or Charlie as a defenseless child who needed protection.

"Sit back down and eat your cupcake, Charlie. I'm sorry for my behavior."

Charlie blinked away tears, then did as she'd been told. She sniffled as she chewed.

"The greatest gift I can give you today isn't a dozen cupcakes. It's the truth."

The girl groaned. "Adults never want to tell me the truth."

"This adult does. I promise not to hide anything from you." She reached out her hand and placed it over Charlie's, expecting the jolt of disgust touching an Ossian spawn would surely cause. It failed to materialize. "You must promise to do the same. Be honest with me, always. Will you do that?"

The girl swallowed the last bit of her cupcake and nodded.

"Okay, then. Let's begin. You have three options: find a way to change the core of who you are, or be used to destroy the universe."

"What's the third option?"

"If you can't do the first and don't want to do the second, then there's only one thing left to do."

Charlie looked down again. "I know already. You don't have to say it. I have to die."

CHAPTER TEN

ELIS

Never in all his hundreds of years did Elis think he'd be spending a Saturday morning adding multi-colored sprinkles to a pan of frosted double fudge brownies. Margot stopped to inspect his work on the way over to remove a batch of butter pecan tartlets from the oven. "More."

"Seriously? I can barely see the frosting through the rainbow. Did Sybille really agree to this plan? She tries to provide healthy food for Charlie. This is enough processed sugar to send the poor lass into a coma."

"What we're hoping for is that it's enough to send her out of a coma, dear heart."

He knew that. Margot's idea was to fight fire with fire. Or, in this case, to fight sugar with sugar. Juliana's kitchen may not seem so tempting if Margot and Sybille's kitchen equaled hers. Not to mention, their baked goods were actual Now World treats, not fake dream goodies that only seemed to smell and taste like the real deal.

He emptied the rest of the contents of the sprinkle container. "Should I take these up?"

Margot slid her tartlets onto a tray. "Sure. Grab that knife and serving spatula too. I'll be right up."

Elis did as she instructed, then exited the kitchen, wandering through the dining room and into the living room. There Nate sat opposite Bore on the couch, absorbed in his beloved soap opera. Propping his elbow up on the arm of the couch, Bore leaned his face against it, sighing deeply. "Elis! Pray thee, wherever art thy remote control? I shall endeavor to rid thine house of this dreadful show with the same vehemence Sybille employs to rid the world of monsters."

Fuck, he hated this guy, which was why it had given him such a petty thrill when he'd hidden the remote in the back of a kitchen cabinet. "Sorry, I haven't. Besides, that's Nate's favorite show you just insulted."

"Tell him to go away, Elis." Nate tried to slam his fists into Bore's knee, but it did no good.

"Nate says to tell you if you watch every episode of this marathon with him, you'll finally grasp why he loves it so much."

Bore stared at the empty chair situated diagonally from him. "Should I have offended thee, I beg forgiveness."

"He doesn't even know I'm sitting on the opposite side of him, does he?"

Elis proceeded towards the stairs. "Sybille gave me a ten-minute warning about eight minutes ago, so if you insist on joining us, you should forget what's on the TV and head up to Charlie's room. Bore, check with Margot first in case she needs help carrying something."

"Spell books? Crystals?"

"Tartlets and gummy worms."

Upstairs, he turned into the first room on his right, a onetime overflow library for Peter's vast collection, now converted into Charlie's bedroom. Sybille and Peter sat on the far side of the bed, Sybille with her eyes closed, hands clasped together on her lap, and Peter mumbling something low under his breath. Charlie lay in the bed, one of Margot's patchwork quilts pulled up to her chin. And all around, on the bedside tables, on TV trays and the top of a dresser, desserts had been arranged with such quantity and variety, Charlie's room had become a pastry factory. Gooey sticky buns dripped icing down the sides of their pan. Cookies stacked a dozen high on the balcony of Charlie's doll house threatened to topple over.

Elis set his brownie tray at the foot of Charlie's bed. Even his refined and highly subjective bloodthirster taste buds were overwhelmed as he imagined inhaling the confectioner's sugar floating around the room like dust particles.

"It smells like the village baker's in here."

Sybille opened her eyes, sniffed the air, and sighed. "If we all live through this, our blood sugar levels are going to be off kilter for days. What was my mother thinking? One child can't eat all this!"

"I was thinking I was being useful, but if you disagree, I can always leave and let you handle things on your own." Margot's mother entered and sat her tartlet platter down next to the brownies.

Sybille pressed her fingers into her temples. The bickering between her and her mother always left Margot defensive and Sybille with a pounding headache, yet neither woman seemed willing to break the habit. It made Elis almost grateful that everyone in his family had been dead since the early eighteenth century.

"I don't want you to leave, Mother. But seriously, look at what you've done here. It's overkill." She picked up a tartlet. "Did you use an egg glaze?"

"Of course, I did. Look, Sybie, all this baking is not overkill. Not if it helps bring her back."

Sybille's face softened. "I know what you're saying, and I appreciate it. The thing that gets me is that I feel like you're undermining my authority when it comes to Charlie. We need her healthy if she's to fight off the Low, and if I can't resist these treats, how can we expect her to?"

Bore and Nate entered the room, the former carrying two large canning jars, one filled with sour candies, the other filled with the much-coveted gummy worms.

Elis gave Sybille a look and made a cutting motion at his neck. There was no need to squabble in the Patron's presence. Sybille knew the routine. She narrowed her eyes but then plastered on a smile. "Nate, Bore, so glad you could join us. My mother has prepared a feast that is sure to help us retrieve Charlie from where she's wandered."

"It is?" Margot raised her penciled-on eyebrows. "But you were just saying the hours I toiled for Charlie's sake translated into me undermining you."

"You must have misunderstood."

"No, you said the exact phrase 'you're undermining my authority.' I heard it." She turned to her audience. "Did everyone else hear it?"

"Thank you for all your efforts, Mother." Sybille cautioned Margot with a stern look. "As you can see, Patron, we are still a well-oiled team, despite our present difficulties."

"In my heart, I knowest it to be true." Bore took the seat Margot offered him. "Do those brownies have nuts in them? My airway closeth up should I consume walnuts or pecans."

"Nut free, dear. I'll cut you a piece, but first, we really must get started. Would you mind passing these plates around. If anyone wants a nibble during the act, feel free to indulge yourself. We must all keep our strength up!"

"About that," Sybille said. "Charlie and Juliana are both kicking it together in my mind. Can we revisit my plan to go in commando and rescue Charlie? One psychic, one trance. Over and done with. Is any of this really necessary?"

"Yes!" Elis answered. "Because it's safer for you, right Peter?"

"Correct." Peter laid one of his fresh juniper bundles across Charlie's chest then reached across, scooped up one of Margot's tartlets, and placed it on the plate Bore had passed to him. "If you enter Juliana's prison and try to take Charlie by force, there will be a confrontation."

"It doesn't matter," Sybille said. "I have complete control over the kitchen and Juliana."

"Charlie's presence there may change the equation. You didn't invite her into your head, yet she's there anyway. How did that happen?" He pushed his glasses up on his nose and then patted his niece's hand. "If Charlie resists and you have to fight her, this may give Juliana enough of a chance to escape, or worse, take over your body."

Elis sat down in the chair across from her, his body tense with a fear rare to him. "I can't see that happen again, Sybille. Let's just play it safe for once. As safe as communicating psychically with a demonic spirit and a part-fae child with evil energy germinating within her can be."

"That's why my plan is ideal." Margot sliced a sizeable brownie and extracted it from its pan. "Here you are, Bore, dear. Let me know if it needs more sprinkles."

"It looketh like sheer perfection." Bore held an empty plate under Margot's spatula and she tipped the brownie off onto it.

"Margot is right," Peter said. "Bore, let me explain. Our plan will allow Sybille to perform her usual task, reaching out into the either in search of spirits. We believe the channel to Juliana's kitchen was opened to the outside world when Sybille exerted herself on a psychic plane during our exploration of the fae timeline. So the idea is to replicate that sort of mental exercise. This will hopefully allow us to talk to Juliana and Charlie over the kitchen's radio."

Bore wheezed. "A glimpse into Lady Sybille's mind."

"Yes, Bore," Sybille cooed. "You get to witness quite a supernatural phenomenon."

"I shall endeavor to lock this moment into the sacred chamber of my memories."

"Bore called my show the pinnacle of idiocy." Nate floated up behind Bore's chair and strangled him with his ghostly hands. Ignorant of his attempted murder, Bore continue to gaze upon Sybille with adoration. Sybille snickered.

"Okay!" Margot clapped her hands. "It's time to begin."

Something niggled at Elis' brain. "And we've kept Laurence away because…"

"Because he would want Sybille to risk herself to save his granddaughter," Margot reminded him. "As fond as I am of Charlie, I have my own daughter to think of."

This answer should have pacified Elis, but instead he found his thoughts wandering down the road to an ethical conundrum. Elis might not care for the man, but shouldn't Laurence be informed that his kin was stuck in a mind prison? He leaned his chair back until his head touched the wall behind him. They'd originally planned on contacting Laurence, conferencing with him all day over Charlie's case. But that was before Charlie had wandered into Sybille's mind. Now they'd made excuses to keep Laurence away until Charlie was brought back. The whole situation sucked. First Sybille, now Charlie. And Charlie's only relatively sane family member was being kept out of the loop. Even if they did get the girl back safely, she was hardly safe.

"I have to think of both of them." Everyone turned to him and he realized he'd said what he'd been thinking out loud. "Well, don't I? Don't we all?"

Everyone gazed at him with pitiful expressions but not Sybille. Sybille smiled.

"Sybille, if this fails and Charlie's still stuck…forget what I said before. Do what you have to do."

"That was my plan all along. I don't need your permission." She reached her hand across Charlie and Elis did the same. Their palms met. Warmth spread through him. "But I'm glad I have your support."

"You don't have mine," Peter warned her.

"Duly noted."

"Oh, for heaven's sake," Margot cried, "let's do this, people!"

Nate hovered over to the head of Charlie's bed. "So, what are we going to do when you get her back? What if being in there with Juliana makes her worse? What if she comes back and has a Low fit right away and it's really awful and she tries to kill you all?"

Peter motioned for everyone with physical hands to join them together. "That, Nate, is why we have plans for you."

"Me? What plans? What can I do?"

"More than you think, my boy." Peter said. "I have no doubt you'll be instrumental in saving Charlie at some point. But for now, sit tight. You are an observer today."

"Wait, I'm a spirit. And I've been inside Sybille before."

Elis nearly choked. "Could you please rephrase that?"

"Why don't you send me into Sybille's mind so I can bring Charlie back?" Nate asked.

"It's nice of you to offer, but I'd prefer to never ever repeat that experience, thanks." Sybille gave him a stern look, her nose pinched and her eyes nearly as piercing as a bloodthirster's. "Let's stick with the elders' plan."

Nate receded into the room's shadows. The air grew still. Elis slowed his breath, trying to match Sybille's. He held Margot's hand in his right and slid his left around Charlie's cold fingers. He gave them a squeeze, hoping for a response. None came.

Sybille's eyelids fluttered as though a baby bird was trying to take flight from underneath them. When she opened her eyes, he was sure they'd have changed colors or taken on some sort of radiance the way his did from time to time, but they were the same warm hazel he remembered from the day she'd been his star volunteer at the county fair.

Now, instead of faking hypnotism, Sybille truly existed in a state of altered consciousness. Margot narrated what was happening to Bore. "She's reaching out into the ether, just as she does when she fishes for the spirits of bloodthirsters. She won't search too hard for one today, of course, as we don't have time for a new client. However, the act is the same."

Nate tottered around the room's periphery. "Shouldn't we all be quiet so she can concentrate?"

"She doesn't need perfect silence, dear, especially now that she's deep into the ether."

"I'm both here and not here." Sybille spoke like a hostage negotiator trying to rationalize with a bank robber. "It doesn't matter if you make noise."

"Besides," Peter added, "the point of this exercise is for Charlie to hear us. If we say nothing, she'll hear nothing."

Elis leaned forward. "Charlie, we miss you. I know Juliana baked you a lot of treats, but Margot did the same. We have all sorts of goodies waiting for you. And she bought gummy candy for you too. You can eat as much as you want if you come back to us. You're making my old bloodthirster heart break, Dorothy Gale. Come back from Oz." He leaned back again. Charlie remained unchanged. "I don't think it's working. Maybe she can't hear us."

Sybille stood with such force that her chair toppled over behind her. When she spoke, her voice was familiar to him, but it was not her own.

"I can hear you just fine, *husband*."

CHAPTER ELEVEN

DEVIN

Sitting with his back pressed against the blood tree, Devin argued for the millionth time why they should send him to the Now World realm, AKA Earth, to get the information they sought from Peter. "Because, Froya, the Esmond's Patron is dumb as bolts."

"Is he?" Froya plopped herself down next to him and lowered her head into his lap so she was turned to look up at the tree's limbs, stretching and joining with the room's sky-pocked ceiling. "I can't tell any difference between you Earth creatures."

"Bullshit! What about the way he talks?"

"All Patrons are trained to speak that way."

"Why? They sound like idiots."

"That's the point. If they sound like idiots, hierophants will feel they have the upper hand. They won't be intimidated by the Patrons, nor suspect any ulterior motives."

"Believe me, it doesn't take a fake accent for the Esmonds to have the upper hand with that clown."

"Maybe so. But I will still require him to get the information from Peter. He's capable of that. He's the reason I found you, by the way."

"Come again?"

"Early in the morning on the day I rescued you from that awful place, he contacted me to let me know he was on his way to, and I quote, 'watch my lady fair slay the world's deadliest dragon.' After he explained what that meant, I asked him how the Blood King had been able to escape death not once but countless times. He wasn't certain how it happened; he'd been told a man named Devin Vargas was behind it."

"But how did that prove I was a fae?"

"I did some digging, as did Ayan and the rest of the coterie. It didn't take long to track down enough of your history to realize you were Warin's son. We'd wondered about you for a long time. Most people assumed you'd died as a baby, that maybe Warin saw how horrific a half-human child was and decided to end you."

"You people have a strange moral logic."

"Well, he didn't kill you, did he? He protected you instead. And he's never given you up."

Froya sprang up and away from him.

"Come on, it's training time." She motioned for him to follow her. They moved along the tree's central vein, leading them to the eastern balcony, where his familiar was currently perched.

Devin took a moment to pat Thunderheart on his head. The bird cooed and leaned into his palm. "Sit tight. Daddy's going to learn some magic!"

He sat cross-legged on a circular cushion, with Froya facing him.

"You've had the experience of forming your first world."

"Can we not do that again right now? That was like being stuck in a Salvador Dali painting. You know, the one with the melting clocks?"

"We will be shifting worlds today rather than creating them. That is a fundamental power of Ichor fae, along with paralysis."

"I was thinking we should start with that one."

"Not until I can trust you not to use it on me."

"You use it on me. It's only fair."

"Fair is a concept I only encountered when I first visited your Now World. You are only an Earthblood. We need to be cautious."

She shifted her cushion closer until their knees touched. Devin glanced past her for a moment, taking in the suns as they trailed slowly towards the sea to the west. Or what Devin thought of as west, at least. They looked as though they might collide and explode at any moment. "A double sun. Like I'm on Tatooine or something."

"Focus!"

He did as he was told, his gaze resting on Froya's lavender eyes instead of the suns.

"As an exercise, we will move through several worlds together. These are worlds created and well established by our people and they're relatively safe."

"Relatively?"

"Then, if I feel you're ready, I'll send you on your own to a world. You'll have a certain amount of time to explore there before I call you back."

"Can that world be Earth?"

"Not yet. It's not safe."

"I get that. But at least let me send a message to my friends. I want them to know I survived execution. Please, Froya, it's..." There had to be a way for him to convince her. "It's hard for me to concentrate on what the Ichor Coterie wants from me, and all this training, and you too, knowing there are people worried about me. All I need is a few minutes. That's it."

Froya looked up towards the heavens the way she did when she seemed exasperated with him. Thunderheart squawked in the background.

"I'll think about it."

"That's all I ask!"

"No, you ask for more than thoughts. But that's all you'll get for now. Let's see how well you do with world jumping first, and then I'll decide. You know what to do. Lift your right hand. Hold my left with yours, twist the fingers on your right. Ready and go!"

The balcony and the twin suns disappeared. Instead, they sat on one large rock in the middle of a field. Yellow and purple flowers dotted the landscape as far as he could see. Only one sun, obscured by a dark cloud, hung in the sky. He squinted at the horizon. "You don't waste time, do you?"

"Neither do you," Froya said. "You were upset by my indecision, yet when I asked you to act, you did. We journeyed together, with me directing the course." A strong breeze blew her short hair from where it had been tucked behind her ear. She let go of Devin's hand to replace the strand, then grabbed him again.

Devin shivered. The air smelled heady, like the flowers knew a storm was approaching and were releasing every bit of aroma they had at their disposal before a deluge ruined them. "It feels like it's about to rain buckets."

"We can leave. But this time it's your turn to direct us."

"Okay, but how? Last time I did, I created that little broken world."

"Go to a world you're familiar with. The capital world or the ranch world. Your choice."

"I'd like to see the ranch again." He frowned. The fact that he had a sentimental attachment to his own prison made him want to hang his head in shame, yet the idea of returning there enticed him. Those were simple days, before he'd discovered the truth. Ignorance had been bliss. "Do you think the farmhouse will be rebuilt if I imagine it to be?"

"That's up to you. Think of it, but not too hard. World jumping is either easy or it's impossible. If you make it too complicated, it won't happen."

They raised their hands. *Farmhouse, prairie, Froya.* They ended up on the bed in the farmhouse's loft. Devin twisted around, his weight on the mattress sending Froya's body towards his. He slid an arm around her belly. "Well now, this is convenient."

Laughing, Froya turned herself to face him. "We don't have time for that, but I will say you're not bad at this for an Earthblood."

"So maybe my teacher can give me a reward?" He ran his hand up her arm and around the back of her neck, feeling her glossy hair between his fingers. He grasped her head and lifted her face to his.

She let him kiss her long enough to make him want to forget about their lesson. He flattened himself against her, toying with the buttons on her shirt. She pulled back, a dangerously flirtatious smile playing on her lips. "You're earning a top of the alphabet grade so far."

"You mean an A?"

"Yes, that's what I said. Top of the alphabet. Now, take us back to the capital."

He inched closer to her again. Simple. Things could be simple here. Nothing else needed to exist. "But I thought we could—"

"Quickly!" Trying to appear unmoved by his advances, she dropped her smile. "Do it and don't think about it."

"I thought I had to think about it, or it wouldn't work."

She held up her hand. "Be smarter than that."

He mimicked her movement, twisted his fingers, and they were back on the balcony, one of the twin suns now half swallowed by the ocean, the other no longer visible at all. "You're right. It's easier to do it like you're playing an instrument. If you think too much about where your fingers go, you fumble. But once you learn the pattern, it becomes muscle memory."

"Muscle memory. Yes, that's right. Only your brain is the muscle."

Froya hopped off her cushion and tossed it so it lay next to his. She sat down and leaned into him, her arm draped across his legs. They watched the second sun go down and the lights of the city twinkle on. Things could be simple here too, only this was a place of knowledge and here, Devin couldn't block out his darkest thoughts.

A silhouette in the sky wove its way towards the balcony. Thunderheart. He landed on the ledge nearest them, a fish dangling from his beak.

"He's been off hunting while we were gone," Froya said.

They sat in silence once more while Thunderheart devoured his dinner. As the fish disappeared down the bird's gullet, so did Devin's hope that he might get to go home tonight. Training appeared to be over.

"You really want to see your Earth friends?"

He sat up straighter. "It would be good to...close a chapter on things, and I can't do that if I keep thinking about how they must be wondering about me. I have a niece, you know."

"Yes, the cursed child. Unfortunate."

"Unfortunate that she's cursed or that she's my niece?"

Froya slid away so she could face him. "I am going to send you where you need to go."

"Really? Are you shitting me?"

"That's disgusting. Why would I do that?"

"Just...say you mean it. You've undone my shackles and you're sending me home."

Froya sighed. "You are home, Devin. Raise your hand. Don't think."

She twisted her fingers and a new world opened to him.

He blinked as he orientated himself. This wasn't the Esmond's house. For a moment, he wondered if he'd time traveled to the mid-twentieth century. He stood in a spacious kitchen, but it was sorely dated, from its gaudy pink wallpaper to the toaster and refrigerator. Country music twanged from an old radio with wood paneling and large knobs on its front. A woman with long, dark hair stood only a few feet away, her back turned to him as she stirred something in a pot over a burner. "Sybille?"

The woman turned and his heart fell. He didn't know who she was, but she wasn't Sybille.

She sneered in a way that he suspected was meant as a smile. "Well, this is quite unexpected. Welcome to Hell, Devin."

Devin

Froya had a sick sense of humor, sending him to this odd little world. Probably some six-year-old Ichor child had made it and she thought it would be funny to stick Devin there to see how he'd fare. The answer was "not well," judging by the dejection building up in him like water in a bathtub.

"How do you know my name?"

"We've met." She pointed to a spot behind Devin. "Aren't you going to say hi?"

He spun around. His niece sat at a round kitchen table covered with a red and white checkered oil cloth. "Charlie?"

The little girl rushed from her chair over to him, throwing her arms around his neck. He picked her up and swung her around. "Are you okay? I've been so worried about you."

"She's fine as long as she's here with me. Outside in the Now World, well, that's another story."

He set Charlie down and placed a protective arm around her shoulder. "Who are you and why am I supposed to know you?"

"I'm offended that you don't remember me."

"He couldn't see you," Charlie explained to the woman. "Which is why you took advantage of him and I almost puked."

"Oh, that's right." The woman ran her tongue over the front of her teeth. "What good fortune that we should meet in a place where the advantage no longer has to be one-sided."

"Wait...are you Juliana?" He shoved Charlie behind him. "Stay back, Charlie, this woman is dangerous."

"She is, but not in here." Charlie pushed Devin's hand away from her and stepped forward.

"Where's here? Seriously, where the fuck—pardon my French, Charlie —where the hell are we? And what's through that door?" He marched over to it. "Is this our exit?"

Opening it, he was met with a dead space devoid of light and warmth. Hand shaking, he closed the door again. "Shit."

Juliana stepped over, carrying a tray of heart-shaped sugar cookies with pink icing. "We're in Sybille's head where she's unjustly imprisoned me now and forever more. Would you like a cookie?"

She held the tray out in front of him.

"No way!" He pushed it back. "I don't want anything that's come from you."

"You shouldn't say that, Uncle Devin. Just because she's evil doesn't mean she can't bake."

"Look, I don't want cookies, or whatever it is you have in the oven right now that smells like heaven."

"It's a three-berry pie."

"Are you serious? That's my favorite." His mouth watered. "Never mind, I don't want it. What I want is to know why you're here, Charlie."

She looked down at her feet. "I'm kinda sick. It's getting worse."

"Jesus, I'm sorry." He moved in towards her and hugged her again. "What does that have to do with you being here, though?"

"I was with Elis and Sybille. She was here in the kitchen too."

"Wait, Elis and Sybille were here?"

"No, just Sybille. But I was in her bedroom when she was stuck in here. And Elis was with her, you know, her body, trying to figure out what to do. I fell asleep and then I was here. I guess Sybille woke up."

He couldn't believe it. Had he made it here only a little sooner, he could have seen her, talked to her, touched her. Maybe she'd have been so happy to see him, she would have kissed him. He pushed that thought aside. "Are you going to wake up soon too, Charlie? Can you give a message to Sybille for me?"

"She needs to stay here." Juliana slid the cookies onto a plate and then held up her spatula like it was a weapon and she was ready to strike. "She runs a high risk of dying out there."

"Don't we all?" Devin stared down at Charlie's heart shaped face. "I want you safe, but Charlie, this place isn't for you. It's Juliana's Hell, not yours."

"But there are cupcakes here."

"Have Sybille make you cupcakes."

"She makes me eat salad."

"Okay, well that's still no reason to stay in this room forever. Your body will be like it's in a coma. Do you want Sybille and Margot to worry about you?"

"No." She frowned. "Or Elis. Elis worries about me the most. He reads me stories."

"He does?" Jealousy bubbled up. His face grew hot. First that damned bloodthirster successfully wooed Sybille, and now his own niece seemed to favor him. "Well, see, there you go. If you stay here, you won't see him again."

"But I don't have Low fits here."

"You don't have what?"

Juliana tapped her spatula against the counter. "The girl told you she's sick. Maybe you should have listened to her."

"No one ever listens to me."

He stifled a protest as the music from Juliana's radio crackled like they'd lost reception and then, without anyone touching it, changed channels to a talk radio station.

"I am both here and not here."

Devin went ridged. "Turn that up! Was that who I think it was? Why would Sybille be on a radio talk show?"

"She isn't." Juliana spun the volume dial. "It seems they're trying to communicate with us again."

Charlie approached the radio. "They want me to come back."

Devin could barely move. Sybille sounded like she was a world away, which he supposed was true enough. "I need to tell her I'm okay. Can she hear us?"

"That would be nice," Juliana said, "but no, I don't think so."

"Can't you try to make them hear us?" He asked.

"How would I do that?"

"I don't know, adjust the dials or, speak right into the radio."

Charlie stuck out her tongue. "It has a speaker, not a microphone."

"So? It's also an interdimensional communication device," he said. "We're not dealing with logic here."

The three of them stared at the radio, which vacillated between static and human speech.

"I don't think it's working," a low voice called out, barely more than a whisper. "Maybe she can't hear us."

"Elis!" Juliana dove at the radio. She pressed herself to the counter and placed her lips right next to the speaker, shouting, "I can hear you just fine, husband!"

More crackling. Juliana hit its side.

"My God!" Elis' voice came through louder now. "She's taken control. How is that possible?"

"I'm standing in my kitchen minding my own business," Juliana hissed, her lips an inch from the radio's surface. "Blame Sybille for putting me in here. It's not like I had a choice."

"She's not in control."

"That's Sybille again." Devin crouched and leaned his ear in, as though being near the radio meant he was that much closer to her.

"I'm still in the driver's seat," Sybille said. "She's just...there too. A passenger."

Elis' snort was loud enough for them all to hear. "More like a backseat driver."

"Sybille!" Shoving Juliana to the side, Devin grabbed the radio with both hands. "It's Devin. I'm here."

A long pause.

"Devin? How are you in my head?"

"Froya sent me here to allow me to communicate with you."

"Froya? How would she know this mind prison existed?"

"Ichor fae can detect all created universes. They're trained from birth on how to move between them." He slumped over the radio, covering it with his body like he was protecting a baby from harm. "Look, Sybille, if you don't see me for a while, I'm all right."

"No. No, it's not all right. Devin, you get out of my head and come home right now!"

"I wish I could. I want to, but Froya is controlling this whole world shifting experience. My path to the Now World has been blocked because she says it's not safe there."

"Hell yeah, it's not safe. That's why I need you."

Devin tipped his head towards the radio, the weight of grief and frustration pulling him towards it. She needed him. Not we, not the group. Sybille needed him. "I promise I'll try to get back to you as soon as I can. I have a lot to tell you about."

The radio crackled. Devin smacked its side the way he'd seen Juliana hit it. Voices came to him indistinct, hazy.

"What? I'm losing you. Sybille, what did you say?"

"Charlie. Is she there with you?"

"Yeah. Yeah, she's here. She's fine."

"My mother says to tell her we made all kinds of treats for her."

Charlie butted in between Devin and the counter, her face at eye level with the radio. "What kind of treats?"

"Charlie," Elis spoke this time. "I miss you. We all do. We have brownies and cookies and whatever these hideous worm things are. You can have them all if you come home."

"She has all of that here." Juliana placed her hand on Charlie's shoulder. "In fact, I'm thinking of keeping her. She's whole here. The Low has no hold over her. Isn't that what you want? For her to be free of the Low?"

"Her body is still here and it's not free of the Low." Sybille did not sound pleased. "We still have a ticking time bomb to deal with and meanwhile, we're without our girl. You stole her and now you need to give her back!"

Juliana threw her hands up. "I'm not the one who brought her here. She came on her own. Devin had some help but now that he's here, I think I'll keep him too. We're an odd little family, but I can make it work."

Devin scowled. "I'm not staying with you. And neither is Charlie." He let go of the radio and turned to his niece. "Charlie, you have to go home. Sybille will find a way to fix you. And as for Elis…you heard him. He's a broken man without you there. You need to find your way free of this place."

She hung her head. "I know. It was just nice to feel like I'm not a monster for once."

Devin tucked his hand under her chin and gently tipped her head up towards him. "You listen to me; you are not a monster. You're my little spy. The smartest girl I ever met."

Charlie sniffled. "You missed my birthday. It was three weeks ago."

He frowned. "I'll be there for your next birthday. And the one after that. We'll get this all sorted. I promise."

"Charlie," Sybille's voice came through again. "Everyone is using me to communicate and I'm tired, honey. I'll be forced to come back from the ether soon. Do you think you could try leaving now?"

"The fae aren't going to let me return home with you." Devin nudged her to the door. "But if you go alone, I bet there'll be a hallway waiting for you on the other side of that."

Charlie stepped forward, one tiny step, then turned and raced back to her uncle. She clung to him and sobbed. "Tell the stupid fae you hate their magic and come home soon, okay?" She turned to Juliana and tried to compose herself. "Bye-bye cupcake queen. Remember, more baking, less evil making."

"I'll put that on an apron."

She turned again to the door, twisted it open, and strode out into a brightly lit hallway. The door swung shut behind her.

Devin leaned against the counter. "Sybille, Charlie's on her way back. She should wake up soon. Oh, and there's something you need to know. It's about the Patron... Not just Bore, all of them... Hello?"

The radio answered him with static before switching to a country hit.

"Well, damn."

Juliana propped herself up next to him, placed her arm around his back and turned herself to face him. There was no room for Devin to back away. He closed his eyes. *Froya at the farmhouse, Sybille in his dreams. Juliana in Hell.*

"Alone at last." She trailed a finger up his chest and then down it again. "Do you want to have a little fun first, or should we skip right to the part where you tell me what the Ichor fae are planning on doing with you?"

CHAPTER TWELVE

JULIANA

Juliana could still surprise herself. She hadn't had an opportunity to touch a man in over one hundred years, and now that an appealing one stood in front of her, she managed to let guilt slide in like an overdue train. She pressed herself closer to him, ignoring her emotions and took in his scent while waiting for him to respond. He smelled like a slow-burning campfire. Wood smoke, embers. The heat radiating from him almost made her forget about Elis.

"What do you know about the Ichor? You're a bloodthirster spirit and you've been dead since forever." He attempted to slide out of her grasp towards the refrigerator. She held him in place.

"I have hundreds of years of knowledge picked up in bits and pieces. What do you know of them, fool?"

He swallowed. "They just wanted me back because my father's one of them. They don't have a plan for me."

"Oh, is this the sort of fun you want to have?" She asked him. "Is it a game where you lie and I tell you you're lying, then you deny it and then I strangle you with a salad tong?"

"I don't think you can strangle someone with a salad tong."

"We won't know unless I try."

"Jesus, I thought you wanted to have sex with me, not murder me."

"The two aren't mutually exclusive." She trailed her fingernails along the tender flesh of his neck, remembering a time where she wouldn't have given a second thought to piercing that neck with her teeth. Shame stilled her hand. She wasn't that monster. Not anymore.

"You're a super twisted individual, Juliana. No wonder Elis stayed with you for so long."

Elis. Despite everything he'd done to her, the mere mention of his name made her want things she should never desire. She eased up on her hold of the fae bastard. "Haven't you learned magic? You should be able to freeze me in place."

"I'm still a novice, and also a dumb Earthblood according to every fae I talk to."

She lifted her hand away from his throat and trailed it down to a spot much lower on his body. "So, I can still do what I wish, and you can't stop me. I'm pure consciousness."

Having proved her point, she removed her hand.

"You sure don't feel like pure consciousness to me." He cleared his throat, grabbed an oven mitt from its hook on a nearby cabinet, and held it in front of himself. "They think I'm slow but it's only because they haven't taught me a lot yet. Froya said she released the block in my head, which is at least a half lie. They still have control over me."

"And you say this Froya, she'll call you back to the Ichor realm soon?"

"Yes. I'm only supposed to visit long enough to tell Sybille I'm okay. And I already did that, so…"

He looked away from her towards the door. It didn't take a psychic genius to tell he was pining for the moment he could walk through it and join his hierophant darling. Juliana's breath hitched. These men in her life chose a human woman over her despite her being superior in every way. She hated that she wasn't beyond an ego lashing.

Maybe this pathetic man was due a lashing of his own…

"The girl made a mistake going back. And you'll make a mistake if you return to be with Sybille. She doesn't love you."

His gaze returned to her face. He scowled. "What?"

"You heard me. You still haven't answered my question. What do the Ichor fae want to do with you? Who are you to them?"

"I'm no one. Just a common Earthblood."

"Earthblood. A half Ichor, half human hybrid is extraordinarily rare.

There's nothing common about you. They must know what you're capable of doing."

He kept his scowl in place. "What do you think I'm capable of doing?"

"You may be unable to perform basic fae magic but you have an ability none of them have. This makes you dangerous. And desirable."

"Considering how you just behaved, I'd say you have the desirable part right. But other than being handy with a stake, I'm hardly dangerous to anyone who's not undead."

"You're wrong. You're dangerous. And so is your sweet little Ossian niece."

"Don't bring Charlie into this conversation."

"You must face the facts about the girl. She is not on your side."

"My *side*? You know what? Shut the fuck up. I don't want to hear your trash."

"It's not trash. If you stopped to think about it, you'd realize I'm right."

"How so, Juliana? You going to enlighten me or what?"

"I don't have time to enlighten someone so deeply buried in his own excrement. But I'll say this. The girl is the Ossian's weapon. She's how they intend to spread their domain over the Earth."

"Come again?"

"I haven't come the first time." Juliana reached for him. He recoiled but didn't stop her. "Remember, Devin, I've had hundreds of years to learn about the world, both the mundane and the supernatural. And for the past century, I've roamed the Earth driven by basic desires. All I do is think. All day, all night. You believe my intentions are evil. I see them as a means to an end. I have no desire to experience the death of the Now World."

"Death? Why would the Now World die?"

"Because to the fae, it's...what's the phrase? Collateral damage. And so is Charlie. The Ossian will use her. No doubt, her own mother knows this and has helped the plan along."

"Raelyn? No. She loves her daughter. She wanted Charlie to leave the Low to protect her, not have the Low eat her from the inside out."

"Forgive me if there are gaps in my knowledge. I haven't exactly been out and about since that day at the cabin, and I've been relying on a nine year old to relate current events to me, but according to Charlie, her mother is an immortal bloodthirster who is now in charge of the Low. Is that right?"

Devin shifted his weight. "That's right."

"So she aimed to take over the Low but also sent her daughter away right at the time when she would be its supreme ruler and her daughter its de facto princess."

"I see what you're getting at, but Charlie would go crazy if she'd stayed!"

"She's going crazy anyways. The Low has taken hold just the same as if she'd stayed with her mother, only now she's in a position to do much, much more damage. And you really think Raelyn knew nothing about this?"

"I think she knew Charlie stood a chance with us on the outside."

Juliana took a deep breath. This man carried more emotional baggage than even she did. "You may have to kill her."

His face reddened, hands clenched the edge of the counter behind him. "Are you insane?"

"She's a weapon. Even she admits it might come down to her death."

"I'm never going to harm her. Not ever, no matter the circumstances."

"Can you ever truly know how you'll act under any circumstances unless you're faced with them?" She cocked her head to the side and examined him. Shoulders hunched. Eyes wide and glossy, like he was trying to hold back tears. What a pitiful fool. He hadn't even gotten to the battlefield yet and already he acted defeated. "Ask your fae girlfriend about this next time you see her. One fae weapon used to fight another. I'm sure that's it. My only remaining question is how they plan on using your ability against the creatures that up to this point you've been helping live forever. Do you even know?"

He opened his mouth. This was it. Perhaps the man had something useful to tell her after all. She leaned in, only to find herself studying the pastel flowers printed on the wall behind where he had been standing.

Gone even without the blink of an eye.

The oven timer dinged. Poor Devin. A fae tool and the unwitting enemy of one of the people he cared for most. And now he wouldn't even get to eat a slice of his favorite pie.

Sybille

Charlie sat on the couch, surrounded by Elis, Sybille, and her family, and a sizable hoard of baked goods. "I told you everything already. Stop asking me questions." She bit into a tartlet.

Sybille stroked the girl's forehead. Charlie's patience was stretched thin, yet she needed to know things only Charlie could know. There had to be a reason both Charlie and Devin were sucked into Sybille's head at the same time. She couldn't let a clue go unsolved. "I know, but it's important that we find your uncle. He can help us help you. I know he can."

"Juliana wants to help too. Or at least, that's what she claims."

"What she claims," Elis grumbled, "is good for the garbage heap."

"I'm not stupid. That's why I said she claims it and not that I believe her completely." Charlie crossed her arms. "She hates bloodthirsters, so she doesn't want the Low to take over the planet."

"Agreed," Sybille said. "Even the biggest liars tell the truth occasionally. Still, we can never trust her, even if we use some of her knowledge to our benefit. Elis, how does she know so much about the fae?"

He drummed his fingers on the arm of his chair. "Even as far back as our early days together, she studied various religious traditions and mystical phenomena. She probably mentioned fae here or there, but I thought it was just folklore she was referring to. Never did I think she was studying something real."

"You're a folklore creature. And you're real."

"That's fair. To be honest, her studies weren't of interest to me. I ignored them for the most part, regretfully." He sat upright, sniffing the air. "Laurence is about to ring your doorbell."

Instead of ringing, Laurence let himself in and rushed over to Charlie. He scooped her off the couch and brought her over to sit with him in Peter's easy chair. As she nestled in, he peered at Sybille and Elis, lips pursed. "You should have told me about her condition as soon as it occurred."

"You're right," Sybille agreed. "That's on me. We got the situation under control and brought her back out without incident. If we'd been unsuccessful, we would've looped you in."

"All the more reason for her to come live with me."

"Her mother entrusted her to our care, not yours."

"Her mother is a soulless monster."

"Who still gets to call the shots as far as her daughter is concerned. You're welcome to visit Charlie every day. We all want you to be a part of her life."

Elis bared a fang. "Not all of us."

She elbowed him. "Elis too. He's just too proud to admit it. For now, she stays put. At least until we have her condition under control. Then we can talk to Raelyn, maybe come to a different agreement."

Laurence looked down at his granddaughter. "Charlie, do you remember where you put the puzzle I bought for us to work on together?"

She swung her feet back and forth. "It's in my room."

"Can you go and get it? Let's start putting it together now, if you're up for it."

She smiled and jumped off his lap. "I am!"

When she'd disappeared up the stairs, Laurence leaned in and said in a small voice, "You do understand that Raelyn is an enemy. She doesn't have Charlie's best interests at heart."

"I consider that a distinct possibility," answered Sybille. "What about you, though? Do you have her best interests at heart?"

Laurence looked like a tea kettle about to boil. "Her well-being, and subsequently the well-being of our entire universe, is the only interest I hold in my heart."

Sybille studied him, saying nothing.

Elis scooted his chair closer to where Laurence sat. "I really wish I could mesmerize you."

"Laurence, if you want to prove your intentions are pure," Sybille said, "there's something else you should know. While Charlie was stuck in my head with Juliana, our wayward and newly christened fae friend also paid a visit. We spoke with him. Or, he spoke through me. Something like that. Then Charlie returned to us and I had to close the channel, so I don't know what's happened to him since."

"That's an interesting development. Did you try entering Juliana's prison to see him?"

"I was advised against it by, well, by everyone."

"I'd have to agree with them."

"And to be honest, I was so tired, I don't know if I would have had it in me to get into the kitchen and then deal with Juliana's freshest batch of homemade bullshit. I'm going to try again after I've had a chance to rest."

Elis stood and began to pace. "Not a good idea. Nope, not a good idea."

Sybille sighed. "He's probably not even in there anymore. Charlie said he was going to be called back to the Ichor realm."

"Right," Elis said. "So what's the point in risking yourself anyways?"

Charlie bounced down the stairs, puzzle box in hand. Elis helped her clear off the coffee table and then dumped all the pieces onto it. The puzzle depicted the universe, with the sun to one side, and the planets lined up in order. The blank space was going to make this puzzle a nightmare. Sybille picked up a random piece and ran her finger around its irregular edges. The piece had a bit of orange along one side and the rest was black. Could be the sun, or mars, possibly. "Laurence, what do you know about inter-universe travel? You know, traversing realities, that sort of thing."

He looked up from where he'd been diligently separating out the puzzle's edge pieces. "A little. I think I see where this is going. But you're not fae, not even part fae. As a skilled hierophant, you can see both sides of the veil. It affords you a bit of navigation ability in realms beyond this one, but you're limited to the ether and headspaces and the worlds beyond death—that sort of thing. Traversing to an Ichor realm, now, that's something else."

"But if you have a roadmap of how to get there, it's a lot easier, isn't it?"

"Again, for fae it is, yes, but…"

"Devin was in my head, Laurence. *My. Head.* He came from the Ichor realm and he went back to the Ichor realm. Does that or does that not give me a map?"

"If we can access it, possibly. That doesn't change the fact that humans can't travel there, not on their own. It isn't allowed."

"Screw what's allowed! They kidnapped my friend. He didn't ask to be taken. They forced him to leave, and according to his own words, they won't let him come back here even though he wants to. So what other choice do I have?"

The weight of Elis' arms as they circled around her made her pulse steady.

"Wait here," he said, "and trust he'll return to us on his own?"

She closed her eyes, then opened them again. "I trust Devin, but I don't trust the Ichor."

"The Ichor want to help destroy the Low," Laurence reminded her. "They want what we want."

"They want to have their competition eliminated. If you stop and think about it, Laurence, everyone has an agenda. And that includes me. First up on my agenda is getting Devin back."

Charlie scooted over and sat on the floor, leaning her back against Sybille's legs. "If anyone can get Uncle Devin back, it will be you. You'll probably fail or maybe even die, but you have to at least try."

"Thanks for the pep talk. All in favor?" She raised her hand and so did Charlie. "That's good enough for me. Laurence, dust off your Ossian skills. You're going to teach me how to breach forbidden worlds."

CHAPTER THIRTEEN

ELIS

ELIS SHIFTED THE BLANKET SO THAT IT WAS TUCKED SECURELY AROUND Sybille's legs. The chill didn't bother him, but Sybille was human and humans were dangerously susceptible to frostbite. "Are you cold? We can ask the driver to turn back."

She laughed. "You've been planning this date for weeks, Elis. And it's been postponed half a dozen times. No, I'm not going to let a little winter wind stop us from our romantic carriage ride. You on the other hand…"

"Me what?"

"You're thinking about Charlie, aren't you?"

He clenched his jaw. Tonight's outing nearly suffered the same fate as his other proposed date nights. Not that Charlie could be blamed. The Low fits struck when they struck, poor girl. Leaving her side so soon after she'd endured an episode had left him on edge.

"Maybe I should call Margot and check in on her."

"Maybe you should give me your phone so you don't do that. Seriously, it's been only a half hour since you last called. They're fine. My mother will contact us the moment that changes. Until then, let's try to enjoy ourselves. It's been a rough few weeks, Elis. I need this. It's not like I can relax and kick back with a stiff drink."

"You drank plenty of margaritas on the beach with me that one time."

"Those were dream margaritas on a dream beach." She sighed. "In real life, alcohol messes with my ability to regulate psychic energy. It often dulls my connection to the ether. I think that's why my mother is so fond of wine. She was never cut out for hardcore psychic work."

Under the blanket, she slid her hand onto his thigh. His muscles tensed, this time for pleasurable reasons. He needed this too. "Let the night carry us where it may, then."

Sighing, she snuggled next to him. Together, they peered out over the dark expanse of the bay as the horses pulled their carriage along the trail leading through the waterfront park. Statues of the city's founders, along with a few other notable citizens in Port Everan's history stood as silent sentinels along the trail, glistening with a deathly pallor under the waning moon.

The calm couldn't have been more foreign to him. After weeks of sickness and worry and strange psychic travels, he'd forgotten what serenity felt like. Maybe he never really knew, but this moment seemed about as close to it as someone like him could get. And it was because of her. He leaned over and kissed the top of her head, cinnamon coating his lips, spreading a spicy heat down his throat.

Desire battled with the serenity until it won over. Her hand stayed firmly upon his thigh.

The carriage came to a stop and the driver hopped down. "Hope you folks enjoyed the ride."

Sybille assured him she had, slipped him a tip, and they were on their way. Walking back to her car, she kept both her arms wrapped around his. "So, what's it going to be? Back to my place to reinsert ourselves into the family drama, or back to yours to create some of our own?"

With her smell still on him, he knew his choice before she gave him one. "Just let me text Margot and make sure it's okay if we don't come back tonight."

She ground to a halt. "You're going to text my mother for permission to have sex with me? Why didn't you ask her all the other times?" She gasped. "Or did you?"

"Of course not. I just want to make sure they don't need our help to manage things."

"Jesus, way to kill the mood." She wrapped her arms around his neck now and pressed herself close. "You need to focus. On me. They don't need you tonight, but I do." She leaned into him and left a trail of nibbles from the back of his ear down his neck.

Nerve endings on hyper alert, he ran his hand down to the small of her back. "As you wish."

"Here's what's going to happen. We're going to get in the car and drive to your place. We're going to forget the world exists. We're going to forget other worlds with blood fairies and bone fairies exist. There will only be you and me and your bed. And possibly the shower and the kitchen counter if we're in the mood for that. Do you understand?"

"I understand that there's a bush right there that would hide us if we wanted it to."

"No, no bush. You're going to have to wait twenty minutes because it's cold out and I refuse to lie on the frozen ground. And no car sex either. It's uncomfortable and we're not eighteen. We can wait."

"Please?"

"Patience is a virtue."

"Is it patience or torture?"

She kissed him, this time nibbling his lower lip, fully knowing what that did to him. When she pulled away, the playful twinkle in her eye left him at her mercy. "You tell me, thirster."

He grabbed her hand and ran. He'd wait. He'd do whatever she wanted, but they were going to run to the car, and they were going to break every speed limit to get back to his place as soon as possible.

Sixteen minutes later, they'd made it as far as the hallway leading from his side door to his kitchen. He pressed her against the wall, hands hoisting up her ass as she wrapped her legs around him. He focused, just as she'd asked him too. Cinnamon and bared skin, clothes they were both willing to sacrifice to the heat burning through them.

He woke to the sound of the garbage truck heading down his alley. They'd made it to the bed for round two, collapsing into it sometime in the morning's wee hours, spent and satiated. Sybille lay at his side, her back turned from him. He wrapped his arm around her and pulled her close. Perhaps round three was in order.

She breathed in. "Good morning."

Elis kissed the back of her neck. "Morning."

"Was I worth the wait?"

"You always are. You're worth everything."

She twisted herself around. Warm eyes searched his. "Are you sure about that?"

"I've never been surer about anything." He wasn't lying, yet as soon as he'd said these words, he felt an inkling of doubt. "What is it, Sybille?"

"I'm happy with you. You know that, right?"

"Of course, I do. And I'm happy with you. I've never been this happy in a relationship before."

"You've only ever had one other relationship."

"That's not true. I did, you know... I dated during the hundred years Juliana haunted me."

"You had sex every now and then. You had sexual relations, not proper relationships."

"So?"

"So you've had one other real relationship in, like, three hundred and fifty years. And that one was, let's face it, the most co-dependent relationship in the history of co-dependency."

"I don't know about that."

"She stalked you as a child, killed you and made you a bloodthirster, then the two of you drank from each other's wrists for two hundred years before she tried to murder you but then instead killed herself, came back as a spirit, stalked you for another century, then re-united your spirit with your body in an attempt to murder you again, then possessed me so she could, once again, try to murder you. Am I missing the psychologically healthy part of this relationship?"

"No, okay fine, it was awful. She's awful, as you well know. But I've learned from that awfulness. I'm ready to do better—to be better—for you."

She lowered her head so that it rested on his shoulder. "I know that. Which is why I'm going to bring this next part up. We have a lot on our plate. Like, a save the world-sized portion. And I need to know I can trust you."

He tried not to bristle. "After everything we've been through, you still don't trust me?"

"I trust you with Charlie. I trust you to help me when I need it. But I don't entirely trust your intentions with me."

"How can you say that?"

"Search yourself, Elis. This is a time for honesty and self-reflection. In another hour, we're going to have to head back to my place, check on Charlie, and figure out our next steps, so this needs to be resolved now."

"What exactly needs to be resolved?"

"The fact that you secretly, deep down, want to turn me into a bloodthirster, just like Juliana did to you."

He wrestled out of her hold and sat up. "No. I would never do to you what Juliana did to me. I didn't know what was happening. She didn't give me a choice."

"Is that the distinction you're making? You're giving me a choice, but in your mind, it's *when* I'll make that choice, not *if*. Which means you do want that. You want me to become a bloodthirster."

"Come on now, love. We could reunite your soul. You'd have a conscience, agency, the ability to control your lowest impulses, but you'd also age so slowly, we'd have centuries together."

"Only we won't. We won't have centuries together. My choice today, tomorrow, and always, will be to never turn into what you are, soul or no soul."

He flinched. "*What I am.* Am I so terrible?"

"Am I? I love who I am. I might complain sometimes, but I love my overbearing family, I love my complicated mess of an existence, and I love my power. I am powerful, Elis. I own that power. As a human, as a woman. I wouldn't trade that for a dozen centuries with you."

"I must admit, that stings a bit."

"I told you this was a time for honesty."

"But you'd still have your power, you'd just have added abilities."

She placed her hands on his cheeks. "I will grow old. I will die. I will not return in this form. My body will decompose, and my spirit will move on. You can accept that and love me for who I am just as I love you for who you are, or you can get the fuck out of my life." She kissed his forehead. "That is *your* choice. I hope you'll choose to stay. If you do, I don't ever again want to hear a hint of you secretly plotting to convince me that I should be turned. Is that understood, bloodthirster?"

Sybille, old and wrinkly. Sybille breathing her last breath. Elis, alone again. He envisioned this with sorrow, but not regret. If he couldn't accept her wish to lead the life she chose, then he wasn't worthy to lead his own life alongside hers. He shackled the beast that still lurked within him and spoke as the human he strived to be.

"Yes. I would choose to stay with you, with every one of your conditions in place, even if you locked me up for any evil thoughts I've ever had."

She let go of his face, relief playing in the lines around her smile. "We can play that game another time. Right now, I need to hop in the shower, and we have to pick up a gigantic triple-shot latte on the way home."

She swung herself off the bed, heading towards the bathroom.

"Just like that? You have these doubts and then you confront me. I tell you what you want to hear, and then you accept it, no follow up necessary."

She paused and turned back to him. "I am a psychic, you know."

"You're not a mind reader."

"No, but I have a good read on *you*. You've changed in the past few months. You have something outside of your own desires to focus on. Someone."

She didn't have to say the fact that she wasn't referring to herself. They both knew.

"It's the way you are with her that made me realize you have the capacity to love in a healthy way. There is nothing purer than the way a parent loves a child."

"She's not… I'm not her father, though."

"Would you or would you not die for her?"

"Yes. I'd die for either of you."

"Well, then, that makes us family. And that's how I knew we could put your baser instincts to rest. This conversation was just meant to get any last inkling of it out into the open so it could be squashed, and to warn you that if you relapse, it won't be without consequence."

He hopped out of bed and joined her, gripping her from behind. "You're the most self-assured person I've ever met." He reached around her front, hands exploring her naked torso and then downwards.

"I am because there's no other way I can be and still deal with the rest of you lot." She let out a groan. "Stop that, or you're going to delay me getting my caffeine."

Ignoring her, he picked her up and brought her back to the bed. "I'll make up for it, I promise."

By mid-morning, they pulled up to the Esmond household, Sybille with coffee in hand. She began to open the door, but he stopped her, hand over hers. All this talk about honesty, but they hadn't even touched on the unspoken tension that, in his mind, was far more pressing. Here they were, in what he considered a committed relationship, and she was about to go off to a different universe to save a guy who was in love with her. His insecurity was strong enough to still her hand, but his courage wasn't strong enough to say what he needed to. He was bound to come off like a jealous fool anyway.

"What is it, Elis?"

"Nothing. I...I love you."

She leaned in and kissed him, no nibbling, just the consistency of tenderness. "I love you too." She looked at him, her expression serious. Maybe she was a mind reader after all. "Don't let whatever happens next make you doubt that."

"What's happening next?"

"I might be away for a while." She paused. "But while I'm gone, there are things here that need doing. Important things. So, I'm giving you a new mission, and it's one you're not going to like."

"Name it and I'll do it."

"You might want to hear what it is first." She leaned in until their noses brushed against each other. "I'm sending you to the Low."

CHAPTER FOURTEEN

JULIANA

JULIANA CLUTCHED THE DOORKNOB, GIVING IT A TENTATIVE TURN. IT SQUEAKED and then clicked as the chamber pushed back. She rotated it a bit more and then opened the door. Just a crack. She wasn't one to admit fear, but if she could be honest with herself, the void waiting beyond that door raised every hair on her arms. She peeked out.

Nothing.

Discouraged, Juliana slammed the door shut before the darkness could claim her. She'd experienced such emptiness before. It lurked inside revivalist tents and on the ends of lit torches. It surrounded her in its foggy embrace within realms within realms. She'd keep her bright kitchen, however a figment of Sybille's imagination it might be. One day, though, a hallway would greet her rather than a chasm. She forced herself to try, every now and then. A crack in the door. The courage to keep going.

"There's no escaping. You must know that by now."

Juliana whipped around. "Well, look at you, the woman of the hour. And you've brought a guest for me. How fun!"

"I'm not a guest and I'm not for you, you miserable, fractured remnant of a ghost."

"Oh, Zareen, I didn't recognize you. New haircut?"

Zareen fumed. Sybille, standing a foot ahead of her cousin, stuck her hand out to prevent her from charging.

"I take it we missed Devin?"

Juliana frowned. "He didn't even get to have a slice of pie."

"Damn. Nothing can ever be easy." Sybille glanced at her cousin. "Zareen came with me because I needed the practice of bringing someone else across worlds, so to speak, in case Devin can't make it back to the Now World all on his own. Laurence thought it was a good idea. Also, Zareen wanted to come so she could yell at you."

"Whatever for?" Juliana cocked her head to the side and faced her accuser with wide eyes like an innocent baby deer. "Do you prefer chocolate hazelnut or vanilla with raspberry filling? I have both!"

Thrown by the request, Zareen's jaw went slack. "What?"

Sybille nudged her cousin. "I told you she's a little off. I mean, she always has been, but now she's full carton of sour milk off."

"Now why would you say these things? I'm just trying to be a gracious hostess. Here, see?"

She lifted the lids from two raised platters. Each held a beautifully decorated cake, one with chocolate frosting, the other vanilla."

"Damn." Zareen edged towards them. "No wonder Charlie liked it here. I'll take a slice of each."

"Zareen!" Sybille pulled on her arm.

"Whatever, Sybille. You told me you ate bread while you were here, so glass houses and all. Besides, I can be mad at her hungry or I can be mad at her with a full belly. Calories consumed in a brain prison don't count anyway."

Juliana sliced into the chocolate cake first, placing a generous helping onto a plate for Zareen. "The sponge was tricky. So hard to tell if it's baked properly with all that cocoa in it."

"It looks amazing!" Licking her lips, Zareen took the piece, ate a bite, and swooned. "Tastes amazing too."

"Really? The hazelnut frosting is made with cream cheese. I was afraid it would be too rich."

"Are you kidding? I could eat a tub of this frosting. Thank you." She put her fork down, wiped crumbs away from her mouth with a napkin, and cleared her voice. "Now it's time to yell."

Juliana slid her knife into the vanilla cake. "Go right ahead. What did I do again? Was it something dreadful?"

"Bitch, you know it was."

Juliana extracted a wedge of cake and balanced it on her spatula. This woman had a right to vent. She'd deceived her in an effort to kill someone Zareen cared for. "Well, I've done so many awful things, I'm afraid I have trouble remembering them all."

"God, I have such a powerful urge to fork you in the eye." Zareen picked up her fork and twirled it around. Instead of aiming it at Juliana, she used it to spear another bite. "Just admit what you did or I swear, as soon as I finish this piece of cake—and that piece you just sliced for me— I'm going to cut you."

"Well, now, this is a side to you I've never seen before. Of course, you were always upfront about your family and what you'd do to protect them, but you were much more polite about it before."

"So, you do remember?"

"I lied to you to achieve my own ends. I made you go to a place that was unsafe for you, and then I possessed your cousin and hit you hard enough to knock you unconscious. That was genuinely unintentional, by the way. I forgot how soft human heads can be." She paused in her admission and stared at Sybille, who had wandered off to a corner of the kitchen, adjacent to the refrigerator. "What's going on there? Why is Sybille staring at the wall?"

"She has her own reason for coming here."

"So this truly wasn't another accident, you both showing up here?" How interesting. "She planned it this time."

"Yes, and I'm sure you want to know why but I'm not going to tell you, and neither is she."

"I'm using the kitchen as a jumping off point to trace Devin back to the Ichor realm so I can rescue him."

"Sybille!" Zareen gasped. "Should she know all of that?"

Sybille traced the outline of vine on the wallpaper with her index finger. "What's she going to do with the information? Bake it into a doughnut?"

"Doughnuts are better fried than baked," Juliana said. "And Sybille is right. I have nowhere to go and no one to tell your secrets to." She walked to where Sybille stood, trying to see if there was something more to this wall than plaster and floral print paper. It was the same spot Devin had been standing in when he blinked out of her world and presumably popped back into the Ichor realm.

Perhaps the door wasn't the only way out of here... "How brave of you to follow him there. You must love him very much."

Sybille turned to her. "He's family to me. Besides, my world needs him more than the Ichor realm does."

"You mean, *you* need him. Is my husband not enough to keep you satisfied?"

She narrowed her eyes and Juliana smiled. She may be a spirit trapped in Sybille's head, but she maintained the ability to get under the psychic's skin. This fact was more delicious than a piece of three-berry pie.

"I'm not going to let you do this to me, Juliana. You will not fuck with my relationships by playing your little manipulative games with me. I love your *ex*-husband and he loves me. But I said Devin is family, and I meant that, and not just to me. He is literally Charlie's family, and we need him to help her. You've met her. Tell me that you don't give a shit if the Ossian use her body to spread themselves over the Earth?"

Juliana blinked. "I'm not as sociopathic as you believe me to be. I feel things."

"Sociopaths are capable of feeling as long as it involves their own self-interest."

"I have no investment in the girl, and she is Ossian. I should hate her for her association with them, though it's hardly her fault. Still, I would like to see you cure her."

"You think a cure is possible?"

"It's unlikely. But I'm the spirit of a deceased bloodthirsty demon trapped in your brain. I'm hardly one to judge what's impossible."

"Then believe me when I say I need Devin's help."

"You need his help, yet I'm guessing you won't tell me why. Do you even know why?"

Sybille hesitated. She looked towards her feet and then back at Juliana. "Maybe."

"There's a simpler way to handle this. Just send the girl back to me. I'll keep her here. She can eat as many cupcakes as she wishes."

"I already told you through your radio that that plan won't work. If her body is with us and she isn't cured, she's a threat."

"Is it all right if I try one of these cookies?"

They both turned. Zareen held up one of the chocolate nut cookies

Juliana had baked just before they arrived. Juliana nodded her consent. "Weren't you going to yell at me?"

"Yes. I'm just waiting for Sybille to stop telling you all her secrets so I can give you a piece of my mind."

"I'm sorry for what I did to you."

"What?" Zareen stared at her cookie. "Was that an actual apology?"

"It was. I betrayed your trust. I had good intentions."

Sybille snorted. "You did not."

"But good intentions do not equal good outcomes. Clearly things didn't work out for the best for me."

"So that's it?" Zareen dropped her cookie. "You're sorry because you got locked up, but not because you hurt me?"

"I suppose I'm sorry about that too."

"You nearly killed me!"

"That's a bit dramatic. I nearly killed a lot of people that day. I only knocked you unconscious. You got off light. And have I even asked for a thank you?"

"You're the worst." After a brief deliberation, she picked up her cookie and resumed eating it. "I think the fact that you bake better than I ever will might make me hate you even more."

Sybille backed away from the wall. "Okay, Zareen, it's time for you to head home."

Zareen furrowed her brow. "You mean, it's time for *us* to go home."

"No, just you."

"Hell no, Sybille. Laurence told you this was a practice run only. We're supposed to do this again at least twice before you'll be ready."

"I'm ready now. Besides, you don't really want to come back here again, do you?"

Zareen eyed the tray of cookies. "Um, no?"

"Well then, go home, tell Laurence I've gone rogue. I'm betting he won't be overly surprised."

"Dammit, Sybille. You're always too stubborn for your own good."

"I'm not concerned with my own good. It has to happen like this. We don't have enough time for all the practicing Laurence wants me to have. Charlie's getting worse every day."

"I know."

"Go. Go back. Make sure they're doing all right, and if they are, head to your place and spend some time with your kids."

"I could go with you."

"It's more important for you to be near home. My mom's all alone with Charlie."

"What? Where's my dad and Laurence."

"They're busy elsewhere."

"Are you going to tell me what the hell that means? Jesus, you've told Juliana more than you've told me."

"She means," Juliana stepped in between them, "that she doesn't want you with her. Your presence will create more risk than reward."

"No one asked for your opinion." Zareen glared at her.

"She's right though." Sybille pressed her hand against the wall. "It's going to be hard enough for me to navigate there, and once I arrive, the risk only increases. Humans aren't welcomed guests. There's no point in putting the two best psychics in the Esmond family in danger."

"There's no point in putting one of us in danger either. Can't you wait for Laurence?"

"Like I said, by the time you get back, Laurence won't even be there. And it's not like I could take him with me. He's Ossian. His presence in the Ichor realm would be justification for an all-out war. That's why I won't let Elis anywhere near this either."

"Or near me." Juliana laughed. "Not that he would make it out of my kitchen once he saw what I've baked for him. And then he'd drop you like a crying baby and choose me. Your mission would be undermined before it even began."

Sybille pinched her lips in a way that reminded Juliana of when she was being berated by the prioress during her days as a novice. "Yes. I'm sure it would happen just like that, Juliana."

"You'd drop a crying baby?" Zareen shrank back. It seemed Juliana could do no right by these women. "I'm glad you'll never get near my children again."

"You'll bring him by some other time, though, won't you?" Juliana remained polite, hopeful. She refused to stoop to their condescending level. "Elis, I mean. He has a standing invitation. Both of you will tell him how delicious my treats are."

Sybille slapped her across the cheek. "Stop slipping into happy housewife mode. It's fucking creepy. Zareen, I'll see you at home." She gave her cousin a hug. "I promise."

She opened the door and gestured for Zareen to walk through. Juliana stood to the side scowling, her hand held gently against the cheek Sybille had struck. She'd given them every opportunity to accept her olive branch, and they'd rejected her. Never would she bake for either of them again.

Zareen stepped towards her cousin. "I'd say this is your last chance to reconsider, but what's the point?"

"The point is that you always look out for me," Sybille said. "Now I need you to look out for my mom and Charlie until I return or Elis and everyone else gets back."

"Wait, they're with Elis? Does that mean…?"

Sybille pushed her through the door and closed it quickly, latching the bolt into place. "Juliana, do you have any baking tips for me?"

Juliana stood up straight. She had many baking tips. Thousands. "Do you really want to hear them all?"

"I want you to write them down. You'll find a notebook and pens in the drawer to the right of where the silverware is kept."

"There's no paper in there. That drawer is for linen napkins and napkin rings in—" She opened the drawer. A thick notebook with a tan moleskin cover and a multitude of colored pens appeared. "Oh, I see."

"It's time for you to share your knowledge. So write a book of baking tips and I'll come back some time to see how it's progressing. I'll even share it with people, maybe try to get it published."

"You would?" She shouldn't trust Sybille, and yet the idea was too appealing to reject outright. "Can I include tips for innocent spirits on how to cope when their bodies have been taken over by demons?"

"I can't believe I didn't think of that! Yes, you do you, Juliana. Just write as quietly as you can now so that I can focus on what I'm doing. Do you understand?"

"You're trying to placate me."

"Yes, but I'm also legit intrigued to see how a book on baking and bloodthirster spirit life pans out."

"So, if I do this, you'll come back and visit? Will you bring Elis?"

"Yes, and probably not."

She grabbed the notebook and selected a sparkly silver pen. "Probably not isn't the same as no."

"That's a girl."

She sat at the table and began to compose her thoughts. She could start with which utensils were most important to have on hand or she could talk about what a spirit should do to remain sane within the ether. Perhaps which utensils were most useful in the ether. She put pen to paper.

After a while, she had a general outline of what she wanted to include. "What do you think of this?" She held up the notebook for Sybille to peruse. "Sybille?"

The radio crackled and clicked on. Two beats of a county song and then a switch over to voice.

"Sybille, can you hear me? What the fuck? I came back and even Nate is gone. Why would our resident spirit have left with them? Aunt Margot's being super cagey."

Juliana spoke loudly into her radio. "You're too late. Sybille is gone so I assume she made it to the Ichor realm or is floating somewhere trapped in between. If you want to yell at someone, it will have to be me again."

"Perfect. Just perfect." Zareen's voice cut out for a few seconds. "… want Nate to visit his bloodthirster in the Low? Does she know how stupidly dangerous that is?"

Juliana considered for a moment. What a constant surprise Sybille had turned out to be. "It would seem she does. And it would also seem that she doesn't care."

CHAPTER FIFTEEN

DEVIN

"Shit! What the—!" These words came out at the tail end of a breath just before he hit the floor at the base of the heart tree. With a groan he rolled onto his back and stared at the tree's branches. Ayan and Froya's unconcerned faces appeared, obscuring his view.

"You shouldn't enter a universe in a high place." Ayan extended a hand and pulled him to his feet. "You might become disorientated and fall."

"I didn't exactly plan it." He rubbed his shoulder where it had smashed against a root. "Besides, Froya brought me back. Blame her."

"I initiated your return, you navigated back." She circled around him, checking to make sure he wasn't too broken. "You'll be okay. At least you got the correct building. I suppose you could have landed in the middle of the ocean."

"You should maybe teach me how never to do that."

"It's all about concentrating without trying too hard."

"So you say."

Ayan headed towards a wide doorway. Beyond it was a hallway that led to the various coterie leaders' chambers as well as the guest quarters Devin was staying in. "I have business to attend to, Froya. Now would be a good opportunity to teach him what he wishes to know. Devin, come see me when you're done."

"Okay, granny."

"If you call me that again, I'll throw a knife at your laryngeal prominence."

Devin placed his hands in front of his crotch. "Did she just threaten to knife me in my family jewels?"

"She means your Adam's apple." Froya placed one hand on his laryngeal prominence and slid the other under his hand to touch another prominence. She leaned in close. "You'll have to tell me where you went and why you smell like a ghost."

"You know where I went, and it's not where I thought you were sending me."

"It gave you what you needed, though, didn't it?"

Not really. He needed Sybille. Sybille in the flesh. He needed more than a passing greeting with Charlie. He flinched as her name came to his mind. "In part."

Froya pulled back and examined him again. "I'm going to mix you a drink. Why don't you go outside and say hello to your familiar? I'll meet you there in a moment."

An argument brewed within him. Her paternalistic way of dealing with him drove him nuts. She excelled at pacifying him more than he cared to admit, though, and whatever she put in his drink wouldn't help the conversation in his favor. "Let's skip the alcohol. I need to be good and sober when I say what I need to say. After that, if you want to liquor me up, it will probably be a mercy."

"Have I made a mistake somehow?" A line formed between her brows. "Are you angry with me?"

"I should be. I am when I think about it and now, I'm starting to think about it, so, yes. Yes, I'm angry with you. And Ayan. And the whole coterie."

"The skin on your face is starting to turn red."

"Yeah, and I'm about to throw Ayan's knives around too. Don't." He motioned to Froya's raised hand. "Don't you dare freeze me, Froya. I'm your goddamn weapon. You can't place that role onto me and then expect me not to be dangerous. That's what a weapon is."

She lowered her hand. "Is that what you're upset about? That you're a weapon?"

"Jesus, yes. That I'm a weapon. That I don't know what that means. That I don't have a clue what I'm supposed to do or how you're going to use me to defeat the Ossian. That you're using me at all. How do you think that feels, Froya? To have your worth measured in usability?"

"Why do you think I work for the coterie? Because they can use me. Ayan has mentored me since I was a child because she saw my potential even then. To be useful is an honor."

"To have your skills recognized, sure. But I'm a weapon. You want to use me to destroy. To kill. And I'm not supposed to have a say in that. Then you act surprised when I'm pissed about it."

"Devin, you will be helping rid your beloved Now World of hideous monsters. Why would you be anything but thrilled about that? No one else but you can do such a thing."

As though she carried the plague, he jerked away from her attempt to rub his shoulder. "Let me ask you something. On the day we met, the day you stood in the middle of the road and drew us out of our cars so you could kidnap me, you called Charlie something. You referred to her as that again just before you sent me to—wherever the hell that was. Sybille's Hell's Kitchen. Do you remember what you called her?"

The patronizing smile she'd been wearing morphed into a scowl, deep lines marring her usually flawless face. "I called her what she is. A cursed one. She has the bones of the Ossian and she carries their power. They will spread their disease through her."

He swallowed. He knew this, but it was still hard to hear it coming from someone in such a clinical tone. "Why didn't you just kill her that day?"

Her expression changed again, forehead now scrunched up in confusion. "What a disaster it would have been if I'd tried. No, I don't have that ability. You on the other hand… What do you think I'm training you to do?"

Silence clung to him. Without a word, he turned and walk away from her, up the wide staircase and out onto the balcony. Thunderheart cooed, flapping over to land beside where Devin slumped himself into a chair. "Fucking A, Thunderheart. They expect me to kill my own family." The last word barely made it out of his mouth before he realized the irony of that statement. Of course they expected him to. He'd done it before. He'd hated doing it and hated himself for going through with it, but he'd still done it.

"You ever have to kill your undead sister? Or maybe contemplate being forced to destroy an innocent child?" Thunderheart bobbed his head like he understood. Like he commiserated. "That's right. It does suck."

Froya pushed open the door and joined him, handing him a tumbler with clear liquid and several ice cubes. "I'm guessing you'll be wanting this now?"

He took it but didn't indulge his desire to drain it in one gulp. "I'm not going to do it. I will never hurt Charlie. Never."

Froya sat on the ledge next to him. "When the time comes, you'll do what's right."

"Why do I think we have a vastly different idea of what constitutes as right?" He glanced at a flash of movement from an adjacent balcony. "What's going on over there?"

Froya turned. "That's Ayan's balcony. She has her channel stone open."

"Her what?"

"It's a large gem. Grows in caves in the southern part of this continent."

"What does it mean to have one of them open?"

"It's one of the ways we glimpse different worlds without actually traveling there."

"So she's glimpsing another world? What world? Is it mine?" A see-through image of a person dressed in a long robe popped up in front of Ayan. Devin gripped his tumbler as he shook. Liquid sloshed over the side of the glass. "Son of a bitch, my world it is. Bore—I never would have guessed what a little traitor he is."

"This is how Ayan speaks with him."

"Does that mean she gave that idiot one of your precious channel stones?"

"He can't do anything with it on his own except request to speak with Ayan. That's probably what happened now."

"I want to know what they're talking about."

"That's private."

"Now all of a sudden you care about boundaries?"

"I care about Ichor laws and what Ayan will do to me if I break them."

Cold steel against his neck, purple eyes raging—Devin knew she wasn't wrong. "All right, but I fully intend to ask her what they discussed. I'll play the adoring grandson card with her if I have to."

"You won't have to. Look." She waved to Ayan who's hand was raised to beckon them over.

They reentered the coterie tree chamber and hurried to Ayan's quarters, an inner sanctum Devin hadn't been invited into until now. He stopped just inside to take in the décor. "I wasn't expecting this."

The subdued color pallet included white marble floors, a grey divan, and wooden bookshelves painted to match the floor. The only color came from the spines of Ayan's considerable book collection. He ran his finger across a row of them, most of which had names printed in unfamiliar alphabets. Amidst these, one title caught his eye. He slipped it out. "Why does an Ichor Coterie member have a copy of *Carrie*?"

Froya glanced at the book. "I brought it back for her from a bookstore in Port Everan. She's a fan of your Stephen King. I think she believes he's an actual king who writes his experiences down in between conducting matters of war and executing his enemies."

"I think he just lives in Maine and walks his dog a lot."

She took the book from him and placed it back on the shelf. "We don't have a lot of fiction here. Our reality is entertaining enough."

"Does she think Carrie actually set a gymnasium full of people on fire with her mind?"

"Why wouldn't she? We create whole worlds with ours. Now, do you want to peruse Ayan's library or go out and talk to your Patron?"

"If I actually have to talk to him, can I take along her heaviest book and hit him over the head with it when I'm done?"

"He's only here as a hologram."

"Damn. What a missed opportunity."

Outside, Ayan's balcony resembled a miniature version of the one adjacent to the heart tree chamber, down to the pelican perch attached to the right of the doorway. Ayan motioned them forward. Bore's transparent image quivered when he spotted Devin.

"Devin, how's your training going?"

Devin froze. Bore still wore his notable garb, but his countenance had changed. He stood upright, proud. "Don't you mean, 'How doth thy training fare, oh noble slayer of beasts?'"

"Ooh, well done!" Bore clapped his hands. "You sounded just like me."

Devin turned to Ayan. "Please explain to me again what the point is of keeping this fool around?"

"The point is that it allows us to maintain a minimum presence on

Earth," Ayan explained. "And that means not letting the humans most capable of understanding us become aware that they're working for us."

"Working for you?"

Bore's image flickered for a second. "Don't you get it, Devin? Sybille's family, and you too, you work to kill the Ossian's soldiers."

"We'd be doing that without you, though."

"Are you sure?" Bore asked. "You wouldn't have a paycheck. Peter Esmond would never have hired you. You'd never have met Sybille. And Sybille's family would have to earn their money some other way."

He bristled against the suggestion that he was only in it for the cash, but there was truth to his words. "Well, shit. So, are you rich, or do the Ichor give you fairy jewels?"

"Either way, I'd be wealthy, wouldn't I? But I do what I do because I get to experience things few other mortal humans can. A glimpse at a fae world, spirit possessions, psychic trances. It's all incredibly exciting!"

"So you're still a groupie. Just a groupie with a mission."

Bore seemed unfazed by his insult. "If you see it that way."

Ayan circled Bore's image again. "We aren't here so the Patron can justify his role in this to you. He's insignificant, but what he stands for isn't. The Patron program goes back several human generations and it's worked so far. It's working right now, in fact. The Patron has an update from your world that I'd like you to hear." She tilted her head towards Bore. "Proceed."

"Okay, so, Devin, while you've been exploring fae realms—I want to hear all about that sometime, by the way. Maybe we can grab a beer when this is all over with?"

"You want me to be your bro now?"

"Why not? We have a lot in common. We're both in love with the same woman, a woman who will never love us back."

"Oh, for fuck's sake!"

"In love?" Froya's grip on his arms tightened.

"Stop it!" Ayan flung a knife through Bore. It lodged in the wall a foot from Devin's head. "Patron, continue and do not let personal matters interfere." She glared at each of them. "That goes for all of you."

Bore took a deep, wheezy breath. "As you know, the Esmonds have been attempting to learn all they can regarding the fae war. The part-Ossian man, Laurence, has proven a wealth of knowledge."

Froya squinted. "Can he be trusted?"

"Yes. Yes, I think so," Bore said. "While he has Ossian blood, he's been operating counter to their intentions for years. And he seems to want to rid his granddaughter of their presence."

Ayan leaned in. "Is that possible?"

Bore sniffled. "You tell me. For the girl's sake, I hope so. I've witnessed her Low fits. They are...terrifying."

Devin pushed his way out of Froya's grasp until he stood shoulder-to-shoulder with Ayan. "I saw Charlie when she was in Sybille's head. She said she's getting worse."

Bore's eyes softened. For someone Devin believed cared only for himself, Bore seemed moved. "I'm sorry, Devin. She doesn't have much time left from the looks of it. That's one of the reasons I contacted Ayan. Be prepared to act sooner rather than later."

The fae women exchanged nervous glances. Froya clucked her tongue. "We've been urging the process along as fast as we can. He's a half fae. Progress has been slow."

Devin ignored the insult. "What's the other reason?"

"Come again?"

"You said Charlie getting worse was one of the reasons you wanted to speak to Ayan. What's the other one?"

"Ones. There are two others. The first is about Elis, the reformed thirster Sybille has taken up with. She sent him back to the Low, and he's not alone. Peter and Laurence have gone with. And the spirit, Nate. I heard Peter talking to him when they got in the car. They're all going together."

Ayan extracted her knife from the wall and returned it to its sheath. "For what purpose are they going there?"

"They said it's to check on Raelyn, the Low's leader, and let her know about her daughter. I think there's more to it than that. It would only take one person to convey that message. And it doesn't explain Nate going at all."

The conversation paused as everyone mulled over what Bore had told them. Finally, Froya spoke. "We'll get to the bottom of that soon enough. What is the final thing you needed to tell us?"

"Right. It's about Sybille."

Devin's chest constricted. "What about her? Is she okay?"

"She's better than okay. She's busy mastering new skills. Reality shifting skills."

"Impossible." Ayan whipped around to speak to Froya. "What do we know of this human?"

"She's a hierophant. Talented." Froya pouted for a moment before continuing. "But limited as all humans are. Medium build. Dull eyes."

"Dull eyes?" Devin could hardly believe anyone would describe any part of Sybille as dull. "Her eyes are beautiful. Like a forest after a rain has ended, leaving everything glossy."

"I agree with Devin," Bore chimed in. "I've been captured in her penetrating gaze more than once."

"Fuck off, Bore."

Ayan stomped her foot. "I mean her abilities. She's a hierophant, but most human hierophants lack the skill to open a portal to our worlds. Are we sure she has no fae blood, no fae bone?"

Froya shook her head. "She has none. Her uncle displays witch power, so they most likely carry that lineage. They aren't fae, though, and if they're anything other than human, it's undetectable."

"And yet she can move easily through the veil and has, as I understand it, trapped an evil spirit in a world she created within her own mind. Devin, you know her well. What is she capable of?"

He narrowed his eyes. "More than you'll ever imagine."

Ayan whipped out her knife again and Devin slid to the side, anticipating her desire to throw it at the nearest available target. "Or she's capable of exactly what I imagined."

Devin turned and then nearly collapsed at the sight awaiting him. Sybille stood framed in the doorway, the light of the twin suns casting an angelic glow around her. Perched on her shoulder was a cooing Thunderheart.

"I wish someone had warned me about that tree," Sybille said, scratching the bird's head. "If I'd miscalculated even a little, I'd have ended up dangling from one of its branches."

Devin grinned. "Yeah, that would have been ridiculous."

"Right? And then I had no idea where you were, Devin. If it wasn't for this weird bird, I wouldn't have known where to look for you. He led me here."

Froya raised her hand.

"Stop! Froya, she isn't going to hurt you. Don't freeze her." He wrapped his hand around hers. "Please."

She dropped her arm to her side. Ayan kept her knife pointed.

"Devin? I'm reading the room here and things are feeling pretty tense," Sybille said. "Are you okay?"

"Humans don't belong here. She's breaking our law," Froya growled.

Devin kept his gaze on Froya, trying to draw her attention away from Sybille. "She's only here because of me. Let me go talk to her."

"She is a threat to the Ichor realm." Ayan held her knife steady.

"I'm no threat to you unless you make me one. And I'm going to tell you right now. If you keep Devin here against his will any longer, I'm about to go psychic badass on you."

"Sybille!" Devin stepped towards her. "Really not the time for that."

"When's a good time? After they've honed you into the perfect weapon? Because I kind of think it will be too late by that point."

Ayan flew forward. "How do you know such things?"

Sybille ignored her. "What the fuck?"

Devin followed her gaze. With Ayan off to the side now, Bore's spectral presence was in full view.

"Why is the Patron in the Ichor realm?"

"Hello—um—how art thou, Lady Sybille?"

Ayan took advantage of their distraction. Raising her arm, she readied her weapon.

"No!" Devin screamed. There wasn't enough time, there was too much space to close. He couldn't stop her.

Ayan launched her knife at Sybille. Its aim was true.

CHAPTER SIXTEEN

ELIS

SNOW CLUNG IN STUBBORN PATCHES TO THE ROCKY FIELDS SURROUNDING Raelyn's manor. The poplars lining the driveway stood like upended witches' brooms. Elis wished he could mount one of them and fly far away. This was a place where nightmares lingered, spreading beyond the bounds of sleep. He'd have thought that bringing down the Blood King would deal the Low a blow. Far from it. Elis' hackles were raised the moment Peter's van crossed its border. It could be his mind playing tricks on him, his deep-rooted fear of this place and what it represented projecting greater power onto it than what was warranted. He tried to calm himself with that thought only to have Peter justify his concerns.

"This place has changed, and not for the better." Peter scrutinized Elis. "You feel it, don't you?"

Elis' fang pierced through his lip where he'd bitten it. He sucked in the blood and swirled it over his tongue like mouthwash. "Do you think it's Raelyn? Has she done something to intensify the Low?"

"Could be. She is a leader to be reckoned with. No doubt she rules with a fair amount of force." He tapped his fingers against the dashboard. "But it could also be the Ossian gearing up for war. The Low is a weapon and an armor all in one. They want this place fortified and ready."

Elis shuddered thinking about that, then forced himself to focus on the road ahead, both literally and metaphorically. His mission clear, there could be no diversions, no missteps, not if the Ossian war was to be diverted. Sybille had put him in charge. If they failed, it would be on him.

Laurence yawned from the back seat. "You should have woken me sooner. We could have used the time to prepare."

"Why? We already know what we need to do." Elis pulled into the center of the u-shaped driveway in front of the mansion and shifted the van into park. He cut the engine. "Just stick with the plan."

"Raelyn will figure it out," Laurence said. "And she won't like that I'm here."

"Let me deal with Raelyn. Besides, who cares if she likes you being here or not? She's not going to be happy about any of us showing up unannounced, but honestly, fuck her."

"I'm afraid my family isn't a good influence on you, Elis. The more time you spend with Zareen and Sybille, the crasser you become." Peter unfastened his seatbelt and turned to face the passengers in back. "But Elis is right. Raelyn is responsible for her choices and is entitled to her opinions. That doesn't change our purpose for being here, nor should we let it stop us. So I suppose I must second the notion: fuck her. Nate, how are you holding up?"

Nate's pale form nearly disappeared into his seat's upholstery. "Not so great. That was a long ride." He extracted himself from the cushions, one limb at a time.

"If we'd had a day or two more," Peter said, "I would've taken you out on shorter jaunts, gotten you used to traveling in a car. You did well, considering. Thank you, Laurence, for aiding him."

"All I did was meditate and then unintentionally fall asleep."

"Your snoring helped center him." Peter opened his door. "Oh, good. Looks like the welcome wagon is here."

On the steps leading down from the front door came two hulking figures carrying scary-looking guns. Peter held his hands up while everyone else clambered out of the van. "Tell Raelyn that Peter is here to pay her a visit. A friendly visit. We're no threat, and we're unarmed."

Elis joined him on the passenger side of the van. "Let me do the talking, Peter."

"Why? Raelyn and I have an established relationship."

Bottomless margaritas and a long, bare neck. Blood with memory and an unnamable taste.

"I happen to have an established relationship with her as well. And Sybille put me in charge."

"Who cares who's in charge as long as we get the job done?"

"And what job is that?" A woman with blond hair stepped out of the shadow of the entryway and pushed through her bodyguards. She motioned for them to lower their weapons. "Now this is a surprise."

Ignoring the still-menacing stance of the bloodthirsters flanking her, Peter stepped forward. "Raelyn, it's a pleasure to see you again."

"Cut the crap, Peter. There's no pleasure in the three of you showing up in the Low without an invitation."

"We wanted to speak with you."

"Haven't you heard of a phone?"

"And see you. A face-to-face seemed critical."

"Again, a video conference would have sufficed. Unless," she peered past Peter and gave Elis a wink, "your ensouled bloodthirster mascot was thirsty for a bit of immortal nourishment again."

Peter stared at Elis, his forehead creased in a deep V. "Again?"

Elis rubbed his chin. "I was hungry. She was…there."

Raelyn stepped onto the driveway. "If you return the favor, my neck will bend for you again, Elis."

He resisted the urge to lick his lips. "I just drank a freshly butchered goat before coming here. Raincheck?"

"Suit yourself." She brushed past him and examined the two remaining members of their band. "Laurence. You know you're not welcome here. What are you even doing associating with these people?"

Laurence scowled. "You know why."

She returned his expression. "Peter, did I give you permission to let this man near my daughter?"

Peter pushed his glasses up the bridge of his nose. "To be fair, you didn't tell us he existed. We didn't know his connection to Charlie until he showed up at our door."

"You should have killed him right there and then. He's dangerous."

"That's rich, coming from you. Besides, he loves Charlie." Elis couldn't believe he was defending the man who'd once conspired with Juliana to murder him, but if he had to choose who had Charlie's best interests at heart, his gut told him it wasn't the homicidal immortal giving an old man a death stare. "He wants to help cure her."

Oh?" Raelyn broke her gaze and turned toward Elis. "Be careful about what Laurence claims he wants. He tried to kidnap her. Did you know that?"

"I wanted her to be safe. She wasn't safe in the Low. *You* know *that*."

"You didn't have my permission to take her."

"I had my son's."

She shook her head. "He's barely concerned himself with her since she was born. Too busy freebasing Crave to care about his only child. Sadly, he's just another junkie, Laurence."

"Whose fault is that! You gave him Crave. You made him what he is."

"The Low made him what he is. But what he isn't is a parent who can determine whether Charlie got to leave with you. You know, as soon as you'd gone, he confessed it all to me. That's why we found you so easily. You should never have trusted him."

"Your hair is the same color as Mary's."

Raelyn stared in the direction of Nate's voice. "You brought a spirit with you. Interesting." She circled around him, a curious lilt in her voice replacing scorn. "Excuse me, spirit. I didn't identify what you were at first. But I'd love to know: who's Mary?"

Nate shimmered and then became more transparent than Elis had ever seen him before. "It's my fault that she died. They killed me too. In the forest. This forest. This is where I died."

"That explains a fair amount." She squinted. "I almost didn't recognize you, Nathanial."

"I prefer if you called me Nate."

Raelyn turned on her heel and headed back towards the house. "Let's go inside and have that face-to-face you came all this way for."

They followed her in, and she showed them to a formal living room complete with lace doilies covering the arms of chairs and tops of coffee tables. Nate spun around as though he'd won the lottery.

Elis eyed a silver tea set. He picked up a spoon with an ornate Egyptian scarab carved into its handle.

"Do you like it? I redecorated when I moved in. Nathanial's taste was a bit too dark for me and I always wanted a formal parlor." She took the spoon from him, held it in front of her and then handed it back. "Now tell me why you're here. Have you found my brother?"

"Sort of." Elis took a seat on the bench of a baby grand piano. "Sybille is working on it."

"That's a no then. I would say this visit is about Charlie, but you've brought the spirit of the beast formerly known as the Blood King with you. I doubt you'd let him tag along just for the scenery."

"This visit is about Charlie," Elis assured her. "But it's about Nate too. We need to figure out what the Blood King's rate of recovery is, and Peter believes Nate can help with that."

"I'd like to know how. But first, I want to hear about my daughter. How is she coping with having her traitorous grandfather in her life again?"

Laurence, still standing near the room's entrance, walked to the back of the divan Raelyn sat upon and gripped its fabric like he wanted to tear it off in big chunks. "You shouldn't be worried about me. Your daughter, on the other hand, is being eaten from the inside out. But I think you already knew that."

Raelyn's smirk faltered. "I'd hoped removing her from the Low would help heal her."

"No, you didn't." The artery on Laurence's neck bulged. Elis ran a tongue over his fangs as the man squirmed, his anger visible in the flush spreading over his face. "You knew it wouldn't. You planned this."

"You think I want to see my daughter taken over by an ominous force?"

"I think you don't see it that way at all. You've let the Ossian dictate your destiny and hers. If they let you remain sitting on your throne, you'll sacrifice your child to their cause, ominous though it may be."

Elis sniffed the air as though he hoped he'd be able to detect danger the way a police dog detects bombs. At any moment, Raelyn would tire of listening to Laurence's truths and call in her cavalry to come and remove them. Or just remove their heads. He imagined the lot of them, sitting around Raelyn's fancy parlor, blood spurting from their headless necks, while Nate floated next to the sideboard guessing which kind of tree its wood came from.

Raelyn remained quiet. Their heads remained attached.

When she spoke, it was barely above a whisper. "I can't control what they decide. It's true: I didn't argue when they told me to give Charlie to Sybille and Devin. I knew what their plan was. But..." She sat up a little straighter. "If you think you can help her, I won't stand in your way."

"That brings up an interesting point, Raelyn." Peter opened the briefcase he'd brought with him, extracting from it a small box. He handed the box to her. She rolled her eyes when she saw its contents.

"You need another blood sample? Haven't you taken at least a dozen from me over the years?"

Peter motioned for Raelyn to push up her sleeve. "What if I told you your blood might be part of Charlie's cure?"

"I'd say you're full of shit."

"Aren't we all, from time to time?"

She rolled the fabric of her shirt up to her shoulder. "You can have another sample, but I have one condition."

Peter grazed his fingers over Raelyn's upper arm until he found a vein. "What condition is that?"

"It's about Nathanial's dimwitted spirit."

Elis glanced at Nate to see if he'd heard her speak about him. Focused on trying, unsuccessfully, to pick up the edge of a lace doily, he made no indication that he was aware of their conversation. "What about him?"

Raelyn's resting smirk-face returned. "You can have my blood, but only if I can have him."

CHAPTER SEVENTEEN

SYBILLE

THE TIME IT TAKES FOR A KNIFE TO PASS FROM THE PERSON THROWING IT TO HER target twenty feet away could be measured in split seconds. Splinters of time. Splintered, like her heart was about to be. Sybille resisted shutting her eyes. If this was her last moment, she would face it with eyes wide open.

And so Sybille witnessed the flash of steel take shape as it grew nearer, then steady, then still. It hung suspended in the air no more than the length of her pinky finger away from her body. She kept her eyes open, afraid if she blinked, the weapon would complete its journey. Frozen by her own sense of terror rather than fae magic, she searched her periphery for the cause of the knife's miraculous withdrawal from the laws of motion.

Devin stood, one leg bent, the other pushed back like he was about to use it to spring forward. He stretched his arm ahead of him in the direction of the knife. On his wrist, a purple jewel shone.

"Grab it, Sybille! I'm not sure how long I can do this!"

Finger's shaking, she placed both hands on the knife's shaft. The tip of its blade stared at her like a one-eyed shark. She tugged it out of its stasis, throwing it to the ground. "When did you learn to do that?"

"About ten seconds ago." He rushed her then, and quicker than a knife could be launched in the air, she found herself wrapped in his arms. Every muscle went from tense to putty as she sank into him, allowing herself a moment to pretend she wasn't about to get murdered by Devin's new family. She soaked in his scent, his warmth, his affection.

"I did not teach you to do that."

Sybille peered over Devin's shoulder at the person who'd spoken. She stood with arms crossed. It was the same woman who'd blocked their exit from the Low, frozen her, and stolen Devin. "We meet again, *Froya*."

Devin pulled back, his eyes wide in surprise. "How'd you know her name?"

"I've been doing my homework." She glanced at the knife on the ground. "I guess you have too."

"Again, I did not teach him that. You should be dead." Froya slid her hand over Devin's arm and pulled him away from Sybille. "But I'm proud of you, Devin. You learned something on your own."

"I'm not proud." The knife-wielding woman fingered a clasp on her belt that Sybille suspected held other pointy items. "You defended this trespasser. Explain yourself!"

"I told you, she's my friend and she came here because of me. That's no reason to go all ninja on her, Grandma."

"Grandma?" Sybille stared at the beautiful woman with orange and black hair and bright eyes the same shade as Froya's. She didn't look a day older than her supposed grandson. Ignoring the woman's menacing expression, she stepped from behind Devin, hand out. "Sounds like there's a story there. Well, anyone who's family to Devin is family to me. My name is Sybille."

Unmoved, the woman stared at Sybille's outstretched hand. At least no one had tried to freeze her yet.

"Sybille, maybe keep your distance?" He tugged on the back of her shirt. "She just tried to kill you."

"Oh that? Forget about it. I'm used to crazy people trying to stick knives in my chest."

Ayan's hair underwent an instant dye job, all the orange highlights receding into blackness. "I will not forget about it. And you are the crazy one for daring to come here."

"What you call crazy, I call brave." Bore's holographic image flickered as he spoke. He appeared to be growing out of a glowing opaque crystal the shape of a deflated football.

"I'll get to you later, Patron. Stay in your Princess Leia hologram mode and don't go anywhere until I have a chance to make you answer my questions."

"I can't answer anything unless Ayan okays it."

"Who's Ayan? And why are you talking like someone finally kicked you out of the Renaissance Faire?"

"I am Ayan," said the knife wielder. "Head of the Ichor Coterie. And your reckoner."

"Okay, so we haven't moved past this." She plopped herself down on a rattan couch and ran her hand over the woven fabric of its cushions. "Look, I'm sorry I came here without your permission. I'm a lowly human, and not worthy of your time, but regardless, I need Devin to come home and deal with a situation that, frankly, is partly the Ichor's fault. So, I'll just grab him, and we'll be on our way."

"What is the Ichor's fault?"

"You know, the whole Ossian trying to take over the world thing."

Ayan snapped and unsnapped the sheath attached to her belt. "That is their doing, not ours."

"Sure, but if you weren't in an eons-long war, the Now World wouldn't be a battleground. And I said partly your fault, not entirely. Believe me, I think the Ossian suck too. They just do it wearing less-clashing outfits."

Ayan charged. Devin put himself in her way, holding her back as best he can.

"Do you want me to immobilize her so she'll be easier to kill?" Froya asked.

"No! I don't need your help killing things, Froya!"

"No one's going to kill things." Devin held her by the shoulders. "Or people. People named Sybille. I won't let you."

Anya stopped struggling.

"See?" Sybille placed her feet on the table in front of the couch. "Devin would like us to be friends."

"I will wait to kill you until Devin isn't around to witness it."

This was getting old, fast. She plopped her feet back on the ground and stood. "Devin, do you have a bag that needs packing?"

"They won't let me go, Sybille. My passage to the Now World is blocked."

"Mine's not. I'll take you with me."

"It won't work unless we let it." Froya again positioned herself close to

Devin. "You would turn up in your world alone. You aren't more powerful than we are, no matter what you believe."

"Then you have to see reason! Devin's niece is sick. I can't cure her without him."

"Hold on." Devin's voice cracked. "Are you saying a cure is possible?"

"Peter and Laurence think so," she said. "I have the rest of Esmond Incorporated working on it. If they succeed in the tasks I've assigned them, we're most of the way there. You're the last piece, Devin."

Ayan stepped forward. Orange had begun to return to her hair, but the woman's wide-legged stance and her array of weapons arranged on her belt were no less menacing. "You're speaking of the Ossian weapon. The girl meant to spread their plague over your universe. She can't be helped."

"She can! We want the same thing here—to kick the Ossian to the curb, destroy their plans. I know you think we're weak, and maybe we are, but we won't sit back and watch our world die." She searched Ayan's face in vain for any hint of empathy. "You're devising your plan—one Devin factors into. I have my own plan, and he's part of that too. Maybe we can work together. The enemy of my enemy is my friend."

Ayan considered her worlds. "My friend is the enemy of my enemy. There is truth to that. But your human plan is bound to fail. Ours is better. So, he stays with us."

She began walking towards Bore, then waved her hand. His image disappeared.

"Hey, I wanted to talk to him!" Sybille scowled.

Ayan's hand toyed with the sheath of a dagger. "If you leave immediately and alone, I'll let you go without any extra holes in you."

"No. I need him to come with me. Just for a bit. You can have him back."

"When?"

"When?"

"When can I have him back?"

She looked at Devin, then back to Ayan. "If we fail. If that happens, he's all yours again."

Devin stomped his foot. "Do I get to negotiate the terms of my own release?"

Ayan ignored him. "How will I know that you'll return him when you fail?"

"*If* we fail."

Devin waved his hand to get their attention. "I'd like a say in this, please!"

"I'll go with." Froya coiled an arm around Devin's waist. "I'll keep an eye on him and then bring him back."

"You are both Ichor." Ayan frowned, but she seemed to be contemplating Sybille's terms. "Your presence in the human's realm can be detected easily."

"If there's any danger that would compromise our own strategy, I'll return with him. Besides, this human's plan could work in our favor."

"Yes, but what is her plan?" Ayan asked, glaring at Sybille.

Sybille picked at her fingernails. "I'll show you mine if you show me yours."

"You speak strangely." Ayan fiddled with her knives again. "Froya, are they all like this?"

"What she means," Froya shot Sybille a dirty look, "is that she won't say what her plan is unless we tell her what ours is."

Devin laughed. "You haven't even told me what that plan is, and I *am* that plan."

"You know what you need to," Ayan told him. "The human needs to know nothing."

"Well then, the coterie leader needs to know nothing about my plans. We've either come to an agreement or to an impasse."

"An impasse."

"Grandma, come on!" Devin gave her his most pitiful puppy face. "It's only for a while. And Froya will be with me the whole time."

Ayan looked back and forth between Devin and Froya, who seemed willing to indulge Devin but only if it meant not letting him out of her sight.

"So help me, if you don't return when I command it, I will go there, I will find you. Sybille." Leaning in to where Sybille sat, she ran her fingers along the base of Sybille's neck. "When I find you, I will slit your throat and use your blood to fuel children's rituals for the next decade."

"God, for a bunch of rainbow-clad motherfuckers, you are a dark bunch."

"I will preserve the Ichor way of life at all costs. Your life means little to me."

"Not to me, it doesn't." Devin clasped his grandmother's shoulders. "Remember, I have a role to play and you need me. If you threaten Sybille or try to make her part of your blood magic, I won't do what you want."

Ayan slapped his hands away. "Leaving to help this human is your one and only choice. Our greatest sacrifices are decided by the blood flowing through our world, our bodies, our hearts. You will do what's right. That is the only path for blood fae."

"Well, now that that's out in the open, can we go?" Sybille asked.

Devin's bird chose that moment to swoop from a nearby perch onto Devin's outstretched arm. "Yep. My bag's packed."

"You're taking your bird?" She cocked her head in the pelican's direction. The bird mirrored her movements.

"Thunderheart's my familiar."

"No kidding?" Thunderheart nestled himself under Devin's chin. "I hope he's housetrained, or my mother is going to freak."

The three departing people, plus Thunderheart, gathered in a circle. Ayan watched from the balcony's edge.

"Okay, here's the plan." Sybille held her hand to shield her eyes as she peered out onto the Ichor city. "I'm going to navigate us through a small world in my brain. That's the route I took to get here so that's the way I have to return. Is that going to be all right with you, Froya?"

"Why do that?" Froya asked. "I'm capable of bringing us directly to your world. There's no need to use an intermediary realm."

"Yes, but I'd rather I was the one in control of this world jumping."

Froya laughed. "You are a novice. Granted, I'm impressed that you made it here, but letting you lead us creates unnecessary risk. One or more of us could become trapped somewhere in between worlds if you bungled things."

It went against Sybille's gut to let this possessive fae woman take the lead. For all she knew, Froya would purposefully eject Sybille into some dark corner of existence while she took Devin on a romantic romp. "How do I know you'll bring us all where we need to be?"

"She will, Sybille." Devin's voice was even. "She knows I'll never forgive her if she doesn't."

"You would eventually." Froya kissed his cheek. "But I promise you, this time I have no opposing agenda. I want to see what you're up to, hierophant."

"Fine, let's just do this then. Do not double cross—"

The world morphed.

"—me."

"What was that, dear? Oh, you're back. That was quick."

Sybille stood in her living room. She spun around. Her mother sat in her recliner, a ball of pink yarn in her lap, crochet hook in her hand. "I'm making Charlie a scarf. Did you find Devin?"

She spun again. "Motherfucker. I'm going to gouge out those purple eyes of hers."

"Sybille, such a horrible thing to say! It's a good thing Charlie's sleeping. Now, did you find Devin or not?"

"Oh, I found him all right."

"Well then, where is he?"

"His fae girlfriend hijacked him again, probably so she can have sex with him on some tropical fairy beach."

"He has a girlfriend? Well, that's nice. He deserves that after what you put him through."

"What are you talking about? I didn't put him through anything. And that's beside the point, Mother. We need him here, and now I have no idea where the hell he is. *Again!*" She kicked at the leg of a chair.

A low ruff came from behind the couch. Margot set her crochet project aside and got up to inspect the sound. "Are you sure he didn't transform into a dog?"

"What?"

"There's a dog here, and it wasn't before you arrived, which means you brought him back with you." She slapped her hands to her knees. "Devin! Come here, boy."

A scruffy brown dog came bounding out to her, tail wagging. Margot patted his head. "There's a good boy." She turned to her daughter. "But this is terrible, Sybie. How on Earth are we going to explain to Charlie that her uncle has fleas?"

CHAPTER EIGHTEEN

DEVIN

DEVIN SAT ON A HILL OVERLOOKING THE DISTANT MESA. PALMS WET WITH DEW, he tore up clumps of prairie grass, tossing the blades into a pile. It was a pointless activity, but a better one than crossing his fingers for the millionth time only to have nothing happen. He wanted to lie down in the grass and never get up again. Instead, he forced himself to rise and walk towards the barn. Pushing open the stubborn door, wood swelled from the humidity, he stepped inside so he would be in full view of Thunderheart's stall.

Empty. Just as he'd guessed it would be.

The facts were irrefutable: Froya had hijacked him again, and this time, she'd stolen his familiar from him as well.

"There you are." Froya's clear voice floated over to him. "I thought you'd be waiting for me in the house."

Grimacing, he kept himself turned away from her and remained silent.

"I'm sorry for the delay. I had to speak to Ayan on my own before I could join you."

Anger roiled through him. His fingernails dug into Thunderheart's stall door. "Why aren't we with Sybille?"

"I thought you might want to see this place again. It has so many pleasant memories, don't you agree?"

"Do I agree?" Now he did turn. His breath quickened; his stomach heaved. "You're full of shit, Froya. What I agreed with is that we would leave with Sybille and we would stay with Sybille. She expects us to arrive at her house. Now we're here instead and she's going to be pissed. And you know what I think? I think that's why you did this. Just for no other reason than to piss her off."

"Why would I care about angering a human?"

"I don't know, Froya. You tell me. Maybe you're jealous because I'd rather be in her world than in yours."

"I'm not jealous of her. Besides, it hardly matters which world you prefer. In the end, you'll do what the Ichor need you to do. I doubt Sybille Esmond will factor into that."

"Right. See, what I think is, you do care where I'd rather be. You care who I'd rather be with. I don't know why you're choosing to lie about that now, but I don't have time for it. I'm going to need you to take me to the Now World or restore my powers so I can take myself there."

"Don't be so upset. I fully intend to bring you to Sybille's. Ayan and I promised you that."

"Then why are we here on this fucking spaghetti-western set instead of in a cozy hundred-year-old bungalow on Port Everan's north side?"

"I know what spaghetti is and there's none here. Unless you'd like some for dinner. It can be arranged."

"Just...fucking hell, Froya. Why. Are. We. Here?"

"Because, Ayan and I felt the need to go over some ground rules with you."

He groaned. "You have to stop that."

"Stop what?"

"Treating me like a child. I can almost—almost—forgive Ayan for doing that, seeing as though she's my grandmother, but you? You're my girlfriend. I mean, I guess that's what we are? We're supposed to be on equal footing."

"How can we be? You're only an Earthblood. You need guidance."

"You know what you're good at besides lying? Proving my point. If we're a couple, you can't keep putting all these restrictions on me, playing with the block in my brain, giving my power back, only to take it away again when you get nervous and think I'm going to take off on you."

"You would never take off on me."

"I didn't say I would. I said you *thought* I would."

"No, I don't think you would because I have the power to prevent it."

"Jesus." He paused to take a deep breath; his eyes looked towards the rafters. "I'm saying that you're being too controlling and that that is what's driving me away. Loosen up on the reins a little."

"You're not a horse. But I think I understand what you mean."

"Speaking of horses. Or pelicans. Where's Thunderheart."

"With Sybille. He's a dog now."

"I'm allergic to dogs."

"Don't eat him then."

"Fucking hell, you Ichor fae will never stop being weird." Leaning back against the wall, he let his mood lighten. Whatever was keeping Froya from bringing him to Sybille, she needed to get it resolved before he completely lost it. Now that he knew the truth about this ranch world, that it was nothing but a mirage built to hold him while the fae calibrated his mind to their liking, it made him nauseous and dizzy. He'd do anything to get away from here, including indulging Froya's skewed perceptions. "Whatever you need to say to me, I'm listening."

She sashayed over to him, her fingers playing with his belt buckle as she leaned into him. "Are you sure you wouldn't be more comfortable in our old quarters? You brought us right to the bed last time we were here."

The usual tingling warmth that would rise and spread whenever her body rocked against his failed to materialize.

"There'll be time for that later." He slid his arm around her back and moved her to the side. "Right now, I don't want to be distracted. And we both know how distracting you can be."

She smiled. "You're right. The war between our people and the Ossian is a serious matter. You're part of it, whether you like it or not."

"I don't like it. Go on."

"Sybille would be dead if it wasn't for me. I want you to remember who spared her."

"I spared her. I'm the one who stopped Ayan's blade midair."

"Yes, but I convinced her to let Sybille live. She has many weapons. She knows many ways to kill. You couldn't have stopped her on your own, but I chose to help you."

"And I'm grateful. I'm sure Sybille is too. Did you have to bring me here to tell me that?"

"When I save someone's life, I have made the choice that their continued existence has value in some way. There is a slim chance that

Sybille will be able to help the Ichor. I've given her the opportunity to try. There's value in that. And in her."

"But what if she can't? What if whatever she's going to do fails?"

"Then we must at least not give Ayan a reason to have her killed."

"Meaning, I have to be back in the Ichor realm, as scheduled, no matter what."

"Yes. It's where you belong." She ran her hand over the stubble along his jawline. Smooth, cold fingers caressed him. "You're one of us, Devin."

"I'm one of them too." He jutted his head away from her touch. The smell of damp hay hit him as he stared at the barn's floor. "I'm as much human as I am fae."

She scowled. "Yes, we can't undo your lineage."

"What happens if I refuse to return with you? What if we need more time than Ayan wants to give us or I just don't feel like leaving?"

Froya broke away from him. "It won't be an issue."

He wiped his sweaty palms against the stall door. "What if I make it an issue? What if I want control over my own life and I say no to you for once? What if I insist on removing the block from my brain altogether so you can no longer control me? What then?"

"You know what then."

"Say it."

She held up her hand. "I'm not a knife thrower like Ayan, but I have other ways. She won't even feel it coming. Unless I want her to."

Before he could formulate a response, she crossed her fingers and the barn transformed into the Esmond's living room.

Sybille sat on the couch, one of her mother's hand-crocheted blankets on top of her, remote control in her lap. At the sight of them, she yelped and turned off the television. "It's about damn time. I was about to try channeling you to see if I could find where you'd gone."

"Really? Because it looked more like you were watching *The Bachelor*."

"I was not! I was just randomly channel surfing. And excuse me for needing to wallow for a moment when the friend I thought I'd saved doesn't seem to have been saved after all and all my plans start to unravel without him. I'm entitled to a little mindlessness."

"You already use far less of your brain capacity than fae do." Froya stared at her like a spider assessing a fly caught in its web. "Why would you want to cease using it?"

"The only thing I want to hear from you," she jutted her finger towards Froya's chest, "is where you were. I wasted the past two hours of my life thinking you'd fooled me again."

"I can't help how you think," Froya told her. "And if you're fooled, it's because you're unintelligent."

"Okay, that's enough of that. Sybille, did you happen to see, um… I guess he's a dog now?"

"Oh, Thunderheart? He's upstairs with my mother. She's giving him a bath."

"Why?"

"Because he has fleas. Also, she thinks he's you."

"Why would she think I'm a dog? And if she thinks I am a dog, is it weird that she's bathing me?"

"She greatly underestimates my skills in world jumping. Thinks I messed up and rearranged your molecular structure. Or something. I tried to tell her she's wrong. Like usual, it didn't work." She crossed her arms and narrowed her eyes. "I'm still pissed, by the way. I don't like feeling conned."

"I took him on a brief detour, that's all." Froya danced her fingertips up Devin's arm. "We had some business to attend to."

She snorted. "I bet you did."

"It wasn't like that!" Devin brushed Froya away.

Froya let out a low purr. "Yes, it was exactly like that. Just like the many, many other times."

"I don't appreciate you sidetracking us, Froya, no matter how much you wanted to play with your newest toy."

"I'm not a toy!" He growled. "More like a pawn."

"Yeah? Well I'm giving you a promotion, Devin," Sybille told him. "While you're here with me, you're a knight. And I'm going to need you to act like it."

A sharp bark came from the top of the stairs. A medium-sized brown mutt with shaggy, wet fur bounded down them. A patch of white in the shape of a heart graced his forehead.

"Devin!" Margot called. "Come back here! You're going to ruin my furniture!"

Margot chased after the dog, who, tail wagging, made his way over to

Devin. Devin caught hold of him as Thunderheart leapt up, placing his paws on Devin's chest so he could lick his face.

"It's good to see you again too, boy." Devin turned his face to the side and sneezed. "You couldn't have changed into a turtle this time, maybe?"

Margot froze upon seeing him. "My god, there are two of you? Sybille, are you responsible for this?"

"Mom, I told you the dog wasn't Devin."

"This," Devin said as he stroked the dog's back, "is my familiar, Thunderheart. He came through from the Ichor realm with Sybille. I got delayed a bit."

"Oh, of course," Margot said. "I think you should know that your familiar likes to eat soap, and as you can see, he does jump up on people when he gets excited. But other than that, he's a good boy. Hello, dear heart." She gave Froya a wide smile. "We've never had a fae guest."

"You've had Devin here before." Froya turned her bug gaze onto Sybille's mother.

"He doesn't count. We thought he was all human. Besides, he isn't a guest. He's family. Would you like something to drink? We have coffee or tea."

Froya's purr turned into a hiss.

"No need to be rude. Did you prefer to indulge in something stronger? I have wine, or whiskey."

Devin followed Froya's line of sight, past Margot, through the dining room. There, in the doorway leading to the kitchen, stood Charlie, her hand shoved into a jar of gummy worms.

"I don't want your human drinks. What I want, as much as it repulses me, is for the cursed one to come forward."

Sybille stepped towards Charlie and placed herself in front of the girl. "Why would you want that?"

"Because that's why we're here. You said you required Devin to fix the girl, so that's what he needs to do. Fix her. Or if that fails…" Froya didn't seem to think it necessary to continue her thought.

"I know what she wants." Charlie's quiet voice echoed up from behind Sybille. Such a tiny sound, but it rattled Devin's bones and sent his blood on a racecourse with no finish line. "She wants Uncle Devin to kill me. He's the only one who can."

CHAPTER NINETEEN

ELIS

THE EDGE OF A DOILY LIFTED AS THOUGH BY A BREEZE. OR SO IT WOULD SEEM to anyone without the ability to see spirits. Instead, Elis watched as Nate managed to touch the linen textile, gently cradling it in his palm before he lost his connection with the physical plain. The doily flopped back over the side of the table.

"I did it! That's the fourth time I've been able to touch something. Something real!"

"See how much fun he'll have here if he stays?" Raelyn opened a narrow drawer under the table and took out a folded cloth lined along the edges with delicate lace. She waved it at Nate. "He's a happy spirit, aren't you Nathanial?"

"I am! Wait, am I staying here? Elis, do I live here now?"

"No! Hell no." He glanced at Raelyn. "Okay, maybe." Raelyn's unabashed glee hurt his brain. Here they were bringing news of how sick her daughter was, and all she cared about seemed to be gaining a new pet. "Peter, how badly do we need her blood?"

"It's potentially game changing, unfortunately." Peter sighed. "Raelyn, what would you even do with Nate if we left him for you?"

She kept her gaze on the spirit. "Same thing you want to use him for. Probe Nathanial's body, see how damaged he may still be."

"Is that all?" Elis asked.

"It's all that matters if you want my blood. Do we have a deal?"

"We'll leave him here." Peter said. He wasn't lying. That had been the plan from the beginning, though exactly how they'd be leaving him probably wasn't what she'd expect. "Now, can we get on with it?" He motioned to her rolled up sleeve.

"I suppose."

Elis rose from the sofa like he was an old mortal man. More decorative than functional, it made his lower back twinge. "Laurence and I will take Nate down to the Blood King's cell. Will you two join us when you're finished?"

Raelyn kept her expression flat, but her voice was firm. "We won't be long, so whatever you think you're here to do, you'll have to do it with me present. And my men will escort you." She rang a tiny silver bell and her bodyguards appeared. "Take them to the dungeons."

"I see you're adjusting to your role as queen of the Low." Elis stepped towards her guards, then paused. "Look, we've been straight with you. All we wanted was to warn you that your little girl doesn't have much time left. We're not here to start a war."

"Don't use my daughter as a bargaining chip, then."

He nearly spat at her. Of course she'd accuse him of committing the sin she herself was guilty of. What an awful set of parents Charlie had been stuck with. Awful, that was, until she'd found her way into the Esmond household. Even if she did succumb to the Low and unleash a hell on earth, at least she'd had time to live in a semi-normal household with people who cared about her. Such a cold comfort to hang his hopes upon now.

"The Wizard of Oz."

Raelyn crinkled her brow. "What?"

"It's Charlie's favorite book. I've been reading it with her. A little girl finds herself alone in a strange land filled with peculiar powers and where evil forces are at work. Forces that want to use her. Use her and destroy her. Seems she can relate to that premise."

Raelyn's forehead remained creased. "Does my skin look green to you? I'm her mother, not an evil witch."

"Funny. I didn't say anything about a witch."

"I'm familiar with the story. Devin and I watched the movie when we were kids."

"Well then you know it has a happy ending. The girl finds friends and she isn't alone anymore. They work together to fight evil. The terrible witch that I'm *definitely not* comparing to a real person gets melted. And her family—those are the people who truly love her—they're waiting for her to heal, to be made whole again." He turned and nodded to Raelyn's bodyguards. "Anyway, I just thought you'd like to know what your daughter is interested in, since you're such an invested and caring mother. Come on, Laurence. Nate, you too. Let's get this over with."

He expected a witty retort, but none came. They left Raelyn to be monitored by Peter, who would draw Raelyn's blood as slowly as he possibly could.

They followed the bodyguards down a hallway with dark wainscoting and mustard and red pinstriped wallpaper. Like the parlor, the décor seemed as though Raelyn was reliving her human youth in the regency era. He had to remind himself that she'd been born less than three decades ago. Her taste seemed designed to mimic the prestige that came with age. Perhaps, despite the growing strength of the Low, not every thirster within its confines was satisfied with its young ruler.

Just before the entryway to the kitchen, one of the bodyguards, a young thirster with a neck the same circumference as his head, pushed open a wooden door. They descended into the mansion's bowels. Each step he took felt as though he was lowering himself into his own grave. He clung to the railing, Nate hovering by his side. Laurence, trailing behind them, panted. Elis was reasonably sure it wasn't from exertion. Anyplace designed to hold someone like the Blood King wasn't bound to be pleasant.

"Leave it to my daughter-in-law to take the Low from an outer to an inner circle of Hell." Laurence paused to cough. "Her dungeon could use a dehumidifier."

A minute later, they stood with the thirster guards in front of a silver-plated door with no window.

Thick Neck punched in a code to a panel next to the door and the click of a bolt rotating followed. He pushed the door open. "Raelyn will be here soon. No funny business or we'll slit the human's throat and take your head clear off."

Elis pushed past him, fangs on display. "Aren't you a loyal one?"

Thick Neck's partner sidled up towards him. "We are Ossian soldiers.

This world will be gifted to us once the Ossian have their way. We're loyal to the bone."

"Bollocks. You'll all die for them, and the Ossian won't shed a tear."

Laurence cleared his throat. "Elis, the Blood King awaits."

That was a bit of an exaggeration. The pathetic, broken monster formerly holding the title of Blood King lay strapped to a hospital gurney, eyes dull and unfocused. Mouth gaped open, a trail of drool escaped between his tongue and jagged, rotting teeth. A stench like that of a dead cow left to putrefy under a hot sun made him cover his nose. He swallowed back vomit.

As soon as he was inside the cell, the bodyguards closed the door. The lock clicked into place. Elis resisted panic. Laurence's skin had taken on a green hue.

Nate hovered over the body that had once ensouled him, the aura that surrounded his form dimmer than usual.

"I can't remember why I got all these tattoos." Unburdened with the sense of smell, Nate leaned in until he was mere inches from his physical counterpart. "What does YOLF mean? And why didn't I go to a dentist even once? Sybille told me dentists are good now. That's why her teeth are so shiny."

Elis joined him as Laurence took up a spot the opposite side of the gurney. "YOLF stands for you only life forever. It's a bloodthirster pun, I suppose. I don't know why he didn't go see a dentist, but I'm relieved for any dentist he didn't see. Laurence, what do we do now?"

"First, we do what we said we were going to do. We have Nate fish around in Nathanial's brain. My god, do they never bathe him?" Laurence took out a handkerchief and tied it around his head so it covered his nose, then fished a flashlight the size of a pen out of his pocket. He shone it in Nathanial's eyes. No response. "It looks like he's still pretty damaged, which is good, but we need to know for sure before we put Nate at further risk."

Nate's quivering form stilled. "Further risk?"

Laurence put his flashlight away. "Take some deep breaths."

"I don't breathe."

"Pretend. That's it. Fake breathing works just fine. Now move your hands so they're above Nathanial's chest."

Nate did as he was told, pantomiming breath as he floated over his comatose body.

Laurence studied the spirit. "Do you feel anything?"

"I feel sad that I lived like this all these years. And I don't even chop down trees anymore."

"No, I mean, do you physically feel Nathanial's body under your touch. A pressure, maybe. And remember, you keep referring to Nathanial in the first person. His actions for the past century are not yours. You aren't him. Not yet."

"I was for a little bit. On the night I possessed Sybille." Nate closed his eyes. "I feel something. Heat. He's warm."

Elis scoffed. "Bloodthirsters aren't warm. They're room temperature."

"To Nate's noncorporeal form, any of us would feel warm. Well done, Nate. Keep breathing while you focus on that warmth. Now gradually bring your hands upward until you're resting them on Nathanial's head. There you are."

Nate caressed the Blood King's forehead like he would a dying lover. "His eyes are so empty."

"Focus on what's behind the eyes."

"Eye sockets?"

"Behind those. Not on a physical level, but on a mental one. Is it warmer than the rest of him?"

Nate shook his head. "I don't think so."

"When you're ready, push further. Find Nathanial's core."

"I used to eat people's leftover apple cores. Is that what you mean?"

"Jesus, Nate." Elis was beginning to think this whole plan would fail. Nate was a loveable oaf, but an oaf, nonetheless.

"Sure, fine. Think about apple cores. Find his seed. Has it begun to sprout?"

Nate shimmered. "Yes. But only a little. It's tiny, but it's there."

Laurence sighed. "That's our answer, then. I think we're in time."

The door opened. "Time for what?" Raelyn entered the crowded space. She eyed them with suspicion.

Elis maneuvered himself so he blocked Raelyn's view of the gurney. "Time to have you increase your security around the Blood King's cell. His brain has begun to heal."

Nate kept his hands upon Nathanial's head. "Not much yet, though. I want to explore him more."

Laurence dabbed sweat from his brow with his shirt sleeve. "Pace yourself, Nate. I would like you to go further though. We have yet to complete the picture."

That was Elis' cue. "I really don't need to see this anymore. Raelyn, how about I cash in on that raincheck now. He tilted his neck.

Raelyn's gaze whipped from Nathanial to him. Cherry red lips turned up on one side. "A little blood sixty-nine? Tempting."

Laurence grimaced. "I'd prefer not to see that. You two think you could get a room and do your…thing while we finish up here?"

Raelyn paused. She had to make a show like she was deciding, but really, he knew she'd go along with his request without question. She'd texted him half a dozen pictures of her bare neck over the past two months, always requesting he send return shots. He never gave in to her, but if she believed he would now, she wasn't going to waste her opportunity.

"Fine, but you'll be locked in here while we're eating. There's nothing you can do about it, so don't try."

Long fingernails latched onto the back of his neck. Like a dog wearing a choke collar, he found himself escorted out of the cell. A few minutes later, they stood alone in her parlor. Relief of being free from that wretched basement room, along with the promise of a feeding, left him giddy. She trailed her fingers from his neck to his shoulders. "We pierce at the same time and drink until we're satiated."

Eyes flaring, he bared his fangs. Memories of the taste of her clouded his senses. For a moment, he wanted only to eat and to let her have what she wanted. It had to be that way. What Laurence and Nate were about to do would definitely not be Raelyn approved. It was either this or they'd need to resort to violence.

A bloodthirster had to eat like everyone else.

Raelyn swept long golden waves away from her neck. Hunger became need. So immersed in meeting this need, he barely felt the artery tear as she bit into him.

CHAPTER TWENTY

JULIANA

THE FAE WOMAN RAN HER INDEX FINGER ACROSS JULIANA'S COUNTERTOPS.

"You won't find one tiny speck of dirt. I scrub them daily. Or nightly. I don't know the difference to be honest. I'm in here all the time and it's always light out. Like I'm being tortured in solitary confinement. Anyways, everything is disinfected, all with non-toxic cleaners. Sybille has an aversion to bleach, even if it can in no way harm the environment because it's only psychic bleach."

"The smell nauseates me." Sybille took out a spray bottle from below the sink. "This stuff uses essential lavender oil. Way better. Juliana, this is Froya, by the way."

Froya examined the tip of her finger like her eyes were a microscope and her finger a petri dish. "Are you real?"

"Excuse me?" Juliana sputtered. "Are you talking to me?"

Froya moved her penetrating gaze to Juliana's face. "This is a psychic realm created inside the hierophant's head. And you made a point to say that things here are not real. The opposite of real is imaginary. Are you imaginary?"

"Of course not!" Juliana pinched her arm. It pricked just like it would if she were in a physical form. "I'm pure consciousness, and so is this room, but I can see and touch and smell and taste. What could be more real than that?"

"Lots of things." Froya stepped over to her and tilted her head, examining Juliana like she was being served up on a platter at a five-star restaurant.

This was how her bloodthirster's victims must have felt before she bit into their flesh, like their worthiness had been weighed and determined to be less than a grain of rice. She pinched her arm harder and turned herself away from the woman's scrutiny. By now, Sybille had made her way to a seat at the round kitchen table. Next to her sat her cousin, Zareen. Both seemed more focused on the loaf of chocolate chip zucchini bread she'd placed on the table than on the reason Juliana had brought them here. And it had been *her* orchestrating the visit this time, not Sybille. Well, she'd put the request in, at least, shouting into her radio whenever it buzzed away from the country station, asking them to pay her a visit ASAP.

"Don't you all want to know why I summoned you here?"

Sybille spread a thick layer of butter onto a piece of bread. "Summoned is a little off the mark. You kept shouting, 'I have an idea and it's not evil, I swear!' and finally, I decided to come here in the hopes of shutting you up."

"I realize you have many reasons to distrust me," Juliana said. "Even though those reasons are nonsensical and a result of below-average intelligence, I want you to know, I do understand."

"Below average. Is that how she compares to other humans?" Maintaining her invasion of Juliana's personal space, Froya removed a wayward string from the shoulder strap of her apron and then ran a hand alongside her cheek. She shivered, something she hadn't felt the need to do in centuries.

"Or," Froya continued, "is that just how she compares to you?"

Juliana trembled again under Froya's touch. It was like being fondled by a purple praying mantis. Any moment now, she expected to have her head bitten off. "Let's put it this way. The humans have no possibility of assisting your people without my help. Would you like a slice of zucchini bread?"

"Do I look to be of the same intelligence as these humans? I know better than to sample food from a psychic realm."

Zareen stopped eating her bread, mid-chew. "What was that, now?"

"Eating psychic food can trap you in a realm. I should know. My people are the ones who figured out how to do it. Even Devin seemed to realize that."

Juliana scoffed. "I assure you, I'm not trying to trap anybody in this domestic nightmare. Although…" She gave Sybille the side eye, "it would be a fine bit of poetic justice, wouldn't it?"

"I'm going to guess you trapping me in here with you wouldn't make a poetic ending for either of us." Sybille swore under her breath. "Getting back to your ludicrous point, we don't need anything from you, Juliana, especially when your idea of help these days is adding an extra handful of chocolate chips to your batter."

"No one wants chocolate chip zucchini bread that's light on the chocolate chips. Oh, no, that reminds me…" She rushed over to the stove, slid on her oven mitt, and retrieved a new loaf to replace the one that was now nearly depleted. "Another minute in there and this would have been overdone. You are all very distracting." She overturned the loaf onto a cooling rack and tried to ignore Froya shadowing her. "Especially you."

Zareen, her plate cleared of its goodies, appeared next to the new loaf, knife in hand.

"You should let it cool for ten minutes, at the very least. Otherwise, it will crumble," Juliana warned her. "That's one of the tips I'm putting in my baking book, not that any of you asked how that project is progressing."

Zareen made no effort to stop what she was doing.

Froya glared at her. "You aren't even as smart as your cousin, are you?"

"You know what?" Zareen raised her knife and cut the air with it. "Fuck you and fuck your self-righteous fae attitude." She cut the loaf in half, placing one of the halves on her plate. "I'll take my goddamn chances. Also, Sybille's already got a plan, Juliana, and it's a good one. Meanwhile, you remain an untrustworthy bitch. Don't roll your eyes at me. You know it's true." She grabbed her plate and wandered off to the table again.

"Some people think I'm an untrustworthy bitch too." Froya sniffed at the dissected bread. "Even ones that should be grateful to me for saving them from a mundane human existence and teaching them to use magic. And all while having incredible sex."

"I have a lot of experience in this arena as well," Juliana murmured in agreement. "Some people are born ungrateful."

"I'd like to know what you have planned," Froya told her.

Juliana stood up a little taller. This fae creature was a bit uncouth, but she spoke her mind and could see Juliana's potential. Most importantly, she seemed to dislike Sybille almost as much as Juliana herself did.

"Whatever plan she might have hatched," Sybille said, "it's going to be ridiculous, dangerous, and impossible to execute. You've been warned."

Juliana clucked her tongue, unwilling to let the psychic spoil her pitch to Froya. "Not impossible, and not ridiculous either. But it certainly is dangerous."

Froya invaded her space again, her hands clasped in front of her. "I like dangerous."

"Well, then, it's simple, really. Release me from Sybille's jail and allow me to possess Raelyn Vargas' body.

Sybille

Sybille pressed her palms into the edge of the kitchen table hard enough to turn her knuckles white. "You have got to be out of your mind, Juliana."

"No, not out of my mind. Out of yours." She cocked her head and sneered in that superior fashion Sybille loathed. "That's my hope, at least."

"I'm not letting you out. You're my prisoner, and you fucking know what you did to end up here."

"Oh yes." Her expression faltered. "I didn't conform to your moral standards. But I've done my time."

"You've been in here for less than three months."

"Really? It seems like it's been years." Juliana took a seat on her left.

Sybille scooted her chair away from Juliana until the wall prevented her from moving any further. "Well then, hopefully years will feel like decades and decades will feel like an eternity."

"Be reasonable, Sybille. I can help you, but not from inside this room. Besides, do you really want me baking brownies in your head for the rest of your life? This arrangement will end at some point. It might as well be at a point in which I can be useful to your cause."

"Oh, hell no, Sybille." Zareen stabbed the table with her butter knife. "Don't trust her. The only cause she cares about is her own."

"I don't need to be reminded."

Froya leaned over the counter. "I'd like to know the rest of Juliana's plan so I can decide if it will happen."

What nerve! The hair stood up on the back of Sybille's neck. "You don't get to decide shit!"

"I get to decide lots of things." Froya ran her tongue along her teeth. "Like with Devin, for instance. I decide when to bring him back to the Ichor realm with me. I decide what magic he can wield, what toys we use. You know, in bed. You don't get to decide any of those things."

"Seriously?" Sybille's stomach heaved. "Why are you bringing that up now?"

Juliana laughed. "So, Devin is your plaything, you lucky fae. This one here," she pointed at Sybille, "had a chance with him but instead she chose to pursue my husband. That should tell you what sort of person we're dealing with."

"He hasn't been your husband for a hundred years, and…" Taking a deep breath, she gazed up at the ceiling. "Why are we discussing my love life? Or yours, Froya? We have actual important work to do."

"That's true enough." Juliana jumped up from her seat. "So, the plan is that I possess Raelyn because she's a dangerous Ossian asset and has put her daughter at risk. She needs to be taken out but, like the Blood King, she's extra immortal. So the best we can do is control her."

"We can turn her brain to mush, like you and Sybille did with Nathanial," Zareen offered.

Juliana shook her head. "That's not a permanent solution. Besides, if I'm in control of her body, I can become a spy."

"For what purpose?" Sybille picked at her piece of sweet bread. Her palms had become clammy. Everything about this conversation unsettled her. "Who would Raelyn spy on? She's the top dog in the Low."

"Yes, but she answers to others."

Froya purred. "The Ossian. You want to pretend to be Raelyn so you can discover their next move before they make it, then report back to me about it. I like this idea."

"I don't." Sybille shoved her plate away, her appetite gone. "Froya, she can't be trusted."

"Trust isn't necessary. She'll do what she says she's going to do because it's in her best interest."

"Of course I will. I'd do anything to be freed from Sybille's head. Besides, I hate the Ossian and want them defeated. Even Sybille will admit that."

"That doesn't mean you don't have ulterior motives," Sybille told her.

"My motives will see this mission through."

"It's decided then." Froya beamed. "We'll proceed with this plan."

Sybille imagined melting this mind kitchen, and Juliana and Froya with it. On a giant mushroom cloud of smoke and radiation and they would be obliterated. "It's a no from me. We will not proceed. And since I control Juliana's imprisonment, that's the final word."

"I can free you, Juliana," Froya said. "It's quite easy."

"What?" Sybille stood up so she'd be at Froya's height. "No, you can't."

"I can and I will, hierophant." She turned to Juliana. "Sybille's cooperation, while helpful, is unnecessary. This is a satisfying plan. I like it, so we'll do it."

Juliana squealed. "Fabulous! Are you sure you don't want some chocolate chip zucchini bread?"

Ignoring her, Froya's hand clamped onto Sybille's shoulder. "If you want to keep Devin in your realm, you'll go along with it too."

"Even if I believed you can free Juliana, I'm not going to the Low. I can't go to the Low. In case you didn't realize it, I have a lot on my plate right now here on the home front. Plus, the Low almost destroyed me last time I went. I'm not going back unless I absolutely have to."

"You don't have to go," Zareen cleared her throat. "I'll do it."

Sybille sputtered. "What? No, no way."

"Sybille, you know I hate Juliana more than anyone, but if I go, I'll be able to keep tabs on her. And let's face it, having someone on the inside with the Ossian might be the difference between life and death. At least, Charlie's life and death, if not all of ours."

"But the Low affects you too."

"I've been learning my father's warding spells. Honestly, I'm not bad at them." Her words were halted, like she hadn't determined yet if they were a lie or not. "They'll help me through."

Sybille hung her head. "Don't do this."

"It will be okay," Zareen said. "I'll watch Juliana while you carry on with the rest of your plan. One of us has to go back to the Low soon anyways. Remember, part of your plan is currently gestating there as we speak."

True enough—that was, assuming Elis and his team had been successful. "Fine, whatever. If Froya can release Juliana from my head whenever she wants, there's not a whole lot I can do to stop this plan anyways. Just...be careful, Zareen. Pull the plug on it and get out of there at the first sign of trouble."

Zareen tore herself away from the zucchini bread long enough to give Sybille a hug. "The first sign of trouble will be the moment I drive over the Low's border. It's going to take a lot more than whatever the Low throws at me to stop us."

Sybille turned to the two supernatural beings. "All right then. Froya, explain to us how getting Juliana from my head to Raelyn's body is going to work without accidentally tearing a hole in the fabric of time and space. And then, let's set this dumb idea into motion."

CHAPTER TWENTY-ONE

SYBILLE

UNEASE SPREAD OVER SYBILLE LIKE SAP BLEEDING INTO THE GROOVES OF TREE bark. Too many variables, too many outcomes. Too much potential for everything to fall apart.

Failure loomed and the unease grew. No amount of deep breathing or energy centering worked. She'd have this knot in her stomach for the rest of her life, which more than likely would be of short duration.

Elis texted with what should have felt like good news. They'd accomplished their mission and were on their way back. She tried to be happy for this small victory, but any positive occurrence felt like something you pinned your hopes on right before that hope was dashed.

"Earth to Sybille."

"Hmm?" Sybille looked up from her romance novel. She'd been reading for the past ten minutes without taking in a single word. Devin sat across from her spot on the couch, reclining in Peter's easy chair while Thunderheart snored softly at his feet.

"Oh." She thumbed back a few pages and placed a bookmark at the beginning of her current chapter. "I thought you'd fallen asleep."

"Nope. Wide awake."

Anxious to hear from the Low team when they arrived home, Sybille and Devin both agreed to wait up for them. It was one of the first times they'd been alone together since Devin's return, yet she'd opted to fake read while her brain ran amok rather than talk to him. "I'm sorry, Devin, I'm just distracted."

"Because of Juliana's bat-shit crazy plan?"

She closed her book. "You think it's a bad idea too?"

"I'd think it was a great idea if it wasn't Juliana who thought it up and made herself the star of it. That woman is twisted."

"Right? You know that she met Elis when he was a child, and she totally groomed him, waited until the right time, and then murdered him and turned him into a bloodthirster so he'd be with her forever and ever. How fucked up of a relationship is that?"

"It's pretty fucked up, and I know fucked up relationships when I see them."

His nostrils flared and he looked down at Thunderheart. Sybille weighed her words before speaking. "Are you talking about Froya? Are you two... How are things with her?"

He shifted in his chair. He might be uncomfortable with her line of questioning, but he was the one who'd opened the door to it. "Things are fine."

The emphasis on the word "fine" gave her pause.

"You don't have to talk about it if you don't want to. I'm sorry I mentioned her and I'm glad things are *fine*."

He set the recliner in its upright position. "Are you?"

"Well, I would be, if I believed it was the truth."

He leaned forward like he was about to stand, froze for a few seconds, then propelled himself forward and took a seat next to her. Woken by the movement, Thunderheart yawned and sat up, followed his human across the room and positioned himself so he was leaning against Sybille's legs. Devin sighed. "It's not the truth. Oh my God, Sybille, she's...she's not nice."

"I gathered that much. But then, why are you with her?"

"Because she controls the block in my brain." He tapped his head. "Literally, she's in control up there."

"I thought they removed that so you'd have your fae powers."

"No, they remove parts of it as they see fit. They keep what they want in place so my powers are restricted. That's why I couldn't just leave them and come back to you all the times I wanted to. And it's why they can take me away again whenever they want."

"So, she's controlling you, and she dangles superpowers and sex in front of you to keep you from an all-out rebellion."

"Right. Those things…and the threat of what they might do to you."

"To me?"

"Have you already forgotten how they wanted to execute you for breaking into their world?"

She hunched forward, unease at full blast. Sometimes she thought her heart wasn't going to last long enough for the whole saving the world bullshit she'd gotten herself into. "I won't be the reason you let Froya control you, Devin. Please don't let me be. I couldn't stand knowing you're with her because you feel like you have to protect me and that's the only way to do it."

He placed a hand on her back. His touch was light, but a comforting warmth spread from it.

"Their powers make them dangerous—to me and to the people I care about," he said. "I can't change that, Sybille. Until I convince my grandmother to give me unconditional control over my brain, I'm stuck with them. Not that it's all bad." He scratched Thunderheart's ear, eliciting a tale wag in appreciation. "They aren't inherently evil. They're creative and they adhere to a moral code. But they think so differently. Their priorities aren't the same as humans.'"

"What about your priorities? What about…?" She bit her lip, her eyes pleading with his. "What about Charlie? What do they want you to do to her?"

He blinked and slid his hand away from her back. His eyes became watery pools. "How much have you figured out?"

"Enough to know they want you on opposite sides of a war. And enough to know I'll be the one standing in the middle of you if it comes to that."

Her breath caught as he grabbed her hand. "That won't happen. I may be going along with them right now, but I won't be used like a pawn."

"There's that pawn reference again. Pawns don't choose to be used, Devin."

"Sybille, I won't—"

The front door opened, and Peter bounded in. "We're back!"

Sybille shifted away from Devin just as Elis and Laurence entered.

Eying them both, Elis came over and sat on the edge of the couch, next to Sybille. He kissed her forehead.

"Well, that was exhausting. Hello, Devin." He lifted his chin in Devin's direction. "How's your new life as a magical being."

"Not that magical. How's life as the same asshole you've always been?"

"Absolutely magical. I've got a dream woman." He nudged Sybille. 'Not to mention, the smartest, most precocious kid on the planet."

"Kid?"

"He's talking about Charlie," Sybille told him.

"Yeah, I gathered that." Devin stood up. "She's *my* kid. My niece. My blood."

Locking eyes with Devin, Elis rose as well, posturing like a schoolboy who'd just been challenged to a playground brawl. "Your blood, my bones. It's not about that. I'm taking care of her. Don't shower me with your gratitude. I simply saw a complete void when it came to the girl having a father figure and graciously stepped into the role. Any bloodthirster with a soul would have done the same."

Thunderheart growled.

Elis jumped backwards. "Well, hello. When did we get a dog?"

"That's *my* dog, just like Charlie is *my* family."

Elis closed the space between himself and Devin. "Then act like it."

"Both of you, cut it out!" Sybille ran her hands through her hair. She'd noticed strands of it coming out in a small tangle when she'd showered this morning. Probably stress. Any more squabbling between these two and she'd be bald by the end of the week.

"Sybille's right." Peter claimed his recliner and motioned for Laurence to take an armchair. "I can offer you both a sedative. Or if you'd prefer something more natural, Margot's got some CBD oil in the kitchen cabinet that might cut some of that tension. Chocolate mint flavored. Should I go grab it or can you both manage to behave like grown men for the next twenty minutes?"

A few more seconds of angry glaring ended with them taking up positions on opposite sides of the room, Elis remaining on the couch next to Sybille, and Devin leaning against the door to Margot's craft room. Sybille started to voice her thanks to Peter for disbursing the testosterone in the room, but her voice caught. At least they were both here with her to hate each other and drive her crazy. How brief this time would be.

Clearing her throat, she wiped at her eyes before anyone noticed the tears. "Okay, let's hear your report. Laurence, you're up first."

Laurence straightened his back. "The situation is promising. Nathanial's brain is still quite damaged, the repair in its infancy."

"That's what we wanted, though, right?"

"Right. His spirit, Nate as you call him, was successfully re-ensouled in Nathanial's body. Now that he's there, he can influence that repair so that the person emerging from the coma bears more of a resemblance to Nate, and less to, well, to a merciless drug lord."

Peter rummaged through his medical kit while he added his two cents. "Remember, there's no guarantee Nate will become the dominant personality. It's a gamble, though a worthwhile one."

"Agreed," Sybille said. "And you were able to obtain the samples you need?"

Peter held up a vial of red liquid. "Blood from Raelyn. Marrow from the former Blood King."

"I'm glad Raelyn cooperated," Sybille said. "And speaking of our head of Ossian operations on Earth, Elis…is she still in the dark on this?"

Elis scratched at his neck. "I distracted her while Laurence and Peter did their thing. She wanted to keep Nate there with her, so I told her we left him wandering in the woods where he claims he was murdered."

This was news to Sybille. "He was murdered in the Low?"

"He and his fiancé, Mary," Elis said. "They were on their way to the church to get married when he stopped to show her the logging site he'd been working at. They were attacked by thirsters, and well…you can imagine. Absolute carnage."

"Poor Nate."

"Anyways, Raelyn bought our story, but she's going to figure out that something's up eventually, especially when the Blood King wakes up and asks her if she needs any trees felled."

"It will be too late by then. All right, Peter, who do you still need samples from?"

"I have marrow from Ellis. That just leaves Devin."

Devin winced. "More needles. You really need marrow?"

"From you? Blood will suffice. Come up to my room and I'll take care of it."

"Gladly," Devin mumbled and followed Peter up the stairs.

Laurence stood and tottered over to the door. "I'm afraid I'm spent for the day, but I'll be back tomorrow evening. Call me if you need me earlier than that."

"I will." Sybille followed him, handing him his hat at the entryway. "Thanks for restoring an immortal's soul for me. I couldn't have done it without you."

He paused, hand on the doorknob. "Something tells me you could. Good night."

Sybille waited until he'd closed the door. "Okay, now I need to get you up to speed. While you were in the Low, I went with Zareen and our resident fae bitch to pay Juliana a visit."

Elis' eyes glowed. "You what? Sybille, I told you it was a bad idea to go see her."

"Oh, it wasn't mine. It was Juliana's idea this time."

"That's even worse."

"I survived. And, surprise, surprise, Froya loved Juliana. Seems they're kindred spirits, and if that's not terrifying, I don't know what is."

"But why did Juliana want you there?" Elis asked. "Is she scheming to escape?"

"Yep."

"How does she plan on convincing you to free her?"

"She planned on making me think she's a reformed woman, but she failed. Lucky for her, Froya can free her and there's not a damned thing I can do about it."

"What? No! Wait…" He spun around. "Is she here? Is she free? Holy shit, is she possessing you right now?" He gripped her by the shoulders, staring into her eyes.

"Elis, she's still trapped for the time being. You can bring it down a notch." She told him Juliana's plan, including Froya's part in it, and how Zareen had agreed to go to the Low to monitor the situation from the inside.

"Juliana in possession of the body of an immortal ruler." His eyes darkened. "That's the worst idea ever."

"Believe me, I'm not thrilled about it, but that's why I need Zareen to go so she can ensure Juliana doesn't double-cross us."

"Of course she's going to double-cross us. That's what she does."

"Not if Zareen's there. She feels like she owes Zareen something. I know it's strange, but it's true. Still, Zareen's going to be so vulnerable. A hierophant all alone in the Low. She could really use a partner for this one. Maybe someone who can blend in with bloodthirsters and has some sway with the target?"

Elis groaned. "No, don't do this to me. I just escaped that wretched place!"

"I made Devin go back right after he'd been there too. I'm sorry, but needs must." She grabbed his wrist and pulled him around to the couch until they were both sitting, then put her other hand on his chest. "Please, do this for me, Elis. She can't go in alone."

"Damn it, why am I even considering this?"

"Because you know how important it is. You can check on how Nate's progressing. And you'll be able to help Zareen deal with your ex once she takes over Raelyn's body."

A crash echoed from the far end of the room as a hardcover edition of the Wizard of Oz came tumbling down the stairs. Sybille gasped. "Charlie!"

Charlie flew back upstairs. Elis retrieved the book. "She must have heard what we said about her mother."

"I'll go talk to her." She squinted at Elis. "But first, undo a button on your shirt."

He arched an eyebrow. "As much as I'd like us to slowly instruct each other to undress, this is hardly the time."

"There's something on your neck, bloodthirster."

He swallowed. "I can explain."

She moved him so he was underneath a wall sconce and tilted his head so his neck caught the light. She pulled his collar to the side. "Elis Tanner, please tell me those aren't fang marks!"

CHAPTER TWENTY-TWO

DEVIN

THE RED OF CHARLIE'S JACKET SHONE LIKE SUNLIGHT BREAKING THROUGH thick clouds. Red swinging up, then down and back to him. Devin pushed her again. Higher. She squealed as her feet lifted to the sky. The bitter cold kept most children inside, but Charlie had begged him to come. Sybille told him his niece visited the park every day. She loved the swings and the jungle gym. They didn't have much in the way of playgrounds in the Low. Sybille's neighborhood park must have stood out to Charlie as a complete anomaly, as standard a fixture as this sort of thing was in most children's lives.

"Stop, Uncle Devin! I told you to stop!"

He caught the chains on either side of the swing, his body jerked forward as he attempted to tame it back down to a halt. His bare fingers scalded as they pressed against the freezing metal. As soon as she was still, Charlie hopped off, Thunderheart running to greet her from where he'd been sniffing trees along the park's perimeter. His tail wagged as she ran her mitted hand through his fur.

Devin straightened the earflaps of Charlie's lumberjack hat. "I was lost in thought and didn't hear you. I'm sorry."

She pushed his hands away. "You're sorry. For not listening to me. Again. I hear sorry from you and Sybille a lot. It doesn't mean much anymore."

He attempted to take her hand. She shrank back and Devin acquiesced. "Sybille said you weren't in the mood to listen when she tried to speak with you last night. I thought maybe you would be today, and we could sort this out."

"What part? The part where you let my mom be possessed by Juliana or the part where you're supposed to be my enemy now?"

He flinched. She'd figured out more than he'd thought. "Still my little spy, I see. But don't worry, I'll never be your enemy, Charlie. I love you."

"But you're a pawn, and the people who made you a pawn think I'm evil."

"Are you cold? I'm cold." He cupped his hands together, brought them to his mouth and breathed warm air into them. It did nothing to remove the chill. "This weather's rough on Thunderheart's paws. We should get going."

She frowned but grabbed Thunderheart's leash from where Devin had left it on a bench and clipped it to the dog's collar. "You don't want to talk about it. I get it."

"I just don't think you should have to worry about all of this. Jesus, Charlie, you're nine."

"Yeah, and you're twenty-nine and still not any smarter." She tugged on Thunderheart's leash, and the two stepped onto the winding path leading out of the park towards the Esmond house. "Grow a pair!"

His jaw twitched as he tried to figure out whether he should scold her or laugh. "You shouldn't tell somebody that. It's not nice."

She stopped walking but kept her back to him. "I'll say what I want and what I want to say is that you're stupid if you think I shouldn't worry about all of this. It's happening to me and I can't stop it. If you get to be dumb, then I get to be mad."

He approached her like he would a wild bird that had accidentally flown inside. "Fair enough. But what I said is true. They can try to use both of us, but we don't have to let them. I won't let it happen. We have plans, you know. More than one."

Her shoulders shook and Devin didn't have to see her face to know she was crying. Concerned, Thunderheart nudged her arm. Devin turned her around and pressed her towards him, letting her sob into the folds of his jacket. "You have to hold on just a little longer. Peter is working on some sort of formula, or antidote, or potion. I don't know what it is, really. But he's good at that sort of thing."

She tilted her head up. Devin's heart ached as he examined the tears that had coated her face. "He better work fast. And besides, you're still planning on killing my mom. Your own sister. But I guess you're used to doing that by now."

"Ouch, Charlie. Words hurt."

"So does spirit possession."

She pulled away from him. He wondered if he should reprimand her for her tone, but sass or not, she had spoken the truth. He'd tried to kill Raelyn long ago. Had he been successful, Charlie wouldn't exist. Now they had another dire plan for her. Even though he hadn't sanctioned it, that fact would hardly matter to Charlie. The adults surrounding her had betrayed her. *He* had betrayed her. Maybe they didn't need any fae war to set them at odds with each other. "We aren't planning to kill her. Sybille's been possessed many times and she's still alive. It's the same thing here. Juliana's, um…she's just borrowing your mother's body for a bit. That's all."

Charlie tugged on Thunderheart's leash. "That's all. Really? Did you believe Sybille's lie when she told you that, or are you just lying to yourself?"

"Charlie! This situation is dangerous. Sybille has to make hard choices sometimes. Your mom, well…she's made choices too."

Traversing over the park's edge, they stopped at a crosswalk and waited for the light to change. Unable to stand still, Charlie shifted her weight from one leg to the other. "I know my mom is bad. Okay, I know! But she's my mom, and I don't think she has to stay bad. She created a chalkboard wall in my bedroom just like I wanted. And she has Chef make me heart-shaped pancakes."

Light changed, they crossed the busy street, walking towards a series of quieter roads. The Esmonds, as well as Zareen's family, lived on a lane three blocks down. "I'm sure when this is over, she'll be back to ordering your cook to make you whatever you want again."

"I'm not sure, and neither are you, and that's like, the tenth time you've lied to me since we went to the park. You suck at this!" She picked up her pace. "You aren't sure that she'll be back or that I'll be around to eat pancakes. You aren't sure that this will ever be over!"

She tore off at a run. Thunderheart, the traitor, didn't even turn around to see if Devin was following, but follow he did, his heart pumping as he jogged down the road. When she made it to the Esmond's street, Charlie veered to the left. By the time Devin turned in the same direction, she'd nearly made it to Sybille's house. He paused then, watching her unlatch the gate and stomp her way up the porch steps, her hat askew again. She unclipped Thunderheart's leash and they both made their way into the house.

Devin remained a few lots down, watching his breath coil out into the bitter air. All he'd wanted was to give her a chance, spare her the horrors of her birthplace. He'd failed. She'd breathed in the Low from the day she'd been born. What kind of messed up savior narrative did he think he was playing at? She was right: he wasn't at all sure this would ever be over.

"Lost in thought, are we?" Her calm voice startled him out of his thoughts. Sybille approached from the direction he and Charlie had come from. She held up a reusable canvas grocery bag with a graphic of a smiling tomato on it. "Margot needed a few ingredients for tonight's dinner, so I walked over to The Organic Market. Jesus, it's colder than the inside of Juliana's cavernous vagina. What are you doing just standing out here?"

"I was at the park with Charlie."

"Let me guess: she brought up her mother and the conversation didn't go well."

"It did not. Also, she knows the fae think she's my enemy."

"Well shit, that was a tidbit I was hoping to keep from her."

"I'm beginning to think that's the wrong choice. She figures out everything anyway, and the thing that gives her the most grief is our dishonesty."

"I get that, I really do. I used to hate it when Margot and Peter would be in deep conversation and then the room would fall dead silent as soon as I entered it. But still, Devin, she's a child. We can't tell her things that are too much for her to handle."

"She has to handle being an instrument of Earth's demise."

Sybille swung her bag back and forth. "Fair point. I'll talk to her again. I wish Elis was still here so I could make him do it. She really does love him."

He clenched his jaw. "Of course. What's not to love?"

"Aww, you're finally coming around." She patted his cheek, and he caught her hand before she could remove it. She stood in front of him, her eyes wide.

"I'm not. And I'll never understand why you ever did."

"Devin."

"He's several centuries older than you."

"In years spent on Earth, maybe, but in emotional maturity years, I still have him beat."

"That doesn't make it less weird. And speaking of, I saw the marks on his neck."

She yanked her hand from his. "So?"

"My sister drank from him. And I would bet money he drank from her. He's totally charged. I can smell it on him. Straight from each other's necks, they fed. It's sexual, you have to admit it."

She laughed, a hollow sound snaking its way out of her throat. "Drinking blood is sexual? What sort of sex are you and Froya having?"

"We're blood fae. Blood is life and sex is part of life. But this isn't about my sex life, it's about your relationship. He's going to hurt you. You're too self-reflective not to know that. So why are you with him?"

She turned her gaze from his face up to the top of the leafless tree. "We all hurt each other at some point, intentionally or unintentionally. I'm choosing to love him with eyes wide open, even if I get hurt from that love. Can you say the same about Froya?"

"I can say the same. But not about her."

She lowered her eyes again, warm hazel to thaw his frozen soul. Silence filled the space between them. This was the moment to say everything that had dwelled in his brain on repeat for so long. But he didn't. It would only scare her away, or that's how he rationalized it. Later that day, he would look in the bathroom mirror and call himself a coward.

The moment passed, and she turned back to the Esmond house. "Let's get inside so I can warm up before I eat the gelato I just bought. Oh, that reminds me, Peter wanted to speak with you."

"Again?"

"He's in his study."

Entering the house, they removed their puffy jackets, and then Sybille departed for the kitchen with no more mention of their conversation. Devin hopped up the stairs, half hoping to encounter Charlie, and half hoping to avoid her. He should be the one to calm her nerves, but he had no idea how to manage it. Knocking on Peter's door, his nose scrunched as an acrid smell hit him. "Peter? You wanted to see me?"

Peter's muffled voice responded, "Come in."

Devin complied. The older man sat hunched over a microscope, a dozen vials resting on the table to his side. "Shut the door behind you. I take it Froya is still gallivanting in Sybille's mind prison preparing Juliana for what's to come?"

"As far as I know. It's amazing she's left me unattended this long." It struck him that Froya and Juliana might have overheard his conversation with Sybille via the kitchen radio, but he couldn't bring himself to care.

He picked up a thick tome with a worn cover, its title barely discernible. *Contributions of Witchcraft to Modern Medicine, 1692 to Present.* Inside, the pages were dog eared and worn at the edges, but the book was in surprisingly good shape considering it had a copyright of 1896. "Hey, Charlie hasn't been around, has she?"

Peter glanced up from his microscope. "I don't think I've seen her since breakfast. Why?"

"She knows you're working on a solution, you know…to her problem. She's pissed off that we haven't figured out how to fix her already. So I thought maybe she came here to see how you were progressing."

Peter swiveled on his stool until he was face to face with Devin. "She hasn't, and that's for the best. I wouldn't want to disappoint her."

Devin's body slumped. He let himself rest on the table's edge while gripping its rim with his hands. "It's a no-go, then. This formula you're working on…it's a failure."

"I'm not sure why you jumped to that conclusion. Have you been sleeping enough? You're projecting a vibe that's both unsettled and exhausted. It's no wonder. There was bound to be a toll for your introduction to fae life."

"I don't know anything about a toll." Charlie was right. He did lie to himself. And now he was lying to a man who would see through it immediately. "I'm as fine as I can be. What did you want to talk to me about? Why would Charlie be disappointed? Can we help her or not?"

"There're no guarantees. The reason I wished to speak to you—alone, mind you, without Charlie here and definitely without Froya anywhere in the vicinity—is that there's been a change of plans."

"For fuck sake, what now?"

"What I'm working at—it's not an exact science. It's more like if science and pseudoscience and alchemy and witchcraft all had a baby together. That baby would be extraordinary. Certainly magical, but with an inquisitive, rational side. And the rational side of this particular baby I'm working on realized right away that I was wrong."

"Wrong about what?"

"Charlie expects to receive a serum that will magically or scientifically cure her. One of those. It doesn't matter which as long as it works."

"Right. Okay, so?"

"So she'll be disappointed when she discovers that she won't be receiving a serum. That's what I was wrong about."

Every part of him felt weighted with exhaustion now. His head might as well be heavier than his pickup truck. Pretty soon gravity was going to flip him onto the floor. "But you just said you were hopeful your serum would work!"

"I am!" He pulled out one of the vials, held it up, examined it, and then swiveled so that he faced his desk again. Out of its drawer, he retrieved a needle. "I've spent the past day examining this thing from all angles. Microscopically, energetically, psychically. And I've consulted with a... colleague. Everything led to the same conclusion."

Peter thrust the needle into the vial, filled it, then flicked it with his index finger to remove air bubbles. "The serum isn't for Charlie." He motioned for Devin to roll up his sleeve. "It's for you."

CHAPTER TWENTY-THREE

ELIS

WINDING ROADS STRETCHING THROUGH VAST FORESTS WHIZZED BY. DÉJÀ VU came at Elis fast, and with it, a sense of futility. What hubris to imagine they could pull this plan off, especially with Juliana as one of the key players.

He glanced at Zareen. She was like a rubber band pulled tight, her lips pressed together, fingers gripping the wheel like the car would fly off the side of a cliff if she eased up even the slightest.

"I'm sorry but the camphor you're wearing..." Coughing, Elis pinched his nose. "It's so strong."

"Thanks for bringing that up again for the twelfth time so it can change the fact that we're trapped in this car together for such a delightful stretch of hours." Zareen claimed the essential oils blend Peter made for her was the only thing keeping the Low from tearing her mind apart. Elis thought it was more of a placebo than anything else. A worthless, hideously smelly placebo that might make him pass out before they arrived at Raelyn's mansion.

"And you know what," Zareen continued, "drivers who have their minds torn apart tend to crash their cars and kill their ungrateful hell-beast passengers. But hey, next time, buy yourself a box of Cinnamon Toast Crunch so you can dream of Sybille. Or instead, what does Raelyn smell like? Desperation and bad life decisions? Maybe you'd prefer that."

"That's a low blow. I was just doing what Sybille wanted me to do—distracting Raelyn so Laurence could pop Nate into his old body."

"Sybille did not tell you to sink your fangs into her neck, I can gauran-fucking-tee that."

"I did what I had to do."

"Goddamn psychopath. But whatever. We have a mission, and I'm willing to overlook your transgressions to accomplish it. I just hope that little comingling episode isn't going to make you soft on our target. What's about to happen will not be pretty."

"My loyalty is to Sybille, as well as to Charlie." He looked towards the passenger side window so she wouldn't see his eyes glow with rage. "And I'll have you know that drinking from Raelyn is an asset to this mission. It won't hamper us."

"We'll see."

She kept her focus on the road, and Elis matched her, staring out into the grey sky engulfing the Low in a winter malaise. "I hate this place. I'm only here because Sybille wanted to make sure you were all right."

"I don't need a babysitter."

"No, but you need someone who doesn't have to lather himself in bug repellant to cope with the Low's energy field. Besides, my cover is better than yours."

"The camphor is to boost energy so I can ward off the Low's attack. The fact that it repels bugs is merely a bonus. And by the way, just what is your cover? Because frankly, telling Raelyn I'm here to appeal to her as a fellow mom for Charlie's sake is pretty believable. A mother will do anything to protect her child."

"Not this mother." A large bird, perhaps a hawk, swooped out of a tree in the distance ahead of them. He watched it as it flew across the road and disappeared behind a silhouette of trees. "On the other hand, I'm here because I just can't get her out of my mind."

"Barf."

"The way she tasted—maybe I've aligned myself with the wrong woman. Sybille won't even let me have a nibble. Perhaps I belong here. With her."

"Are you trying to convince her or yourself?"

He scratched at the abrasions on his neck. "I don't care if I ever see

Raelyn Vargas again. But like I said, my completely wholesome experience of feeding off her can be used to our advantage. She'll believe my excuse."

"You should play the Charlie angle too, though. She knows you care about her daughter."

True though that was, her words unsettled him. Charlie wasn't an angle to be played. "She'll be pissed if I come down too hard on her about Charlie. It strikes a nerve."

"That's exactly what we want, though, isn't it? We need her thrown off."

Silence followed, but soon it was cut short as the theme song to *The Love Boat* filled the car. The tension in Zareen's hands eased. "Oh my god, is that your ringtone?"

"Not for everyone." He connected the call and put her on speaker. "Hello Sybille, I'm surprised this call went through. Reception is horrid."

"We're ready to—" Her voice cut out.

"Hello?"

"Yeah, can you hear me?"

"Now I can. You're ready to what?"

"Froya and I are ready to do this crazy thing that we absolutely shouldn't do."

"Fabulous. We're about ten minutes out. Give us time to talk to her."

"Will do. Text me when it's a go. And, Elis, she's going to put up a fight when she realizes what's happening. Keep your distance. Be careful."

"I will. You too. I love you." He glanced at the phone. Call ended. "Damn, I don't know if she heard me."

"Does it matter? I'm sure you show her every day how much you love her by not biting the necks of sexy bloodthirster ladies."

He closed his eyes, breathing through his mouth to minimize the camphor stench. "I wish I could mesmerize you so you'd understand where I'm coming from."

"Thank God you can't."

Ten minutes later, they were being shown into Raelyn's Regency-era sitting room by one of her guards.

Zareen slid her hand along the bottom of a gilded frame featuring a bucolic landscape. In it, a gentle river flowed between fields of grazing cattle. In the distance, purple mountaintops cut jagged lines along a deep blue sky. "This place creeps me out. Like she's creating a fantasy that no one will believe besides herself. It's delusional."

He yanked her hand away from the painting. "Keep your voice down! She could be listening."

"I certainly could be."

They jumped at the sound of her voice. Elis cursed himself for once again letting Raelyn catch him off guard. He had a role to play, and fear was not the emotion that role was meant to be grounded in. "Zareen doesn't like your décor for some abhorrent reason. I can't understand it, as certainly your taste is refined for a lady of your generation."

Zareen made a point to scrunch her nose at a gaudy golden vase sitting on top of the piano. "To be fair, my current style ascetic veers more along the lines of preschool chic. You know what it's like, right Raelyn? Having a child makes it pretty hard to keep a refined home."

Raelyn narrowed her eyes. "Are you implying that I've relinquished my daughter so I can collect antiques?"

"What? No! Of course not!" Zareen's cheeks turned the same shade as the sun in the landscape painting behind her. "I only meant that you're familiar with the chaos of parenting. I understand completely why you wanted Charlie to leave this place."

"You do?"

"Yes, and my opinion isn't the same as Sybille's. She's not a mother, but I am. I know that your actions were meant to save Charlie. I don't buy the whole willing participant in the Ossian Fae's evil plan badge of shame Sybille wants to sew on you."

Elis had to admit, Zareen was selling her story with gusto. Raelyn, on the other hand, needed more convincing. "If that's what you believe, why are you here? And you!" She pointed at him. "Back for thirds?"

"Thirds?" Zareen whispered.

"Yes, actually. I thought maybe you and I could—"

"He's here in his capacity as asshole of the century, which you'll probably be into. I'm here as a fellow mother, and I'm hoping you'll hear me out."

"I'm more interested in what Elis has to say at the moment."

"You're more interested to hear this undead shit-for-brains crushing on you than about the welfare of your own daughter?"

Raelyn moved like a snake slithering over grass until she'd positioned herself in front of Zareen. Even though Zareen stood half a foot taller, there was no mistaking which of the two women held the upper hand. Zareen shrank back under Raelyn's scrutiny.

"I've given her the best chance I could, but Charlie's fate is not in my hands," Raelyn said. "Yours, however, very much is."

Raelyn drew a hair from Zareen's cheek and tucked it behind her ear, then slid the back of her hand down Zareen's face. "You smell like you'd taste amazing."

"Raelyn!" Elis caught the young thirster's gaze and motioned her to release the trembling Zareen. "I'm sure there will be time for a human snack later, though I can't imagine why you like camphor. I nearly staked myself having to sit in the car with her for the past four hours."

Raelyn inspected her blood-red fingernails. "If you could get to the part where you explain yourself, including why Nathanial's oddly cherubic spirit hasn't returned from his forest walk, that would be a wonderful way not to waste my time.

"Right. I don't know about Nate. Maybe he got lost? I can check for him later."

"Is that all you have to offer me? You're here so you can 'check on him later?'"

"No!" He'd promised Charlie he'd help cure her. If he failed at this mission, he'd be failing her too. He had to sell this, as much as it repulsed him. "You need to know, Raelyn, I've come back to you because I couldn't stay away. Please don't let this woman distract you from that fact."

Raelyn stepped back and draped an arm over the stone mantle of the parlor's fireplace. Its glow tinged the back of her dark leggings. The illusion positioned her in the center of a black hole. "Do you expect me to believe either of you really just decided to come here on your own? Your reasons are pathetic and unbelievable."

Elis placed his hands in his pockets, trying to appear casual. His fingers closed around the syringe Peter had given him. Not enough to knock out a powerful immortal like Raelyn, but it would stun her for a minute. That was their window. "You're right, Raelyn. Zareen is here because she's delusional, and so is Sybille. But that's them. I made up an excuse to come along because I needed to see you again, to tell you how wrong I've been. Taking up with a human was a poor choice on my part, and I regret it now —she doesn't understand what it's like to be us."

He stepped towards the fireplace, towards the black hole of Raelyn. "I'm sorry it took me a while to realize it. I mean, you did help abduct me. It was a lot to process."

"I also helped you escape."

"I know. You saved me. Now I'm just asking for a chance." Another step. She seared into him, bloodthirster eyes ablaze. He forced himself to maintain eye contact. "Forget about this woman. Forget about Sybille. Forget about everything."

He pressed himself into her, taking his free hand out and wrapping it around the curve of her lower back.

Her gaze softened. "I don't forget things."

"I meant in a metaphorical sense. And just long enough for me to sweep you off your feet."

His carefully placed smile collapsed as she kneed him in the crotch.

"Don't you dare, bloodthirster!"

He crumpled over as pain traveled outward towards every part of his body. "Ow! Why did you do that?"

She punched him in the jaw, then grabbed a scruff of hair and pulled his head up so he was again at eye level. At the periphery of his pain, he could hear Zareen whimpering for Raelyn to stop. "I'll give you a chance, Elis. Just not the chance you were expecting."

She forced his head back until he lay flat on the ground. Centuries of undead strength couldn't compare to her immortal power. She swung a leg over him and straddled him like a horse, her weight baring down on his chest. "You can have the chance to be my prisoner. There's a cell open right next to Nathanial's. When I'm hungry, I'll always know where to find you."

He squirmed under her hold, desperate to get his hand back into the pocket where the syringe still sat. She kept his arms pinned to his sides.

A flash to his right. Zareen slammed a metal serving tray against Raelyn's head. Its only affect was to anger her. Zareen pushed the woman, who had no choice but to let go of Elis' arms so she could deal with her assailant.

Using the distraction to his advantage, Elis dug out the syringe, but not fast enough.

"No!" Raelyn lunged for it, her hand closing over Elis' as she struggled to pry it away from him. Zareen pulled on her hair, hard enough to yank some of Raelyn's weight from him. Her fingers loosened their grip. Desperate to make his only moment count, he flicked off the syringe's cap and thrust forward. Raelyn leaned her body to the left, her hands now at the sides of her head, trying to stop Zareen from pulling her hair out of its scalp.

He thrust again, and this time, needle met flesh. He pressed the plunger, releasing the contents into her chest. Raelyn screamed.

"Sorry, this would have been less painful in your arm. Keep hold of her, Zareen." They waited for the tranquilizer to work its magic.

As Raelyn began to sway, her eyes rolling back into her head, Elis heaved her off him and scrambled onto his feet. "We don't have long."

He grabbed his phone from the coffee table and dialed Sybille's number. "We've got her. Tell Froya to get her purple arse here now."

CHAPTER TWENTY-FOUR

JULIANA

Dipping her gloved hands into the bucket of sudsy water, Juliana drew out a cotton rag, wringing the excess liquid from it before she plopped it onto the floor. On her hands and knees, she scrubbed the linoleum in wide circles. Several spots between the oven and the island opposite to it troubled her: grease stains that didn't want to come clean no matter how much energy she put into the effort. The pointlessness of it all wasn't lost on her, but she persisted with her chore regardless. Soon she would be free of this place and of the domestic compulsions that came with it.

Circle, circle scrub. She daydreamed as she cleaned. Once she'd been released from Sybille's prison, like hell if she'd ever consent to bake another blueberry muffin or chocolate chili tart again. Never would anyone find her crouched over a work surface, kneading or mixing, or wiping away crumbs. Once she'd taken over Raelyn, her servants would bake whatever she desired, and they'd clean up afterwards as well.

"I can hear you plotting, spirit woman."

Juliana twisted from her kneeling position to find the fae woman, Froya, examining her last tray of brownies as she eavesdropped on Juliana's thoughts. Froya sniffed them. They'd come out of the oven less than an hour ago, releasing the aroma of melted chocolate into the air.

Soon, no one would be here to eat them. Plus, she'd nearly finished her baking book with tips on spirit living. All those hours of work and she hadn't the slightest idea what would come of her manuscript once she departed the kitchen. She cringed when she realized these thoughts upset her. "Can you blame me for plotting, Froya? Sybille has turned me into someone whose greatest desire is to make food for humans."

"Food makers are highly revered on Ichor."

"That's not the point. It isn't what *I'm* supposed to desire. She's trapped me in her brain, but she's also manipulated my consciousness, and consciousness is all I have!"

"Not for long. Are you ready for your new body?"

Juliana pushed herself off the floor, rag discarded, and stood. She removed her rubber gloves and lay them over the edge of her water pail. "I will do what I promised you I'd do. And then I expect you to help me remain free of Sybille, just as we discussed."

Froya stepped around the newly cleaned corner of the floor. "I don't care what Sybille wants other than when it aligns with what I want. We all have a common desire to defeat the Ossian. If you help me do that, you're welcome to keep your new body or select a new one, provided it's not fae. We would kill you if you tried to possess one of us."

"I don't doubt it."

"Fine then. If Sybille wishes to capture you again, she'll have to do it without my help."

Juliana removed her ruffled apron as she contemplated these words, her lips pursed. Froya wouldn't help Sybille, yet she wouldn't protect Juliana either. It wasn't ideal, but no matter. Once she'd taken possession of Raelyn's body, she would need no guard. "All right. How do we go about breaking me out of here?"

She began that sentence standing in Sybille's mind kitchen and ended it in a fancy parlor filled with bucolic landscape paintings set in gilded frames. She floated to the left of a silver tea service. On the floor in front of her lay Raelyn, Blood Phoenix of the Low, primary servant of the Ossian. It wasn't her new host body that made her flutter, however. Her eyes widened despite herself at the sight of Elis Tanner. Scowling, he crossed his arms and took a step back so that Zareen blocked her sightline.

"Jesus, Elis, really? The rest of us have had to face her," Zareen grumbled. "Welcome to the party, Juliana. Froya, let's get this over with."

"Gladly." Froya crouched down next to Raelyn. "Her mind is already wakening. We'll fail unless we do it quickly."

"So, what do we have to do?" Zareen began shuffling through her messenger bag. "I brought candles and incense. A couple of crystals."

"Human hierophants with your worthless knickknacks." Froya sniffed at a stick of incense, grimaced, and dropped it. "I have limited time to spend in this awful place before the Ossian take note. Step back and let me work."

Pouting, Zareen did what she asked. Elis folded himself onto a divan.

Placing a hand over Raelyn's face, Froya made a circular motion. Juliana flashed back to the kitchen. Circle, circle scrub. This body, like the linoleum floor, could be cleansed of its contaminant.

"Juliana," Froya called to her. "Move towards us."

Juliana glided over. Strange after her time in the kitchen, where her high-heeled shoes click-clacked on the surface, to be able to move without sound, without vibration. "What now?"

Froya continued her circular motion over Raelyn and lifted her left hand towards Juliana, repeating the motion.

The pull happened without thought, without effort, without time. Blurry, then clear. A ceiling.

"That's it? It's done?" She blinked. A physical motion in which eyelid covered eye for a moment before returning to a neutral open state. She tested her jaw. Opened wide, snapped shut. She'd already spoken words using this mouth, this jaw, air from these lungs, and it had been easy— graceful even. She wiggled some fingers. *Her* fingers. Lifted an arm. *Her* arm.

It felt natural to exist in this body.

And just like that, the effortlessness ended. Her chest contorted; her breathing became shallow.

In the corner of her brain, Raelyn woke. And she wanted out.

Juliana would have felt sympathy for her, given her own imprisonment, but Raelyn was a monster and monsters were not to be pitied. They were to be destroyed. And if that couldn't happen, then they must be leashed.

"Hush, little girl. Stay in your corner."

She said this to her struggling hostess, but it confused the dimwitted human in the room.

Zareen scoffed. "Did you just call me a little girl."

Juliana struggled to a seated position. "Raelyn doesn't like me in her body." She pressed her fingers to her neck. The slow, steady beat of a bloodthirster's pulse pressed back.

"Can you control her? If not, you're of no use to us," Elis said, his voice flat and accusatory, like he expected her to fail.

"Of course I can control her. I took over her body with ease."

"No, *I* took over her body *for you* with ease," Froya reminded her. "I've suppressed her abilities as best I can, but she's strong. Be careful. I have to go now, so I won't be here to help you."

"What? You promised you'd see this through." Zareen marched in Froya's direction. Froya raised a hand and Zareen froze in place. "Stop that! You can't just freeze people when they say something you don't want to hear!"

"The fact that you're unable to move right now says otherwise. And I did do as I promised. I helped Juliana possess Raelyn. But I can't stay here." She wrinkled her nose. "The Low is no place for an Ichor fae. My presence will stir up the Ossian. If I remain here, you'll be fighting a bloodthirster army."

"Been there, done that, not keen on doing it again." Elis shuddered.

"But I need you to help keep Juliana in check," Zareen said.

Juliana bristled. It figured that this impulsive human would believe Juliana to be the weak one. "I can keep myself in check."

Zareen scoffed. "I doubt you even know what that means."

"I have more self-control than you. I've seen what you can do to a loaf of zucchini bread."

Froya pulled on Zareen's arm before she could lunge at Juliana. "If you can't handle this, hierophant, go home and leave Juliana to carry on by herself."

Elis shook his head. "You know, I'm here too. Why are you talking like I'm not even present?"

Froya made no attempt to hide her disdain. "I do feel bad that you'll have to deal with that oddly emotive bloodthirster man, but that's Sybille's fault, not mine." She shivered. "I can't spend another minute in this place. Succeed or fail. I won't place bets either way. I'll be waiting."

She raised her hand again, fingers pressing together and then she was gone. The room seemed strangely empty without her. Juliana stretched her limbs. "It's good to be young again. Elis, why don't you come and help me up. I understand you aren't wholly averse to touching this body."

"Gross! Who told you that lie? I've never been less attracted to anyone than I am to that body you're wearing."

"Try selling it a little less next time to make it remotely believable, dude." Zareen wrapped her arms around herself and sulked.

"Get yourself up, Juliana. Start earning the allowance we've given you," Elis said. "There are guards standing down the hall at the entrance to the basement. Command them to let me go downstairs. Alone."

"As you'll recall, I'm good at giving commands." On her feet for the first time, she swayed, catching herself on the arm of a chair before toppling over. Raelyn wore riding boots—not at all like the three inch heels she'd grown accustomed to in the kitchen. Funny how a solely noncorporeal existence could be messing with her physical experience now. "Elis, I truly could use a hand."

"And I could use a getaway with the woman I love—which isn't you or Raelyn by the way. If you can't walk on your own, you'll have to lean on Zareen. But don't make it obvious. You have to sell Raelyn to her minions."

Juliana perked up. "I have minions?"

"This is an ideal situation for you, isn't it?"

"If you think being stuffed into an immortal bloodthirster's body is ideal, you've forgotten how much I loathe your kind."

"My kind, sure." Elis stepped towards the door. "Except for me, who you seem to forget you tried to murder, and now can't wait to have your hands all over."

"Old habits, I suppose…" She took a deep breath, then steadied herself, slowly letting go of the chair. "Okay, I'm ready." She took a step forward, then another. "Let's take you to see how your science experiment is coming along."

Elis

The moon had made way for the sun. Dark hair, now light. Elis lowered his eyes rather than peer at the woman's long tresses as they swung back and forth while he trailed behind her.

In some folkloric traditions, the sun killed his kind.

Juliana in an immortal body. Juliana, the sun. It was wrong, so wrong.

Juliana tilted her head to acknowledge Raelyn's goons. They flanked the door to the basement. He glanced down the hallway. It was a straight shot to the front door, where another burly bloodthirster stood at attention, waiting to pounce at the first sign of trouble. If only they knew how badly they'd fucked up. Their mistress had been drugged and body snatched less than fifty feet from them, and they'd failed to notice.

Juliana smiled at her men. "I'm sending Elis Tanner to the cells."

Her men stepped towards him. The one closest began cuffing his wrist. "Hey now!"

"Not as a prisoner." She stilled the guard's hands. "He does belong behind bars, but for today, I've given him another task. He's to examine our current prisoner. Let him pass."

The minions wore the same wide-eyed expression. The one who'd grabbed Elis shook his head. "I'll watch him closely, Phoenix."

"No, I need you both up here. An Ichor fae was spotted in the Low. You can imagine what a security issue that is. Elis will be fine by himself, but my property needs protecting."

The mention of an Ichor fae sent the guards into a tizzy. One of them radioed someone else with the news. After another nod to Juliana, they headed to converse with the front door guard. They exited with hurried steps, thoughts of having to babysit Elis gone in the face of a much greater threat.

Juliana opened the basement's door and shoed Elis through. He scrunched his nose as the familiar mint aroma wafted off of her.

"Did you see how they didn't even question me, Elis? They rushed to do as I asked."

Zareen snorted. "You've had a queen bee fantasy going on for a long time now, haven't you?" She waved to Elis as he flicked on the light to the basement, then closed the door on him. Their voices became muffled, then trail off altogether.

As he descended, Elis covered his nose to keep out the basement's musty odor. Raelyn's fancy remodeling projects hadn't included ridding the lower level of black mold. No wonder Laurence had nearly hacked up a lung down here. The stench mixed with the remnant of Juliana's smell was enough to make him long for a camphor bath.

Punching in the key code he'd memorized when the unsuspecting guard had used it yesterday, Elis slid open the door and peeked inside where the smell was at its most toxic. He heaved, his face sweating as he took in a ragged breath. "Nate? Are you awake?"

No response. The broken thirster lay on his gurney, looking just the same as he had when Elis had been here last. Pulling the door open all the way, he entered the cell and stood at the sleeping man's side. Touching Nate's arm, he traced the outline of a squiggly tattoo depicting two crossed skeleton keys. Nate's skin felt hot to the touch, but his face gave no indication of fever. If anything, his expression seemed relaxed and unbothered, lips curving up in a gentle half smile.

He gave Nate a jostle. Still no response.

"I need you to wake up, Nate. I hope you've had the time you need because I'd rather not have to carry your giant arse up those stairs on my own."

He paused, listening to Nate's slow, steady heartbeat. His eyes fluttered under their lids. That seemed a hopeful sign. "Come on, that's a good lad. Wake up!" He gave Nate a gentle slap on the cheek. A weight hit his right shoulder as Nate's arm clamped down upon him. Elis staggered to the side, and before he could steady himself. Nate jumped off his gurney, slamming Elis into the wall. Cold concrete crumbled against the back of his head as warm hands tightened around his throat.

Nate's eyes shone dark as obsidian; his nose flared like a bull's. Elis hit at Nate's tree trunk arms in a futile effort to make him loosen his death grip. As his vision blurred, he realized what a luckless bastard he was, being pummeled and strangled by not one but two immortals in less than a day.

He tried to gasp, but Nate's hold prevented him from taking in even a miniscule amount of air. White appeared at the corners of his sight, then spread inward.

White sun. It would do him in after all.

On the verge of unconsciousness and with little vision remaining, Elis watched Nate's face switch from anger to recognition.

"Elis? Why do I have hands?"

Nate let go of him so he could examine his newfound hands without the interference of having Elis' neck lodged between them.

The sweet release came too late. Elis slipped to the ground, freed from Nate's grip as well as from the burden of consciousness.

CHAPTER TWENTY-FIVE

JULIANA

THE UPSTAIRS TO JULIANA'S NEW MANSION SMELLED LIKE FRESHLY SQUEEZED lemons. She craned her neck to see into a room to the left of the staircase, but nothing out of the ordinary stared back at her. Boxes stacked in the room's center partially hid a double bed with a worn green quilt. "It looks like a spare room," she said to Zareen.

Zareen peeked in to see for herself. "So where'd Raelyn keep her Ossian communication device?"

Juliana glared at her. "How should I know?"

"Um, don't you have access to Raelyn's memories?"

"Raelyn isn't being very cooperative." Her eyelid twitched. "To access her memories, I'd have to ease up on my control over her. Neither of us wants that."

"No, we do not."

"We must rely on our own prowess to find what we're looking for. Next room?"

They stopped midway down the hall at an ornately carved wooden door. It seemed promising. "I bet this is the master bedroom." Juliana's hand shook as she turned the knob, knowing that her new luxurious accommodations awaited her. She pushed open the door and her mouth dropped. Zareen snickered behind her.

"This can't be right." There was nothing luxurious about this space. No four-poster canopy bed replete with silk sheets and velvet throw pillows. Instead a simple bed with a white compressed wood frame that looked as though it had to be pieced together when it arrived in a box took prominence in a room that was remarkable only for its numerous posters of Justin Bieber. "Is this the daughter's room?"

Zareen ran her hand over a sequined pillow. The motion changed the image on the pillow from Justin circa 2009 to Justin circa 2015. "Nope. Who would have thought it? Raelyn is a Belieber."

"I don't know what that is."

"If I was a psychologist," Zareen said as she circled the bed, "I'd have a field day with this. Justin would have released his first album right around the time Raelyn ran away, but he'd been on YouTube before then. Maybe she followed him from the beginning. He was so innocent, just like her. Then she becomes an addict, then a bloodthirster, then a dead bloodthirster, then a resurrected whatever-the-hell she is, and then the head servant of the Ossian. Yet she still clings to Justin, to innocence, to a time before everything changed for her. My God."

She brought her phone out form where she kept it holstered in her bra. "I have to take pictures to send to Sybille. She's going to die!"

"We can only hope." Juliana walked the room's perimeter, searching for something that didn't quite belong, but nothing belonged here as far as she was concerned. She maneuvered back towards the door. "We should keep searching. I don't know when the guards will be back."

They went into a bathroom next, then a room that seemed to be used as an office, a metal desk barely visible under the clutter of papers and books. The office's windows overlooked the home's circular drive and its sweeping front lawn.

"I found something!" Zareen's voice carried to her from the room next to the office, where Juliana still stood, watching a guard walk the lawn's perimeter, a large gun swung over his shoulder and a stake held in his right hand. She turned from the window and joined Zareen in a bedroom with three of the walls painted silver and a fourth a chalkboard black. Colored chalk had been used to create an image of a stick figure woman with blond hair sitting on a throne, a halo hovering over her head. Something told Juliana that Charlie wasn't the one who'd taken the time to draw the image. A small bed with a purple frame and a rainbow blanket complimented a matching dresser and desk.

"This must be Charlie's room." Zareen pointed to the bed. "And look what's here."

She stepped over to a bedside table and motioned for Juliana to join her. On the table sat a disk-shaped crystal, cool white light emanating from it

"A nightlight?"

Zareen frowned. "Maybe. I think that's what you're supposed to assume it is. Maybe Charlie thought that's what it was. But remember who Charlie is to the Ossian." Her shoulders went up, and she scanned the room. "Shit, they could be listening to us right now."

"Don't be absurd. There's probably a way to make it open a signal to them." She picked up the disk. It was lighter than it looked. Feeling around its edges, she could discern no switches or buttons to push. She ran her hand over its top as though it were a dog she was petting and then nearly jumped out of Raelyn's skin. The object's glow increased. She placed it back on the table and exchanged a look with Zareen.

"Hello?" She spoke at it the way she had with her radio when she'd been trying to communicate with Sybille. "It's your Earthly Ambassador, Phoenix of the Low. I ask to speak with you. Please."

"It was really hard for you to tack on that 'please' at the end, wasn't it?"

Juliana snarled. Zareen just could not cease her poking and prodding. She contemplated ripping off her tender human head and drinking blood straight from her spurting arteries. It would be as easy as slicing through butter on a warm day. But Juliana wasn't Raelyn. She hadn't been a bloodthirster in over a century. Sliding back into a thirster body was hardly a reason to relapse into old patterns. Still, the urge to silence her forever grew every time Zareen spoke.

"Remember who you're talking to, Zareen."

"How could I forget, *Ambassador*? You're so full of yourself!"

"I am full of love for myself, but that's not the point." She lowered her voice. "I mean, if they speak to us, you need to convince them that I'm Raelyn just as much as I do."

Zareen's shoulders dropped. "Fine. Whatever you say."

They waited for something more to happen. Juliana imagined a holographic image of the Ossian appearing above the crystal. That's what happened in that movie—one of the few motion pictures she'd seen. *Star Wars*—that was it. She'd come to visit Elis sometime in the eighties and he'd been watching it on his television using high-tech equipment that would probably be considered obsolete by now. He'd been proud of it and even humored her questions about the movie, which she by and large did not understand. But she had felt a sort of kinship with the young princess with the silly hair. She needed help but she could only appear as a grainy image of herself. She couldn't be touched, not in that form. Juliana could relate.

Sometime during this *Star Wars* revelry, the Ossian made their move, but not in the way either she or Zareen had expected. No princess hologram, no booming voice cutting through worlds. Something much more startling.

The silver bedroom flooded with white light until everything in it had been erased by its brilliance. She gasped for air as though she was drowning. For a moment, Juliana thought her new body was failing her, but then the light faded. As her eyes adjusted, she could again make out her surroundings. She'd been taken from the silver bedroom on a beam of light and deposited in a landscape of bones.

Or rock. Rocky bones.

"Oh my God, I'm going to be sick." Zareen bent forward, knees knocking together. "This is worse than the Low. It's like the Low on acid."

"It is a confounding place, I'll admit." They stood upon bone morphed into unrecognizable shapes as though everything that ever touched this place eventually calcified. Such a thought. The two of them could become like pillars of salt here. Her heart tugged in Raelyn's chest. Only one would be grieved for back on Earth if that happened, and it certainly wasn't her.

Beyond the bony surface, there was nothing. A black sky. Starless. It was as though they were standing on the moon. There appeared to be no atmosphere here, but that couldn't be. Zareen would have frozen up and shattered into a million pieces by now. Even Juliana in her immortal body would have felt more than this sickening unease. And it was warm here, not cold.

"Hello!" She called into the void.

Zareen moaned on the ground beside her.

"Get up." She pulled on her ailing companion's arm. "You'll be fine, or you'll hover near death. Either way, might as well be on your feet in case I need to use you as a human shield."

Shaking, Zareen rose, then slumped against Juliana's shoulder for support. Juliana grimaced but held her up. It figured that Sybille got to go to the Ichor's rainbow dance party realm while she ended up stuck minding a weak human in an incomprehensible space station boneyard.

"Stop shaking, Zareen. You're giving me a headache."

Zareen's grip on her tightened. "I'm not shaking. I still feel like I'm going to lose my lunch, but the shaking—that's not me!"

An earthquake. Or a bone quake? The ground beneath them, Juliana now realized, had begun to tremble. The vibration spread through her. With it came a sound like the buzz of several household appliances all running at the same time. A cacophony of indistinguishable hums.

Zareen straightened up. "You hear that, don't you? Please tell me it's not just me!"

"Yes, I hear it. Now shh."

The cacophony deepened, then diminished until Juliana could make out patterns. Those patterns soon formed meaning. Voices. Words.

This woman will die if she stays. Do you want this to happen?

Why do you wish to speak to us?

Do you know what will happen if you fail?

Juliana hesitated, not sure which question to answer first.

"I wish to speak to you because the girl—my daughter—she's nearly ready. For what you have planned."

She waited. No one answered, so she continued. "I can't recall what will happen if I fail. And by fail I assume you mean the Ossian lose to the Ichor and Earth doesn't get turned into..." She looked around. "Into this delightful place. Could you remind me?"

Zareen groaned and leaned in towards her. Juliana gripped her waist so she wouldn't collapse. "And as for this woman, I should probably get her back to our world before she dies. So, if you could respond, we'll be on our way faster than butter melts on a hot griddle." She grimaced at her own food-based metaphor. *Damn Sybille and what she'd done to her.*

The vibrations started up again. "They're creatures of sound," Zareen said. "The Ossian are formed from vibration. That's how bones become denser too. Did you know that? It's from vibration."

"That makes no sense to me."

"Does it have to? You can literally feel them. They haven't just created the ground we're standing on. They are the ground. They're everything here."

Juliana's mind reeled against this idea. "If they're creatures of sound made manifest as bone, why did they create bloodthirsters? Monsters that crave blood."

They crave what our enemy thrives on, the world boomed. *They take it.*

Sound formed patterns again and patterns formed speech. Juliana spun around. Standing before her was a bone being—not a skeleton exactly, more like if each bone had been layered by cartilage and more bone in ways that shouldn't be. The Ossian stood at least seven feet tall. A thick substance Juliana assumed was marrow oozed from its neck, a sour smell accompanying it.

"Who are you and why is everything so weird here?" Zareen swayed against Juliana.

The Ossian spoke. "This is Ossian. You are not Ossian."

Zareen snorted. "That's fucking right."

Juliana pinched her arm. "Do you want to die here? Don't use profanity!"

"Your daughter is Ossian," the creature said. "You know why."

She didn't, but Raelyn evidently did. She'd have to feign knowledge if she was to pull off this bit of subterfuge. "Of course, but this weak human," she jostled Zareen around the shoulders, "is my new assistant and I promised her she'd get to hear it from you. She was willing to die in order to come here and see you in person!"

Zareen stomped on Juliana's boot but gave their Ossian attendant the best ingratiating smile she could muster. "Yes, it's my dying wish."

The ground shook again. Juliana's vision shook with it. The Ossian stood firm, a sentinel for its (his, her, their?) people. "We rebuilt you from ash. You are Ossian. We let your daughter be born with her mother's Ossian bones and her father's Ossian heritage. She is Ossian."

Zareen gasped. "Holy shit. If I wasn't about to collapse from breathing whatever's passing as air here, that little tidbit would have me on the floor."

"See? It's quite incredible—what I am, what my daughter is." Juliana wouldn't let herself think too hard about the contaminated body she inhabited. Ossian bones. She'd become her own enemy. "Remind my servant about what will happen if my Ossian spawn fails to take over the Earth for you."

The shaking grew until a fissure formed in the bony surface separating Juliana and Zareen from the Ossian being. "If she fails, Earth is lost to us."

In that case, failure sounded like the best possible outcome.

"And then," said the Ossian, "we take back our bones from you. All of them. You will be an empty husk ground into the dust."

"Wait, is there a downside to this?" Zareen asked.

Juliana swallowed. "Charlie's bones are Ossian too."

"Yes." The Ossian stepped towards the fissure. "We will take her bones back as well."

It stepped off the ledge that had formed at the fissure's edge. The vibrations ceased. In their place, a rumbling echoed out, like a motorcycle picking up speed.

"It seems like no matter what, poor Charlie is being sacrificed. Damn these stupid fae!" Zareen stepped away from Juliana long enough to make this proclamation. "We need to tell Sybille and Devin what we just learned. So, how the hell do we get out of this boneyard?"

She turned to face Juliana, but her eyes darted away from her and upwards, widening as they did so. "You've gotta be kidding me!"

The rumbling built to a crescendo. Juliana turned to see what Zareen was so frightened of. Her own breath caught. The boneyard churned like an ocean during a hurricane. A tsunami of Ossian bone had built to a moving wall as tall as any building Juliana had ever seen. It appeared ready to crash down under its own weight. They stood in its wake, the giant fissure blocking any chance of escape.

The only thing left to do was to wait for the Ossian world to swallow them whole.

CHAPTER TWENTY-SIX

ELIS

A LOW BUZZ COMING FROM THE ROOM'S ONLY LIGHT BULB INVADED ELIS'
consciousness. His hand fluttered to his throat, but the skin felt as it always
did, smooth and whole. He swallowed. No pain. Still, when he opened his
eyes, he realized he was lying prone on Nate's gurney. The towering man
stood over him, his breath like rotten meat. Elis flinched.

"I didn't mean to strangle you," Nate said, his voice raised at the end
like it was more a question than a statement.

"You did mean to, but let's just chalk that up to disorientation, mate.
You've been without a body since the turn of the twentieth century. I know
firsthand how jarring the re-ensouling process can be."

"Am I a bad guy now?"

"Come on now, it will take more than an intentional strangulation to
make you bad. Why would you even think that?"

"He has dark thoughts. The Blood King. Nathanial, that is." He worked
his jaw for a bit before finding the courage to say one more word. "Me."

"Ah, well, yes I'm sure Nathanial has perfectly evil thoughts. But
remember, this isn't like when I merged body and soul. Peter and Laurence
have given you the tools you need to have an easier transition, one in
which you, Nate, can stay in the pilot's chair. Nathanial can have a role on
the flight crew too, but he must never be pilot."

"Flying had just been invented when I died."

"Right." As sweet as Nate was, there were moments when Elis could envision himself giving him a good slap. "You're ship's captain then. Nathanial swabs the decks. You must never let him take the helm."

"No!" Nate crossed himself. "Never ever."

Elis hopped down from the gurney. "I'm going to assume you've moved beyond the whole strangulation impulse. If not, let me know right now so I can locate a tranquilizer gun."

"I said I was sorry."

"You did not. You said you didn't mean to strangle me and even that wasn't true. But let's not quibble. We need to make sure Juliana and Zareen succeeded."

"Juliana?" He glanced around the cell, like she might be hiding in the ventilation system. "I've heard terrible things about her."

"Whoever you heard that from was very smart."

"I think it was you."

"There you have it." He led Nate out of the cell and towards the steps leading up to the ground floor. "Juliana remains terrible. However, she, like us, would love to rid Earth of the Ossian fae, so we are relying on her communicating with them while she's possessing Raelyn's body in order to gather any information at all that may help us defeat them."

Nate clomped up the stairs behind Elis. "I guess to someone as smart as you, that makes sense."

"Not entirely, but it is what's happening, nonsensical or not." Elis pushed on the door. Daylight streamed in. Both winced. "You'd think we were two of those Hollywood vampires who burn up at the first exposure to sunlight."

He closed the door behind them. "I have no clue where to look for them."

"I might. Some of the Blood King's memories are mine now. I know the house pretty well, and I'm almost positive when Nathanial communicated with the Ossian, he kept the crystal orb upstairs."

"Wait, Nathanial was in communication with the Ossian?"

"Yeah. More than that. They bring you to their world when they want to make you understand them. They hated him, though. He liked messing with them."

"So that device is a transporter, not just an interdimensional phone?"

"I thought you knew that." Nate craned his head to the left. "Hey, I think that guy's name is, like, Paolo or Paul or something. Hi Paul."

Nate waved to one of Raelyn's guards, who went from a stationary position near the front door to tearing across the floor, rushing towards them. He held a stake up as he slammed Nate against the wall. "What are you doing out of your prison?"

"Paul, don't hurt me. Don't you remember? We're friends!"

"My name is Jason, and we were never friends. I worked for you and you treated me like shit."

"Who's Paul, then?"

"The hell should I know?" Jason grabbed Nate by the scruff of his shirt. The stake moved closer to his chest. Elis debated whether he should intercede. A stake through the heart would barely phase Nate. Elis on the other hand, didn't relish the idea of being turned into a pile of ash.

"There's no need for violence. Perhaps if you understood that the Blood King isn't the same as he once was. The traumatic brain injury he endured has made him much nicer."

Jason responded by tapping his comm with his non-stake hand. "Calling all members of Phoenix Guard. Backup requested. Proceed to the mansion's main corridor." He glared at Nate. "I'm putting you back in your cage."

Nate's face crumbled. "I don't like it down there. You can't make me go back."

"I think I can. The Phoenix Guard can handle you."

"Nate," Elis said, "His friends are going to be here any second. Can you deal with him, or do I need to risk my recently strangled neck for you?"

"No, it's okay, I've got this."

"What are you—" The words died on Jason's tongue as Nate flicked the stake out of his hand, grabbed his wrist and twisted him around, slamming his head into a mirror mounted on the wall. It shattered, bits of it lodging into the thirster's face.

"Elis, could you get the door for me please?"

Elis obliged, opening the door to the basement. He waited for Nate to toss the guard down the stairs. When the thud of him landing at its base echoed back up, he closed the door. "Right. We better find Juliana before you have to dispose of Raelyn's entire security force.

"That was fun, though."

"No worries, lad. I'm sure you'll have more opportunities to toss people down staircases in about two minutes. Why don't you show me where you think that crystal orb might be?"

They dashed up the front staircase. Nate paused on the second-floor landing. "The orb had to be kept in the Northeast corner of the house. I don't know why but that's what the Ossian said to do. So that would mean it's in that room." He pointed to an open doorway at the far end of the hallway. "Let's go."

Elis pushed through the threshold first, Nate right on his heels. "Zareen? Juliana?" The room, which Elis immediately inferred was Charlie's, stood empty of his team, but full of cold white light streaming from a rock next to the bed. His stomach twisted. Charlie's room containing a portal to the Ossian realm seemed like poor parenting even for the likes of Raelyn. He pointed to the crystal. "That's it, isn't it?"

Nate crouched so he was eye level with the device. "It is. I'm guessing that Juliana and Zareen are on the Ossian world right now, and that's bad. That place is awful. It smells like fish guts."

"No offense, mate, but you smell worse than rotting fish. Remind me to show you how a shower works as soon as we get this situation sorted."

Nate sniffed at his shirt, then turned his attention back to the orb. "The Ossian used to make this crystal vibrate like Sybille's phone when she leaves it on the table. Kind of like what it's doing now."

The orb began to shake so hard, Elis imagined it would fall off the table. "Are they going to transport us too?"

Nate began pressing the sides in what seemed to be random patterns. "I hope not."

The orb continued to shake. Its light dimmed. Elis wondered if that was a good or bad sign. "As much as I'd love to get out of the Low, this is not the way I want to make our escape. Stop it, please."

"I'm trying!" Nate began hitting it. "I think something's happening."

It began glowing brighter again. The room filled with light as it bounced off the silver walls. It reminded him of when he'd gone to a club in the late seventies, disco ball casting rays of blinding light across the dance floor.

When the brightness fell, Elis expected to find himself in whatever crazy Ossian realm they'd sucked him into. Instead, Charlie's unexpectedly cheerful bedroom appeared before him, just as it had looked before the Orb activated itself.

"Oh my God, we're back." Zareen's weary voice spoke from behind him. He turned to find her being held up by Juliana. Zareen took in a strained breath. "Elis, I've never been so happy to see your handsome monster mug. But holy crap did those Ossian fae tell us some wild stuff. We need to get home."

Elis wrapped Zareen's arm around his shoulder and eased her off Juliana, who peered at him with Raelyn's wide, calculating eyes.

"She's right," Juliana said. "The situation with Charlie? It's much worse than we imagined."

Sybille

Sybille poured lemon ginger tea into Margot's favorite rose cup and placed it on its saucer in front of Devin. She slid the honey jar over to him and then sat in front of her own steaming mug of coffee. She'd sequestered him away from everyone else in the household, hoping to suss out what had sent him into a tailspin. Not that there wasn't plenty of depressing events to choose from that might cause one to assume the fetal position, but if she was going to get everyone through this in one piece, she needed Devin upright and functional. She slid her hand under the table and gave his knee a pat. He jolted, knocking the table and sloshing the tea over the side of his cup.

"Sybille?" He looked at her and then down at his tea, seeming to realize they were both there with him.

"You've been acting out of sorts ever since you went off with Peter. I need to know if he said something upsetting to you."

Devin spooned a generous teaspoon of honey into his cup and twirled it around until the sweetener dissolved. "You could say that."

Sybille brought her hand back to her own lap. "I knew it! It's the potion for Charlie, isn't it? It's a failure."

The teaspoon clattered to the table. Devin gripped his cup with both hands so hard, Sybille thought he might shatter it. He stared at her with hopeless eyes. "There is no serum for Charlie. There never was."

"What?" She sprang up, ready to face her uncle to find out why he'd deceived them all yet again. "I'm going to throttle him."

"Sit down, Sybille. You don't know the whole story." He tapped her chair.

She sank back into it. "I'm listening."

"There's no cure for Charlie. At least, there's no cure that Peter or Laurence can come up with to give to her."

"Then what the hell has Peter been working on all this time?"

"A serum, just like he said. But not for Charlie." He stared at his lap again. "For me."

"For…you." She took a big swig of her coffee. "Why?"

"Look, I'm not going to pretend to understand it completely, but the hope is to reverse engineer me."

"Reverse. As in, you can make bloodthirsters immortal but now…?"

"I can kill them. Like, kill kill. The permanent never coming back from it death. Or that's the theory."

"But what does that have to do with helping Charlie."

"Even if the Low takes her over completely and turns her into some sort of Ossian world generator, I'll be capable of stopping her."

"And by stopping, you mean killing her."

He let go of his teacup. His fingers danced against Sybille's. He slid them into hers and gripped her like she was the surface of a mountain he was scaling. "I won't do that."

"Of course not." She squeezed him back. "I can't believe Peter wants you to."

"He doesn't. He wants me to find a way to spare her, but he also doesn't want her to unleash an Ossian plague across the planet."

"He must have known when he went about concocting this serum that it would put Charlie at greater risk."

"Think about it. Peter's been working behind our backs for years. He has backchannels to both sides of this Ossian war. Do you really think he made this serum all on his own? He told me he'd consulted with a colleague about it. Who do you think that was?"

"Laurence helped him."

"Laurence helped him create something that would make me capable of killing his granddaughter?"

"Okay, maybe not."

"Definitely not. No, this was Froya's doing. Probably at Ayan's direction. This was part of Ayan's plan all along, ever since she heard what I'd done to make the Blood King immortal and then suddenly couldn't wait to meet her long-lost never before cared for grandson."

"Are you saying Peter's been feeding them information this whole time? Does he have an orb too?"

"No, but we know who does, don't we?"

A warmth grew between their palms. It was pleasant to fixate on that instead of the dawning awareness gnawing at her consciousness. "The Patron." She closed her eyes. "He's helped orchestrate this. He told the Ichor where to find you, and he told Peter what they wanted him to create in order to stop Charlie…at any cost."

She opened her eyes to find him staring at her. "No wonder you're so depressed, Devin. This whole situation just keeps getting more and more awful."

"I hate it. I hate all of it. How Charlie's been used. How I'm expected to be her executioner. I didn't ask for any of this. A few months ago, I thought my dad was a lowlife dive bar owner. Now I have magical powers but I'm a dog on a leash. Even Thunderheart has more freedom than I do. I can't use my powers whenever or however I want. I can't go where I want. I can't… I can't be with who I want."

Sybille's cheeks heated. She should've pulled her hand from his, but she didn't. He hadn't shown this level of vulnerability since he'd confessed to killing his sister, but now there was an added intensity to him. His whole body exuded something she could feel but lacked the vocabulary to say out loud.

"Devin, I know this sucks, but focus on what's happening. There's a power building inside of you. You need to stay aware of it so you and only you can decide what to do with it."

He kept his gaze on her. "I hate Froya. She manipulated me, lied to me. She treats me like a pet. She helped turn me into this."

"Into what? You're still Devin. You're still the best field agent I've ever had. You're still my friend."

He laughed, a long humorless laugh that became strangled at the end. "Am I?"

"Yes!"

The door leading from the kitchen to the dining room opened. Sybille tried to let go of Devin's hand, but he continued to hold on until he saw who had just entered.

"Tis thy fairest lady Sybille. Perchance you to speak with thy lowly servant for a moment?"

Rising from the table, Devin dropped her hand, formed a fist, and punched Bore in the face.

CHAPTER TWENTY-SEVEN

DEVIN

DEVIN RUBBED AT HIS KNUCKLES. USING BORE'S BONY NOSE AS A PUNCHING bag hurt his hand like a son of a bitch but damned if it wasn't worth it to see Bore's shocked expression. One hit. That's all he allowed himself, and it was all it took.

"Why'd you do that?" Bore cried.

"Being fae and all, I could have turned you into a snake, but that would have done a disservice to all the perfectly nice snakes in the world. Be thankful all I did was give you a bit of a tap."

"A tap? You broke my nose!" He grabbed one of Margot's dishtowels and held it to his bleeding nostrils.

"My mom just bought that. She's going to be pissed." Sybille looked ready to strike too, but whether it was Bore or himself she aimed to hit, he couldn't tell.

Peter, who had entered the kitchen behind Bore in time to witness the showdown, placed a hand across Bore's back and swung him around towards the dining room. "Let's go to my lab and get you cleaned up. Devin, why don't you come with us so we can talk through some matters and maybe do a bit of conflict resolution."

Conflict resolution. It was just like Peter to gloss over his own involvement and play the role of benevolent peacemaker. "I'll be right there. Give me a minute."

As soon as they were out of the room, he turned to Sybille. "I'm sorry I hit him."

"Don't be. I've been wanting to do that for years. I mean, I did hit him when I was possessed but that doesn't totally count."

He inched towards the door, then stopped. He should follow Peter, but who knew if he'd ever get another moment alone with Sybille. Ever since Peter had injected him, a boldness had taken over. He felt different, detached, like he was watching himself say words and punch assholes, and it was sort of him doing it but sort of not. He wondered if this was how Sybille felt when she was in the throes of possession.

"Do you remember back at the cabin in the Low when we needed to find Elis and we knew we'd be facing a terrifying enemy soon?"

She cleared her throat. "I remember every moment of that day."

"Me too. Especially the part where I wanted to tell you things. I started to, but…"

"I stopped you. I told you there would be time for grand declarations later."

"But there never was. We succeeded in what we needed to do, and then Froya found me. Besides, your heart…" He should stop right there. What point was there in drudging all of this up? "Your heart was elsewhere."

Sybille's eyes moistened. "Devin."

"Look, Sybille, we're probably going to die or be separated again or who knows what so I'm going to say what I want to say, and I don't need you to respond, okay? I know you love Elis. I hate the guy and it will always be creepy to me that you're with this centuries-old creature, but whatever. I can't change that situation any more than I can change the fact that I love you."

The room spun, then steadied. He'd said it out loud, finally, and it didn't kill him, nor did it change anything.

Sybille let loose a few tears but remained silent.

"I don't care if it is the wrong time to say it, because it will probably always be the wrong time. There will never be a right time, not for you and me, and I accept that. Some things just need to be said, and as it turns out, Peter's serum is helping me figure out a lot about myself. It makes me want to right whatever I've done wrong. Not telling you how I felt—hell—two years ago is a wrong and now I've made it right. If I die or you die or we both die, there will always be that."

He nodded as though he'd confirmed his own statement and then backed towards the door. "You know, next I'm going to tell Froya to shove it. I'd rather be alone for eternity than be her toy any longer."

He opened the door, only to stop when Sybille stilled him. She spun him around and pulled him into an embrace, wrapping her arms around his shoulders and pressing her face next to his. "Damn you, Devin Vargas."

She kissed his cheek, then broke away. "Get out of here. Go apologize to Bore. Find out if he and Peter are keeping more secrets from us, and…" She held his gaze. "I need you to remember that you're one of the most important people in my life. You said my heart is elsewhere, but if you think you don't carry a piece of it wherever you go, you're wrong. Now get out of here before I start crying again."

She shooed him out the door. As he approached the living room, Thunderheart jumped off the couch and joined him. Ten seconds later, he walked into Peter's study. Bore held a bloodied cotton ball to his nose while Peter conversed in a corner with Froya. "Sorry about your nose, Patron," he said offhand as he strode past him to get to Froya. "I'll try to find more nonviolent ways to deal with your complicit ass next time. And you!" He pointed at Froya. "I am done with you."

Froya blinked her purple eyes as she cocked her head. "You've done what with me? Quite a bit as I recall. Did something confuse you?"

"No, nothing about you confuses me anymore. You're completely transparent and hateful. I'm over you and your manipulation. And I want my mind back."

"Did you misplace it?"

"Shut up, you know what I mean. Remove my block, Froya. I deserve to be in control of myself."

Froya stepped around Peter's desk and approached him, invoking a growl from Thunderheart. He stood by Devin's side, teeth bared.

Devin patted the dog's head. "Good boy."

Froya shot Thunderheart a nasty look. "I need Ayan's permission to remove the block, so you'll have to take it up with her."

"Bullshit. You have the ability to do it, so do it!"

Peter stepped in between them. "I know this is a sore point, Devin, but it's not our only one. Charlie is worse, and I fear what will happen when Elis returns with my daughter and Juliana, who is temporarily residing in your sister's body. She's bound to react badly, feeling that her mother's been compromised."

"Imagine that." Devin could only shake his head as he sulked. He couldn't argue that Raelyn was a dangerous asset to the Ossian, but letting Juliana take control of her body was reckless at best. "All right, so now that we have one horrible idea in play, let's see what else you people have thought up. Froya, would you like me to drown kittens after I've disposed of my niece? Maybe burn down a few churches while I'm at it?"

"If doing so diminishes Ossian power, then yes. Please drown as many kittens and set as many fires as you wish." Froya fiddled with the Ichor crystal embedded in her wrist.

"Are you communicating with someone?" Peter asked her.

"Yes." She slid her arm back to her side. "You should be a lot more grateful to me, Devin. We could have let the Ossian take over your precious human world. We've risked ourselves to help you."

Devin's body pulsed. "Liar. You've risked little for a whole hell of a lot. You aren't fooling us. We've all been on the frontline fighting the Ossian for years, not even knowing that's what we were doing. Meanwhile, you came to Earth as a goddamn tourist and then went home to your perfect blood tree magic pelican world and left us to figure out shit on our own."

"That's not entirely true." Froya pointed to Bore. "I recruited Patrons, including this one. We've been paying your salary and have dribbled information to Peter Esmond through the Patron program since before you were born."

Devin aimed his death glare at Peter, who frowned and then responded, "I must emphasize that the information was cryptic, rarely helpful, and never complete." He pushed his glasses up the bridge of his nose. "My reasons for going along with the Ichor are mine, and I won't share them now. However, I assure you, Devin, I won't keep anything from you or Sybille regarding the Ichor or the Ossian. Not anymore. It was a mistake I made based on false pretenses, and I won't make that mistake again."

"What false pretenses?"

"I already said I won't share now. Bore, come here please." Peter motioned him over and Bore, cotton ball still pressed to his nose, complied. "I'm not excusing his behavior, but you do understand why Devin was angry?"

Bore bit at his nails. "I supposeth I do."

"For fuck's sake," Devin said. "Stop speaking like that, man."

"Calm down." Peter pressed a hand against Devin's chest. "Froya, I think it's safe to say you'll be bored stiff at my attempts to mediate between these two. Why don't you go and finish your communications with your people? You can use Margot's room."

Froya pushed off the wall she'd been leaning against. "Fine, but if you think they'll turn violent again, let me know. I'd love to watch." Devin shrank back as she placed her fingertips against his cheek and ran them down to his chest. "You'll change your mind about me. I can make you change your mind."

"I'm beginning to think I punched the wrong person."

Scowling, she left the office, slamming the door shut behind her as she went.

Peter turned back to Bore. "She's gone. Now tell Devin what you told me this morning."

"Okay, okay look. I'm not a bad person. I wasn't trying to deceive you, but I was sworn to secrecy when I was selected to be Patron. Ayan said I was helping rid the world of monsters and that I'd get to see paranormal stuff. She was right. You killed a lot of bloodthirsters. Sybille and her family released a lot of innocent souls. But I never totally trusted the fae, not since the day I met Froya at Comic Con."

"You met Froya at Comic Con?"

"I told her that her cosplay was excellent, but I wasn't sure what fandom she was from. Her response was that she could fulfill my wildest fantasies, and I mean, come on. Who in their right mind wasn't going to pursue that?"

He winked. Devin envisioned punching him again.

"Get to the point where you don't trust her."

"It was, like, so much information. I thought she was LARPing, you know? Live Action Role Playing. She refused to break character, and before I knew it, I was playing along. I assumed it was a game. All this talk of fae wars and bones and blood. Bloodthirsters. Those weren't real, they couldn't be. Pretty soon, she convinced me to join the Patron program, and after training I was assigned to the Esmonds.

"Here's the thing. She said it the first day we met, and only said it the one time. I wasn't meant to remember it—it was insignificant. She said,

'The Ossian and the Ichor both have a presence on Earth, but neither can flourish while the other is here.'"

"They both have a presence." Devin slapped the table. "So as soon as the Ossian are defeated, the Ichor will take over?"

Bore dropped the cotton ball in the garbage and felt around his nose to make sure it wasn't still bleeding. "You keep saying 'the Ichor' like you aren't one of them, like you still won't accept your role in all of this."

"My role," Devin said, "is to be their weapon of mass Ossian destruction."

Bore shook his head. "I talked to Peter about this and we both agree. Your role is to win Earth for your people, but it doesn't end there. When the war is over and Earth still stands, your job is to rule it."

CHAPTER TWENTY-EIGHT

SYBILLE

LAURENCE HELD ONTO HIS GRANDDAUGHTER'S TREMBLING BODY AS BEST HE could. Charlie struggled against him as she flopped like a fish on the braided oval rug in front of the couch, face flush with heat, voice gravely.

Sybille didn't want to see the pain etched into the little girl's brow nor hear her plaintive cries for help that none of them seemed able to provide. She forced herself not to look away.

Laurence recited lines to an appeasement spell he and Peter had worked on.

Leave us in peace
We will nurture the darkness
Wherever you may go.

Margot joined his recitation, her melodic voice lifting the words, if not the mood, as she also attempted to feed Charlie teaspoon portions of a thick brown syrup. It smelled like the thyme cough medicine she'd given to Sybille as a child.

Charlie tossed her head back and forth like a belligerent toddler as Margot maneuvered the spoon towards her mouth. After several failed attempts, Sybille brought her hand down over her mother's arm. Margot lowered the spoon in defeat. Her home remedy would do little now anyways. Anything they tried—spells, tinctures, reasoning—all were doomed to failure. There was a chance Devin would be able to use his powers to save Charlie, but no one, least of all Devin, was confident about that. Her only hope was that Elis would arrive home with his mesmerizing abilities plus good news from Juliana's spy mission.

The uncertainty chipped away at her resolve. Pain shot from her shoulders to her temples. She felt like she was coming down with the flu, her body heavy and feverish with worry. Minutes ticked by, and every part of her began to ache. Her hope was pinned on Juliana. They were all doomed.

The doorbell rang. Sybille rose from where she'd been crouching next to Charlie. "That must be Elis. Keep hold of her, okay?"

Just as she was turning the doorknob, Margot called out to her, "Dear? Why would Elis bother to knock? He has a key."

Too late, not that a locked door would have kept this visitor out. "This isn't really a good time, Ayan."

Even though she knew it was futile, Sybille began to close the door, only to have it freeze open. Her right arm stiffened, refusing to bend or move. "Holy hell, you made your point. Now, let me go!"

Ayan slid inside the house. "That was very rude of you Sybille. Here I went and politely followed your custom of ringing the doorbell to be allowed entrance to your home, which is more than what you did when the situation was reversed. And then you tell me I'm not welcome?"

"You wanted to have me executed, and you threw a knife at my chest. Am I supposed to act warm and fuzzy?"

"You're supposed to be appreciative of the fact that none of my knives found their way within your flesh."

"No thanks to you! Devin's the only reason you're not my murderer. Jesus, I thought fae were supposed to have good memories."

"I remember how inconsiderate you are." Ayan swept past Sybille. In the living room, she paused to assess the situation. "Gods, I hate the human world. This is the girl, I take it."

Her attention on Charlie, she flicked her hand in Sybille's direction. Sybille fell against the door as the freeze hold abated. The door clanked closed. Rubbing life back into her arm, she righted herself and joined Ayan in the living room.

"Don't come any closer," Laurence said to Ayan. Crouching by Charlie's head, he pressed his hands to her temples while Margot sat opposite of him, a hand on each of the girl's ankles. Charlie continued her struggle.

Ayan clicked her tongue. "This child should never have been born. Her suffering is one of the many reasons the Ossian don't belong in this world."

Sybille bristled. "Why are you here, Ayan? To remind us of how incompetent we are at trying to fix a problem you helped cause?"

"This feud over Earth began long before me. And the Ossian made the choices that led to this impending battle. They placed this girl in your midst and decided her life was worth the price they wished to pay. I didn't cause this." She stretched her hand towards Charlie. "But I can't prevent it either. I just tried to freeze her to provide you with more time, but it didn't work. Would you like to know how bad that is?"

"Not really." Sybille swayed, the weight of fae powers swarming around her adding to her already dizzying state of anxiety. "So, you came to see if you could stop Charlie yourself? That's bullshit. You already knew you weren't capable."

"No, but my grandson is. I'm here to see that he does what's necessary. Do you think I'd be in this horrible world if I didn't have to be? The future won't secure itself."

"What the hell does that mean?"

The front door burst open and Elis emerged from the foyer. "We're back. And we have news. Oh, hello, who's this?"

Ayan had her knives out before he'd completed his question. "Ossian soldier, you've drawn blood from innocents for the last time!"

Elis looked confused. "Come again?"

Seeing Ayan aiming her weapon, Sybille scrambled to stop her, only to find herself pinned to the ground under an invisible weight. She prepared herself to witness Elis' heart being torn in two, but Ayan never managed to throw her knife. Instead, Charlie's groans turned to shrieks. She launched herself out of her grandfather's hold and onto Ayan's back. Unprepared for this attack, Ayan lost her grip on her knife, which skittered across the floor towards the staircase. The fae's concentration broken, Sybille scrambled to her feet.

Charlie pulled on Ayan's curls and spoke the first distinguishable words she'd uttered all evening. "If you hurt him, I will tear open your throat with my teeth and let the dog lap up your blood!"

"Charlie!" Elis inched towards her, but Sybille blocked his path.

"She's about to lose it, Elis." The hair on her arms stood up as the room became electric. "Can't you feel it? Look at her." Charlie's skin had begun to flake off like paper after it burned. Under it, her veins darkened to a deep indigo.

"I have to help her."

Sybille's lip quivered. This is what she wanted, wasn't it? To have him make this desperate, dangerous attempt. Even if it came to no good, Elis had to try and she had to let him. She stepped aside.

"Charlie," his resonant voice filled the space, "you've fought this before and won. You can fight it again. You're meant to rule Oz, not be conquered by it."

To almost anyone else, his hypnotic intonation would have been heard as a command. Charlie gave no indication that she even knew he'd spoken.

Electricity sparked against Sybille's skin. She felt like they were all inside of a grenade, and the pin was about to be pulled. She yanked him out of the fray again. Defeated, he sagged towards her. "I can't save her. I failed."

Charlie kept up her demonic temper tantrum. Ayan had just enough sense to appear scared at her assailant's growing strength. "It's too late for you, child."

She let Charlie pound on her back as she touched the crystal embedded in her wrist.

"What are you doing?" Sybille asked.

"I'm calling for my grandson. It's time he ends this."

Elis

Elis barely had a moment to wonder how many people were going to attack him today before a nine-year-old possessed with the energy of the Ossian fae came to his defense. Gutted by his inability to do a bloody thing to help Charlie, he had just figured out who the fae woman with the

Halloween-colored hair was when the living room filled with more people, including Devin and the lavender-eyed Froya.

His bloodthirster heart thumped under the warmth of Sybille's palm. She pressed him back towards the wall and as much away from the chaos as the room would afford. It irked him to remain on the sidelines, but any of the fae, including Devin, could ash him faster than he could mount a counterattack.

"That's Devin's nan?" he asked Sybille. She didn't look a day over thirty, but then, he himself was a prime example of how looks could be deceiving.

"Ayan, yes." Sybille shushed him with a stern look, fingertips pressing hard against him, but her concern at keeping him removed from the spotlight seemed unnecessary now that Charlie had asserted herself.

As Devin tore Charlie from Ayan's back, Laurence and Margot rushed to hold her down again. Freed from the child, Ayan's attention turned, not back to Elis, but towards another newcomer.

"Who is this?" Ayan circled Nate. Knives in both hands, she ran them along his waistline as she twirled around him. "He's like the other one, isn't he Froya? Only not as repulsive."

"Thank you! Could you please tell me why my body isn't able to move right now?" Nate smiled, his rotting teeth on display.

Ayan sniffed. Her lips peeled back and she let out a hiss. "Perhaps I should rethink that."

Froya joined her, tongue pressed between her teeth. They seemed immune to Charlie's screeching parrot-level antics not ten feet away from them as they continued to scrutinize Nate. Froya squeezed his bicep. "Strong. A bloodthirster with a soul like that dark-haired man, yes, but this one has Devin's power within him as well. Like her." She pointed to Juliana, who hung back by the front door, watching the spectacle in front of her. Elis glanced her way and shook his head. *Stay back. Do not engage.*

Ayan didn't give Juliana more than a passing glance. "She has the soul of another. It's a possession, not a rejoining. She will be easy to dispatch when she's no longer useful to us."

"Excuse me?" Juliana stepped forward and then froze where she stood. "What's happening to me?"

"I froze you just like I froze the other immortal," Froya told her. "Your place isn't to challenge us. You're our servant."

"I am nobody's servant." Her voice shook.

Froya continued her examination of Nate. "What do you want to do with him, Ayan?"

Ayan lifted her knife to Nate's throat. "We should slice him open. I can take some organs back home to have our people run tests. His blood will be harvested too, of course."

"Of course," Froya agreed.

"Am I still alive when you harvest my blood?"

"You are not truly alive now." Ayan kept her knife pressed to him. "Tell me, soul, why trap yourself in this undead body? It's a tool for the Ossian. Do you wish to be a monster?"

Elis wondered why she hadn't taken the time to ask him that question before trying to end him. He would have had a better answer than Nate, who simply said, "Monsters get to be scary instead of scared. I've been scared for a long time."

"Scared? Why?"

"Because they killed Mary. I loved her."

"Who killed her?"

Nate's eyes softened. "Bloodthirsters. And then they turned me into one of them. One of the worst ones of them."

"I see. So, you seek vengeance for your lover's death."

"Yes."

Taking advantage of a temporary lull as Charlie caught her breath, Devin called over, "We need him, Ayan. Nate is strong, like Froya said. He's on our side. The Ossian solider he used to be isn't in control now. Nate's got him locked down, don't you?"

"He's very grumbly inside my head, but I don't listen to him," answered Nate. "He doesn't remember Mary the way I do. I remember what they did to her."

"Revenge is a motivation I understand, as is the desire to have a successful outcome in our battle for Earth." Ayan lowered her knives and sheathed them. "You are both an enemy and an ally. We'll watch you closely and decide when to dissect you. Until then, you won't be bothered by us. Froya, you may release him."

Nate wobbled as he gained back control over his limbs. He grinned again, and Ayan placed her hand back on one of her knives. "Do something about that stench soon or I'll cut off your whole jaw just to be rid of the foulness. Devin, why is the child still screaming? You are the only one who can do something about it, so do it. Now!"

"I can't!" Devin cupped Charlie's head in his hands as she wailed. The room's charge grew, sparks flying everywhere.

"You must!"

"Wait!" Elis gripped Sybille's hand and lifted it off him. "I have to tell everyone something, and if I don't do it now, things are going to get very bad very soon."

Face pinched, Sybille let him go.

"Juliana and Zareen have been to the Ossian's world."

The assault of sparks intensified as everyone strained to hear him speak over Charlie's screams.

Elis continued. "You can ask them yourselves, but they learned a lot while they were there, as was the plan. And one of the main things to note is that if Devin doesn't kill Charlie, she's going to explode little bits of Ossian world-making Low bone all over Earth, and we're all going to die."

"I'm not going to kill my niece!" Devin shouted.

"For once, I agree with you," Elis said. "Because if you do kill her, you will likewise release the Low into the world. She is made from Ossian bones. There's no removing the Ossian from her. She is," he swallowed. "She is Ossian. No matter your strategy, the result will be the same and it will be unstoppable."

Ayan's knife was out and gouged in the wood panel next to Elis' head before he could blink. "Lying Ossian scum! You're trying to deceive us so we fail!"

"What do you know?" Zareen leaned against the wall next to Juliana. "Have you ever been to the Ossian's wasteland? Because I have. And I almost died there so that Juliana and I could bring you back this information. Everything Elis has said is the truth!"

"So, what are we supposed to do?" Sybille asked. "Charlie—she's almost gone now."

Devin, still holding Charlie, handed her off to Nate. "How is it that Charlie, a human who's only supposed to have remote Ossian heritage through her grandfather's line, has Ossian bones?"

"You know the answer to that, Devin," Juliana said. Strange, Elis thought, how Raelyn's voice had morphed into hers so quickly. Raelyn's pitch, Juliana's inflection. "Your sister knows too. She's always known, though she tried to hide it from me as soon as I possessed her. Your abilities resurrected her, yes, but the Ossian contributed to her reconstruction, right down to the bone.

"This body gave the Ossian the advantage they needed to put things into motion. If you want to end this, it starts with me." She stretched out her arms. "Looks like you get to murder your sister again."

CHAPTER TWENTY-NINE

SYBILLE

FAR BE IT FOR SYBILLE TO OBJECT IF JULIANA CHOSE TO SACRIFICE HERSELF TO help save the world, but no way was she buying the altruism act.

"All right, everyone!" She called out to the crowded living room. "I'm dividing up this spectacle. Anyone who doesn't do as I say—that includes you two." She pointed at Froya and Ayan. "You can get the fuck out of my house.

She turned to Nate. "This is your big moment, hon."

Shocked, Nate pointed a finger at himself. "I have a big moment?"

"You do," she said. "You're strong, powerful. Pretty soon, no one besides you will be capable of containing Charlie. You need to take her into the kitchen. And do not let go, no matter what. Do you understand?"

He clutched Charlie against his mammoth shoulder, expression solemn. "I let go of Mary. They pulled her away from me and I couldn't hold on." His eyes reddened. "I won't let that happen again."

"Good man. Laurence, Mom, Peter—go with Nate and do whatever magic woo-woo, science, mantra chanting, whatever it is you still have left in your bag of tricks. Buy us some time."

Laurence, looking defeated and feeble, shook his head. "I don't know what else to do."

"Think of something. Go!" She shooed them back through the dining room. "Bore, get your traitorous ass over here too."

Bore, who had planted himself in a corner behind Margot's favorite rocking chair, stuck his head up. "Me? Why?"

"Because Charlie may start turning Earth into an Ossian world at any moment, and when she does, my kitchen will become ground zero. If that happens, I want you to be one of the first to die."

Ayan perked up. "You too have a vengeful side, hierophant. Maybe you aren't entirely horrid."

Sybille waited as Bore marched himself past her into the kitchen. "I'm going to see if I can help them with Charlie. Meanwhile, I expect you all to figure out how to salvage this situation. And Juliana: if you want to play the sacrificial lamb, you better put your head on the chopping block and keep it there."

"I'll watch her, Sybille." Zareen said.

"You all will." She looked at Elis, then Devin. "We're all walking away from here today, you got that? Do what you need to do."

She turned and pushed her way into the kitchen, where all hell seemed literally to be breaking lose. Sparks flew everywhere. One landed on her bare wrist. She flinched, but the ember soon turned to dust. No, not dust. She tried to rub it away, but it stuck, hardening into a lump of bone.

Nate held Charlie but it was clear even the immortal lumberjack was struggling to maintain control. As the other adults chanted around her, Charlie began to chant with them, her voice garbled and mocking.

"Leave us in peace and we will nurture the darkness wherever you may go." She laughed and then resumed shrieking.

Laurence grabbed onto his granddaughter's arm. "Please, Charlie. Fight this!"

She repaid his command with a hiss. Her body convulsed and bone sparks flew straight from her hand onto his. Laurence recoiled, his own screams as loud as hers.

His hand flared blue. The smell of burning flesh made Sybille gag. Laurence slid to the ground as the flames flickered and cooled, leaving a hard coating where a hand had been. Bone, mangled and twisted.

Sybille covered her mouth. Bore whimpered as he pressed himself against a row of cabinets, inched his way towards the backdoor, and made his ungrateful exit.

Coward.

Poor Thunderheart, who had probably sought refuge in the kitchen before any of them had invaded the space, huddled under the table, big brown eyes begging for an end to the madness.

"Okay," she said as she tried to formulate strategies in her head. All of them made little sense and ended in the annihilation of the planet. "I see we have things under control here, so I'm going to check on the others to make sure the right person is murdered. Just..." She looked to her mother, who pursed her lips and hung her head. "Just try to hold on."

The sound of splitting wood accompanied by a violent shaking caught her off balance before she could exit the room. She heaved to the side, slamming her shoulder into the edge of a countertop. She had just enough time to realize this was no earthquake when the ground gave way under her feet.

Juliana

She did not wish for death. As Juliana lifted her arms, feeling the electricity in the room like a current circulating through her, she knew this wouldn't be the end of her. Raelyn's body resurrected by Ichor blood and Ossian bones—that could go if necessary. Juliana's consciousness would remain.

She was eternal. Beyond death and life, beyond everything. She'd grown fond of Raelyn's form. It was young and lithe and knew no equal in both beauty and power. As soon as she'd prompted Devin to work his fae magic upon her, she began to seek an out. Devin, despite the fae women's efforts, seemed to be stalling as well.

"We went to great lengths to make sure Peter Esmond could make you the weapon necessary to defeat the Ossian," Ayan said as she pushed Devin forward. "Now this woman has control over this Ossian body, and you can easily destroy her. What are you waiting for?"

"She's my sister! I've already killed her once."

"If you'd finished the job then," Froya said, "we wouldn't be in this situation now. So, finish it. Remember, Sybille's life depends on your success. Besides, your sister hasn't been your sister in years."

"She's still here, Devin." Juliana lifted her hands higher. "It's her strength that has allowed me to break free from the fae spell, so I can move and fight. You don't have to kill her."

"Yes, you do." Pushing Froya aside, Elis came and stood next to him. "Her death may be key to weakening the Low within Charlie, making her Ossian bones go dormant."

Devin shook his head. "I don't see how."

Juliana did. She knew her ex had figured things out correctly, but no matter. She remembered Charlie—not the writhing, spitting, hissing girl, but the Charlie who visited her in her kitchen, who'd eaten her treats and appreciated Juliana's skill in making them. Intoxication mixed with memory. Memories of that Charlie and memories of Raelyn's daughter. Charlie as a baby, held close to her breast. Charlie as a toddler, Raelyn chasing after her as her blond head bobbed and laughed down the Low's forest trails.

Juliana, never a mother and always without a loving home all the centuries she'd existed, pulled from Raelyn's memories, letting Raelyn rise just enough to send Juliana a message.

If it's her only chance, let me die.

"What did you say?" Devin closed in on her, the fae women at his heel.

She'd thought those words in her head. She hadn't said them out loud. But someone had.

"Raelyn, that's you, isn't it?" Devin croaked. "Are you sure about this?"

Juliana turned when she felt Zareen's presence at her side. "Juliana, Raelyn is surfacing," Zareen said. "She wants us to save her daughter."

Juliana's lip trembled. Raelyn's lip. Her lip. Hers but not hers. The room swam and the floors shook. Zareen pulled on Juliana's hands, trying to keep them both upright. Whatever was happening with Charlie in the next room, it was happening fast.

"Juliana!" Zareen's voice was firm, insistent. "Devin wants Raelyn's permission. Does he have it?"

It was all she could do to hold on to Zareen's words long enough to make sense of them. Her mind shook along with the room as another wave of vibrations hit. Raelyn rallied again, the vibrations pushing her up towards consciousness.

Zareen waited. Zareen, who had a loving husband and children who adored her. She too was willing to place herself in grave danger to protect them. Juliana wanted to feel that sort of sacrificial love again. She'd sacrificed for Elis, she'd loved him that dearly, but that had ended in betrayal and abandonment.

Maybe it was time for another sacrifice. But she would rather die than be the lamb.

She clung to Zareen as she made her decision. "Don't let go of me!"

"I won't," Zareen promised. She took Juliana's hands and squeezed. "And Raelyn?"

Juliana grinned. Truth, like always, was on her side. "Raelyn consents to her death."

This was the easy part—letting Raelyn speak her truth. That beastly woman deserved to die, just as all bloodthirsters did. How Juliana would miss her powerful body, though.

"We're ready, aren't we, Zareen." Zareen's full lips rounded into an O. Juliana kept hold of her as Raelyn gave her final words. "Do it, brother. Then save my child."

CHAPTER THIRTY

DEVIN

Never enough time. No time later, no time now.

The ground shook and Devin shook with it. His blood coursed like the rapids he'd rafted on the Colorado river as a teenager. He'd had all the time in the world back then, it seemed. Before Raelyn left home. Before her life had taken a downturn, and his life had been pulled along with it.

Now he'd been carried out to sea, thrust into a world of blue water and blue sky, no land in sight. He had a decision to make and no firm ground to stand on.

Then she spoke to him.

Not Juliana. *Raelyn.*

She granted him permission to take her life, to strip her of what only two beings on this planet, as far as he knew, had had. True immortality. He'd gifted that to her with his own unwitting blood sacrifice years ago, and now he was the only one who could undo it.

Ayan's fingers tingled where she touched his neck. A gentle touch. Supportive, almost. He could think of her as a relative in that moment, someone offering support…but not without a catch. Still, he let her touch him. He couldn't be choosy, not now. "You have what you need," she told him. "This is how the end begins."

She placed one of her knives in his hand, then stepped away.

Raelyn nodded. No. Juliana nodded. Both women swarmed at the surface of Raelyn's mind, but Juliana still held control. That thought should have made him hesitate. It should have made him fearful. He could second guess all he wanted, but time was a luxury of those without the supernatural ability to save the world from evil fairies.

He raised the knife and sliced open his palm.

A collective gasp echoed through the shaking room. No one else could do what he could do. No one else understood, not even Froya. Not even Ayan.

His blood, a river; it flowed from him, held aloft by powers he had only begun to grasp. He pressed forward, palm raised.

A blood river struck Raelyn. He grabbed her jaw with the untorn hand and forced her mouth open. Despite her verbal acquiescence, he expected a fight and he got one. Two women, knowing death was near, couldn't help but struggle as his blood threatened to drown them.

"Get back," he yelled to Zareen, who still held Juliana's hands.

"No!" Juliana choked and sputtered. "Stay!"

Zareen's eyes glossed over. "It's so warm. I can't let go."

A surge of energy coursed through Devin. "Don't you fucking dare, Juliana! Don't do it!"

He increased his assault. Raelyn's body lifted into the air, and he pinned her there, hovering above the floor, but her hands still clung to Zareen.

Screams threatened to shatter him. Far off screams from Charlie, nearby screams from Raelyn, and then from Zareen as Juliana used the bridge she'd created to claw her way from a doomed body to the nearest available host. And a final scream, from Sybille, as she crawled her way through the quaking house towards him.

"No! Devin, stop her!"

Devin had his hands full, though. Elis, hampered by the tremoring ground, staggered over and attempted to pry Zareen away from Juliana's grip.

Raelyn's body seized as Juliana left it. She collapsed to the ground. The shaking diminished but it didn't end. So much was happening around him, yet only bits and pieces filtered through to him as he held his dying sister against his chest.

Blood poured from her mouth, from her eyes and ears. His blood, her blood. She looked at him and her eyes were those of a child. The immortal and the bloodthirster had already passed. She gurgled, trying to speak. He bent over to hear her.

"Charlie," she whispered.

"What? What about Charlie?"

He leaned in closer, listening. When he straightened again, her eyes turn upwards, dull like a doll's.

Pain had a stillness, a solitude. The shouting from everyone around him couldn't penetrate it, not for what seemed like an endless stretch, as though all the time he'd thought he didn't have had been thrust into this one moment.

Sybille's voice brought him back. "Fight her! Fight her, Zareen!"

He bent away from his sister's body. Sybille and Elis held Zareen, who tossed and turned with her unwanted guest.

Gentle fingers on his neck again. "Grandson," Ayan spoke. "There's still the girl. You must act now while she's weakened, or this monster's death will mean nothing."

Act now. Kill. His sister and Charlie—they were nothing but monsters to Ayan. They were his family, not hers.

Picking up her knife, he twisted, grabbed her hand and turned her around so that he held her from behind, blade at her throat. "My enhanced blood is on this knife and if it pierced your flesh, who knows what it might do to you."

Froya looked ready to pounce but she held herself back at his words. "What are you doing?"

"Give me my fucking mind back. Remove the block or I'll slice Grandma open before you can freeze me or make me forget my whole life or take me to your stupid love ranch."

Froya raised her hand. "You aren't ready."

He pressed the knife against Ayan's neck. "I was ready enough to kill my sister. Ready enough to hand you a victory against your enemy. Ready enough to do what you say. But not anymore. If you want me to deal with Charlie so you can, I don't even know what it is you're going to do here on Earth, but if you want that, then you take the block out of my head right now. Or so help me, I will slit Ayan's throat, and then I'll sit here and let Charlie vomit Ossian matter over both of you."

Froya's eyes flickered. She looked to Ayan. "What should I do?"

Ayan didn't pause to think about it. "Free him. Whatever happens then will be his own doing."

Froya stepped forward.

Devin shuffled back, keeping Ayan close. "No tricks, Froya. I've got enough of my own mind to slow down your magic. Long enough to press a knife into her neck."

"I promise you. No tricks. Touch your crystal to mine." She offered him her wrist, palm side up.

His crystal, embedded in the wrist of the hand he'd sliced open, was caked with blood, but Froya didn't flinch when she touched hers to it. He breathed in as he broke away from her. "Holy shit."

Never did he imagine he'd be able to feel the difference so immediately or so profoundly. Memories of lives he hadn't lived wove in alongside knowledge of magical powers he'd yet to embrace. He accepted them now. He accepted himself.

An Ichor fae with an Ossian niece. The Ossian, an enemy, always.

"Do you know now?" Ayan asked him. He blinked and stared at her, wondering when she'd moved out of his grasp. She wrapped her long fingers around his chin, aiming his face towards hers. "Do you understand why it must be done?"

He jerked away from her touch, looking instead to what had been his sister's body, now a pile of ash, then to Sybille as she continued to focus on her possessed cousin. As though she could feel his gaze, she lifted her tearstained face, questioning him with her maddingly beautiful eyes. If he could make her see what he saw, make her know what he knew, maybe then she'd understand.

"Yes," he answered Ayan, his eyes still on Sybille. "I know now."

Breaking eye contact with Sybille felt like being thrust into the cold void of space. He shrugged off Ayan next. "You and Froya stay here. I don't want any of you—especially Sybille—to see what's about to happen. Keep her in here. Can you do that?"

Ayan smiled. "Of course."

He'd spoken softly, so only the fae women could hear him, but Elis' keen ears had picked up on it as well. The bloodthirster stopped him in the dining room, positioning himself between Devin and his goal.

"I heard what you said. Charlie...you can't." Elis stopped to compose himself. "I promised I'd fix her. I wanted this plan to work so badly and I failed."

The loathing he normally kept bubbling under the surface for the bloodthirster dissipated. He placed a hand on his shoulder. "No one has failed. Let me through so I can say your promise has been kept. Go help Sybille with Zareen. She needs you. I'll let Peter know what happened."

He left Elis standing there. In the kitchen, Charlie continued her struggle. Her mother's death had, as Ayan said, decreased the Ossian presence in the world, and hence in Charlie. But it was far from gone. Elis had been wrong on yet another crucial point. Bones were life to the Ossian just as blood was life to the Ichor. Charlie's Ossian bones had not gone dormant. Such a thing was impossible.

"My mother." Charlie struggled as Nate clung to her. "You killed her!"

She knew. Of course Charlie could feel it, like a part of her had died too.

"Yes, I did."

Peter stopped him as he approached. "She's still dangerous, maybe even more so. She—"

"She's about to destroy us all without need of her mother's strength, and only I can prevent it? Yeah, I know. Elis thought killing Raelyn would be enough to subdue her completely. I wanted him to be right enough that I almost believed him."

"Froya removed your block?" Peter asked.

Devin stared past him. "I'm free. To leave, to fight, to kill." He could create worlds with his thoughts, infuse them with life using a drop of his blood. He could do so many wondrous things, but despite what everyone believed, he couldn't prevent Charlie from going supernova and destroying Earth. Not without ending her the way he had her mother. And even then, Charlie wasn't a bloodthirster. She wouldn't ash when she died. The risk of the Ossian taking advantage of her death fell heavily upon him.

He had few options remaining.

"You need to know that your daughter—Peter, I'm so sorry."

Peter's face reddened. "What's happened?"

"Go see if there's something you can do." He moved to brush Peter to the side, then paused. "Tell Sybille it's my choice this time. And this time... tell her not to search. She won't find me."

"Devin!" Peter grasped the mala beads he wore around his neck like they would somehow ward off the surrounding insanity. "What are you going to do?"

"I forgive you for all your fuckups and secrets. Now go to Zareen. She needs you!" He maneuvered around Peter, who rushed in the opposite direction, towards his daughter.

Devin eyed the remaining people in the Kitchen. "Get back, Laurence! Margot, you too."

For once, people seemed to be taking him seriously. Margot leapt away, pressing herself against the refrigerator like she was guarding her condiments and left-over chicken salad from a hungry burglar. Laurence, coiled up on the floor whimpering, used a clump of ill-formed bone where his hand should be to press himself away from Charlie's feet. He attempted to say something but collapsed instead.

That left Nate, who stood upright with Charlie in his arms, his face firm and resolved and coated with bits of bone. Soon enough, even this tree of a man would fail to contain her. "Nate, release her. It's okay"

Nate wavered. "Sybille told me not to let go. This is my big moment."

"It is. But you've done your part. Charlie would already have turned us all to ash and bone if she didn't have an immortal giant keeping her together. But Nate, man, you're half coated in bone already. It's time I take her the rest of the way. Sybille will understand."

Nate hesitated before letting one of Charlie's arms swing free. She used it to propel herself towards her uncle, but Nate still held on to her other arm. He grimaced as he fought against Charlie's inhuman strength.

"Let her go, Nate. Charlie, if you're mad at me about your mom, I understand. Now's the time to make me feel all the pain you feel."

Another moment of hesitation passed before Nate released her. Charlie cried out as she ran at him, throwing herself into his awaiting arms. "I hate you. I hate everything!" She beat his chest and he took it. He deserved it. He'd killed her mother twice, and now he'd been turned into an instrument of war meant to eradicate her. But this world, the world he'd been born into, the world he loved, the world that had created people like Sybille—it didn't deserve what Charlie was about to do to it.

"I can't control the Low anymore! I need to die! Juliana told me it might be the only way and she was right!" She continued to hit him, her face a marble crisscrossed with inky veins.

"No, you don't. You can't, Charlie. You can't die."

Sparks flew from her fists, landing on Devin's shoulders like ash from an exploding volcano. He winced as each one planted itself onto his skin, tiny calluses that dug into him, setting down roots.

This was how it began then. How fitting if he became one of the first to fall. He could almost give in to the temptation to let her do what she was about to. Let the Ossian win. He wouldn't care—he'd be dead. Death wasn't the worst thing he could think of. But if he died, so too would everyone else. Margot, Laurence…Sybille.

He couldn't give in, couldn't let this world end, not like this. If he died, that's what would happen…at least, that's what would happen if he died here.

Death could serve no purpose, or it could serve a higher one.

More sparks. His body would be made into bone soon.

His grandmother's words floated into his head as masses of bone grew up from the floor. "Our greatest sacrifices are decided by the blood flowing through our world, our bodies, our hearts. You will do what's right. That is the only path for blood fae."

The time for choices was behind him. There was only one path, and he already walked upon it. He treaded it with weary footsteps, though, Charlie's Ossian nature working in opposition to his own.

He didn't know how he would do what he needed to do, only that he had to find a way. A keening bark cut through his despair. Thunderheart emerged from where he'd been hiding under the kitchen table.

Even Charlie paused as the dog approached. He got up on his hind legs as though he was trying to protect her. His Ichor crystal glowed, and he whined at Devin.

"I'll be damned. You want to help." He recalled Froya's lecture on their crystals, how they made world jumping easier, especially when several crystal wearers were in proximity and all headed to the same destination. "You sure about coming with?"

Thunderheart barked.

"You really are a good boy."

Devin shifted Charlie to his hip so he could support her with one hand. He lifted the other and touched his crystal, coated with the blood from the open wound on his palm, to Thunderheart's. Power surged through him.

Giving Nate a final nod, he thought of Sybille—Sybille surviving and her world surviving with her.

He could live with that. He could die with that.

Letting space and time fold in, Devin twisted his fingers, removing his loyal familiar and his brave little spy from this beautiful, messy world forever.

CHAPTER THIRTY-ONE

ELIS

ELIS GASPED LIKE A TEENAGE GIRL WHO'D SEEN THE REFLECTION OF A GHOST IN her bathroom mirror. He'd been standing in the dining room staring at the door to the kitchen, the one Devin had gone through. It opened and Peter rushed out and past him, but he hadn't moved, had stood there, stunned and silent and then...nothing. He'd collapsed, or so he'd gathered after the fact, after he'd awoken. He crawled backwards then, through the living room and away from Zareen's possessed body, which was now being attended to by Sybille and Peter. Pressing himself against the wall by the stairs, he tried to calm himself. His heart raced. Raced like it hadn't in centuries. Not even when he'd been aroused by Sybille or terrified by the horrors they faced had it pounded like this. His breath shallow, he tucked his knees up to his chin and covered his face with his palms.

This couldn't be happening.

Sybille scrambled over to him. "What's going on, Elis? I need you to stay the fuck present right now, okay? Juliana has a firm hold over Zareen. I don't know how to make her leave. And I have no idea how Devin is going to manage Charlie, and—"

She cut herself off, paused, then spoke again. "The ground stopped moving."

He'd noticed that too, but when exactly it had stopped, he couldn't recall. "Whatever Devin did, it worked." He peeked out from between his hands. The house was still, but everything felt off-kilter.

Sybille touched his forehead. Her face filled with concern. "You're warm. Can bloodthirsters get fevers?"

"My heart."

She brought her hand down and pressed her palm against his chest. "My God."

He closed his eyes, hoping that if he focused on the sounds of commotion minus the visual stimulation, he might return to normal. A few moments later, he realized Sybille had been speaking with someone else, and he hadn't been paying attention at all.

"What do you mean gone?" Her words came out strained, like it hurt to say them.

He opened his eyes. "Who's gone?"

Sybille slumped against him, shaking her head. Margot knelt in front of him. "Devin took Charlie. She'd begun to…to transform. He removed her from Earth to save us. But where did they go?"

Now not only did his heart pound faster, it threatened to break. "I still have two chapters of the Wizard of Oz left to read to her."

Sybille began to sob. He closed his eyes again and kept them closed until someone nudged him on the shoulder. Not Margot, who seemed to be helping her brother carry a heavily tranquilized Zareen/Juliana combo out of the front door.

Purple eyes glared at him. "Ayan believes the Ossian threat has passed. You're our test—you and the Blood Prince."

"Blood King."

Froya smirked. "You set a low bar for kings on this world. How do you feel?"

"I feel fine." He looked down at Sybille, whose head still rested against his shoulder.

"He's lost his bloodthirster abilities," she said to Froya. "But you already guessed that, didn't you?"

"Well, I hadn't!" Incredulous, Elis sat upright, his body trembling.

Froya tilted her head from side to side. "The only reason he isn't a pile of ash is because he has his soul. Ayan is in the kitchen with your king. I expect his case is similar."

Sybille sat up as well. "What about the rest of the bloodthirsters? What about the Low?"

"The old humans have already agreed to go there to investigate." Froya said. "We are hopeful that the Low will have been neutered and the Ossian soldiers will have all fallen."

"All...fallen." Elis' heart raced again.

"Meanwhile," Froya continued, "Devin has failed to return to Ichor's home world."

"How can he?" Sybille asked. "He has Charlie with him."

"He can create a world for her and then leave her in it."

"Leave her to die, you mean."

"Yes. But he would live and only his terrible little universe would suffer."

"He'll never abandon Charlie."

"Then he's probably dead already." Froya frowned and looked away from them. "Whatever the case, if he doesn't show up at home soon, he'll have broken our agreement. He knows the consequence."

"What consequence might you be referring to?" Sybille rubbed at a lump of bone jutting out of her wrist.

Elis barely took in their words, the beating of his heart reverberating like someone was banging on a drum inside of his ear. "Are you telling me..." He shouted to hear himself over his mind's wild imaginings. The women stopped their conversation.

"What you're saying is, bloodthirsters are all dead, and I'm...I'm human again?"

Sybille

She sat at the tiny desk wedged into her kitchen's corner staring at the wreckage. Every now and then, she took a sip of chamomile tea. The stove, thankfully, still worked, but nearly everything else in the room was trashed. In its center, just feet away from where her mother usually stood minding a kettle of simmering tincture, the fractured floor sprang up with jagged edges of calcified wood, like coral growing over the boards of a wrecked ship. Pots and pans and dishware lay scattered across the room. Pieces of the ceiling dangled overhead, threatening to come undone and clunk someone on the head. The damage was substantial, but it was also limited. Margot had checked on neighbors before leaving with Laurence and Peter to bring Zareen's compromised body to the Low. Not one of them had felt more than a slight rustling.

Sybille placed both hands around her warm mug. The pressure behind her eyes made her vision swim, but she could cry no more. She might be in shock. This seemed a reasonable state to exist in for the time being, or possibly forever. Charlie and Devin were gone, probably turned to bone in whatever strange fae world they'd landed in. The fae women had left without telling anyone what the Ichor planned to do now that their competition on Earth had fallen back. She knew what they'd wanted —to install Devin as a puppet ruler, controlling the world through him. With him gone, it was too much to hope that they'd simply leave Earth be.

If they did return, she hadn't much of a resistance to mount. Zareen was possessed, and Elis... Elis was upstairs passed out in her bed snoring like the human male he now was. Unable to sleep, she sat here instead, tallying the cost of her house's damage, wondering if Bore would still pay her family now that there were no more bloodthirsters to kill.

As she finished her tea, an idea ignited. The bloodthirsters might be gone—she wouldn't totally believe this until Peter reported back to her from the Low—but what of their spirits? Perhaps they were still trapped, unaware of what had happened to their monstrous bodies.

Maybe she still had spirits to seek.

After a few minutes spent following her breath and relaxing her mind as best she could, Sybille opened the channel, dipping herself into the ether for a peek.

Her empty mug went crashing to the kitchen floor to join the rest of the clutter as she flung her arms around, trying, instinctually but without logic, to stop in the physical world what was happening in the ether.

They'd been waiting for her.

"Stop!" She shouted to them. How many? Impossible to say. One after another approached her, pleading, begging.

"Sybille?"

Half in the ether, half in the Now World, Sybille struggled to recognize the voice of the speaker.

"Nate?"

He shook her shoulders. Bone like barnacles obscured several of his tattoos. His neck was made thicker than ever with its calcified additions. "Close the door, Sybille. Close it now!"

"I...I don't think I can!"

She grabbed for the grounding stone her mother kept on the desk and clutched it to her, trying to will the room back into focus. Nate stood next to her, his eyes darting around the room as spirit after spirit materialized, brought out of the ether despite Sybille's will to stem the tide.

"They're desperate, Nate. Groundless." Dangerous too. Their bloodthirsters were dead yet still they existed in this state of limbo. Why?

"Who are they all? Some of them don't look very nice." Nate sank into one of the few unbroken chairs left in the room. "How many bloodthirster spirits are we going to have to deal with? It seems like a bunch of them."

"A bunch?" She took a deep breath as the spirits continued to stream through her consciousness and out into the room. Tasting iron, she touched her upper lip. Her fingers came away coated in blood. "They're all coming, Nate. Every single one of them."

THE END

Thank you for reading! Did you enjoy?

Please Add Your Review! And don't miss more paranormal novels like, FORGOTTEN MAGIC. Turn the page for a sneak peek!

SNEAK PEEK OF FORGOTTEN MAGIC

Magic is elemental. It's a full-bodied thread in all that we are. To me, to all my folk—witches and wizards of every make and the other supernatural creatures that co-exist in our ley line-loving world—magic simply *is*.

It was magic that lived deep inside me, hidden beneath the wretch of who I'd been, of what I'd done ten years ago at age eighteen. My father would call me a hypocrite— if we were still talking. He'd tell me that keeping myself from the covens in New York and from my family back in Crimson Cove, keeping myself from the life he taught me to be proud of, was a coward's way.

I was a witch only when it served my purposes.

Like now, slipping inside the dreams of such a talented writer. My client, Ivanna Ride (pseudonym, of course), was the hottest thing in erotic romance. She outsold and out published even the most popular authors and she did it on her own. There was no major house working behind her. Just Ivanna, her clever English-nerd husband, and me, Janiver Benoit, graphic artist extraordinaire. Well, that might be pushing it. It was magic that made me extraordinary and it was my gifts that helped me slip inside Ivanna's mind and discover the theme, the vibe, the truly disturbing imagery she saw when she dreamt of her characters.

This time around it was Kjel, the 1050 A.D. Viking warrior in love with an enemy clan leader's daughter. Blood and war and lots of sex. That's what I had to make come to life on the cover of her book.

Walking inside Ivanna's mind was like taking a stroll through a Renaissance Fair—on acid. The mist around me as I stepped into her dream was thick, a clotting smell that stuck in the back of my throat and choked me with the heavy scent of lavender. It hung in my sinuses, made my dry mouth collect with saliva. But on the back of that scent was something I recognized only vaguely as sweat. In Ivanna's dreams, there was sex. It became apparent that's what she had in mind, literally, when her REM cycle kicked into high gear.

Kjel—or who I took for Kjel—stood barefoot atop a bear skin rug in a rugged stone hut, glaring down at some whimpering, silly girl who looked more turned on than frightened. She was the enemy's daughter knocking on the door of womanhood, looking at Kjel like she wanted him to guide her way through it.

With a shudder of sound and the shift of light, the scene changed and the small room with its dirt floor became a boudoir with fine, cerise linens and a massive four-poster bed. The girl's face transformed to mimic something like Ivanna's. At least, how she'd looked this afternoon when I listened to her babble on and on about the pending Kjel series and her vision for the rest of her books, her promo graphics, and the blog tours she wanted to organize.

I'd listened to her politely, nodding where appropriate as this mid-forties woman tucked strands of curly brown hair behind her ear. Damn. Was it petty of me to notice that there was gray flirting in those strands near her temples? She guzzled on an iced coffee as she talked, never once asking for my opinion or curious about what ideas might have come to me when I'd read the manuscript. That didn't bother me, though, not really. My clients typically didn't want to know what I thought. They just wanted to make sure I made magic happen on their covers and their promo materials.

Funny how close that was to the truth.

I'd listened to Ivanna for nearly an hour, sipping my own Venti English Breakfast Tea, more interested in the chipping black paint on my fingernails and the wadded napkin Ivanna had used to wipe her mouth. That would be the souvenir I'd take to give me access to her dreams.

Magic, no matter what fantasy authors or Renaissance vendors tell you, is just an old school name for the things mortals want proof of to believe. Everything we do has to be logical, must have an explanation.

It is true that there has to be basis for every spell or hex. There has to be something elemental that connects our target or, in my case, client, to the magic we twist. It isn't simply supernatural. It's dependent on the natural. Magic elevates it. That's why I needed Ivanna's napkin. It was something she'd held, something that she'd left a bit of herself behind on, and it was the element I needed to slip into her dreams.

But I didn't like doing it—dreamwalking. Not like this. It was an invasion that made me feel cheap and simple. Intruding into someone else's private dreams? Seeing the things they'd never freely admit to desiring? I was like some kind of perv trying to make my clients happy by copying their own imaginations.

Still, it paid the bills. So I stalked in the shadows in my client's dreamworld. Kjel and dream Ivanna were starting to go at it. Bleaching my eyeballs was the first order of business when I woke up, which needed to happen right now. I had work to do.

I started that slow awakening, the controlled transition that would bring me out of Ivanna's mind and back to the "real" world. It was a simple enough process—a little focus on my breathing, on the things around me. I drew upon a picture in my mind's eye of my tiny apartment, of myself lying in only a black tank and red boy shorts, my dark hair covering my face, tattoos and runes dotting around my ankles, thighs, up the side of one bicep. The black ink was shaped in ancient languages, looping around my arm, connected to a black and gray rose on my left shoulder.

Things were calm, my mind working effortlessly to bring me back safely, away from Ivanna's Viking wet dream and her saccharine world. I was nearly there, watching myself sleep, turn beneath my white sheets, knocking over an empty tumbler on my bedside table—not the bourbon, thank God—and then, the alert of a video chat on my laptop blasted across the room.

Jani! Jani! The alarming scream of my brother's voice shot through the slow retreat my mind made. Sam's voice became a grating, loud yelp that made my chest constrict as my heart sped.

Jani! Jani, for the gods' sake, wake up!

And I did, jerking from my sheets, sending my pillows shooting onto the floor and the thick gasp of air in my lungs coming out like a yelp.

"Shit!"

The bell alert from my laptop lying on the floor next to my bed kept ringing, that low, constant loop that announced an incoming video call. Sam hadn't actually spoken to me, but still had a way of scaring the hell out me, nineteen hundred miles away. My brother could call to me, unannounced, whenever he wanted, but especially when I was unconscious. The annoying sibling connection was a nuisance I'd never be rid of.

"Stupid, intrusive…" My laptop flopped against the mattress when I picked it up and jammed my finger on the surface to accept the call. I didn't bother letting my big brother explain a damn thing. "You asshole, I was in someone's dream."

"Well hey to you too, little sister."

A quick glance at my cell phone to cut off the insistent text I knew Sam had sent me and I caught the time. Shit, someone was probably dead.

"Who died?" My brother's small chuckle was the only thing that made me relax enough to leave the bed and tug on my jeans.

"No one yet, though I'm pretty close to killing your brother-in-law." My brother always blamed me when shit hit the fan, and from his tone, I'd guessed that this time the shit had slammed into the proverbial fan in buckets.

Still, that wasn't my fault. "Ronan is your brother-in-law too, Samedi."

"Yeah." The frustration was heavy in his voice at my using his full name. "Well Mai is your twin, *Janiver*, and since it's her husband that started all this shit, it should be you that gets us out of it."

Mai was younger than me by only four minutes, but somehow we were years apart. I always picked up the pieces when she let her world fall apart —like it was now, with her in the middle of a bad breakup with her lazy, perpetually cheating husband. Still, it wasn't my fight.

"You've got the wrong twin."

I cut Sam off from whatever excuse I knew he was going to use when he cleared his throat by shaking my head and reaching out to grab the bottle of bourbon that had been sitting on the table beside my bed. I took a deep pull on the bottle, despite the glare my brother gave me. "Ask Mai to work out this mess."

"She can't. She's gone off the rails."

That meant trouble. It was habit, something my twin did when she couldn't handle the messes she'd made for herself.

"What…" A small exhale and I readied for the bad news I suspected was coming. "What do you mean?"

"She's back at Papa's and won't come out of her room."

"Circe help us."

The bourbon didn't burn when it went down, despite the long swig I took. My throat had grown numb to the sting of liquor a long damn time ago, and the small little noise of judgment Sam made got completely ignored. When you numb yourself in order to forget, something that had become one of my more practiced habits, you tend to get used to both the bite and the judgment, no matter where they come from.

Mai's hiding away—my twin's way of forgetting—wasn't the worst of the situation. Not by a long damn shot.

"She caught him with that same stripper from last year."

"The one with the pixie cut?"

"Yeah, whatever, but this time he didn't bother begging Mai not to kick him out." Sam leaned on his arm, rubbing the back of his neck. His complexion was darker than mine or Mai's, taking on more of our mother's Haitian creole features than our blue-eyed father's French, but like both me and Mai, Sam had full lips and hazel eyes. We were all a good mix of both our parents. "Papa thought giving Ronan a job would maybe keep that asshole from running off for weeks at a time." Sam looked tired, like he hadn't bothered with sleep in days. My stomach tightened at the thought, and I couldn't quite ignore the weight in my chest that settled there. My brother had enough to deal with. He didn't need Mai's jackass of a husband doubling up his anxiety.

"Bet that was pointless."

"You got no idea." Sam released one long exhale and scrubbed a hand against his fade at the back of his head. He'd abandoned the short afro he'd grown out the last time I saw him and looked more like himself. "He totally fucked us over."

"What do you mean? What happened?"

"If Papa hadn't let Ronan take care of so many clients when they came calling, none of this would have happened. He just botched up too many jobs, was too sloppy, and I was too busy to notice that his haplessness had become a serious problem."

The whole time he had been talking to me, Sam had kept looking at his cell phone. It wasn't like him to let a text distract him. The string of beeps coming from his phone was odd, but the expression on his face was almost funny. *Almost.*

"The whole damn town is talking about it. Papa says if we can't pull in a big client, our name will be ruined." Another heavy sigh and Sam threw down his cell. "Not to mention all the damn attention we've been getting from the mortals."

Watching Sam, seeing the tension bunching up his features, I suddenly realized that this conversation was the longest we'd had in a year. In the past, we simply fought all the time. Even after our mother died five years ago, we hadn't managed a civil conversation. But then last summer, his wife, Adele, and their unborn child died in a car crash. The kid that killed them had been confused, barely legal, and since their deaths Sam and my conversations had simply become short and to the point. But this was different.

"Has Ivy or his men been snooping around?" I'd held my breath after asking that question. Ivy Beckerman was Crimson Cove's chief of police. We all suspected he wouldn't blink twice if he caught any weres shifting into their animal forms or spirits haunting the edge of the cemetery, never mind any chance encounters with a wizard doing something beyond human comprehension. There was something about the man that made him different from the other mortals. They only saw what they wanted. But Ivy was smart, observant; he saw things that the others didn't. So far, though, he'd kept his questions to himself.

"No, not so much," Sam said, once again focusing on his phone when it beeped, offering only a glance my way when he spoke, "but he did come by asking who busted in the store window." Sam waited for that to make an impact.

"What the hell happened to the store window?"

"Some asshole pissed off that we hadn't done our best to hide whatever bullshit they didn't want the mortals to see, we think. Thanks to Ronan, we got a sledgehammer through the front window."

That was unnerving. My father had managed to keep up the façade of running a respectable antiques store for decades. It was a decent way to front his real business—making sure the mortals never caught wind that a good majority of the Cove's residents weren't mortal at all; Papa was what the supernatural community called a "fixer."

"How bad is it really, Sam?" That question came in front of a small, silent prayer that I could help my family from the comfort of my fifth-floor walkup in Brooklyn.

I should have known better.

Another of Sam's exhales came out slow, this one with a labored drag of frustration, maybe the small hint of defeat. "Carter Grant has pulled his coven's contract with us. He doesn't want to be involved in any accidents we can't quite cover up."

"Shit." That revelation warranted another swig and another disapproving shake of my brother's head. If the Grants, a founding family and one of the oldest covens—and the one family our ancestors had pledged fealty to generations before—cut ties with us, then things were about as bad as they could get.

"We've asked a couple of the other Finders to help out, Jani, but none are as good as you. Papa says you're our last resort."

Whatever I was ten years ago—Finder of Lost Things, twin of a mighty healer, daughter to a man who swept our lives away from mortal eyes—I'd packed up in a steamer trunk my father swindled from a Tulsa antiques dealer and hopped a bus to New York. I'd been eighteen and thought Crimson Cove had seen the back of me. I hated being wrong.

It probably was tearing Papa up to know Sam was going to ask me to come home. He'd always maintained that once you left, that was it. No need to drag up the past with a trip down memory lane. Besides, he'd always told me "nothing but heartache for you here, Janiver." But after the bomb my brother dropped, I had little choice.

"I'll take the red eye."

"About that, Jani..." Another alert. This time Sam read the message then immediately snapped his gaze back up to the screen. "You don't need to worry about getting a ticket." My brother swallowed, shifting his attention away from the camera like he'd rather do anything than explain himself.

Damn it. This definitely required more bourbon.

"Thing is, someone is coming for you."

"Who?"

"In a few minutes, actually."

"Samedi, who?"

"Should be there. Now."

"Son of a bitch."

Please don't let it be him, I prayed.

I wanted to handle this issue my family had and be done with it. I had no intention of *reconnecting*.

Please, please, don't let it be him.

"He was already in the city."

"What are you talking about, Sam?"

"Look, Jani, something happened, with the Elam."

The Elam? The talisman through which all the magic in Crimson Cove converged, which kept us hidden from mortal eyes and in check?

"Someone attacked and took it..." Someone had *stolen* it?

"You don't lead with *that?* My God, Sam..."

"I know...it's just... Look...we really, well, we tried finding anyone else to help find it, but shit, sis, you're the best and there is so little time and he was there in New York and..."

"Balls..." I said, already knowing what point my brother was skirting around.

This was bad. Very bad. No wonder my family was on the edge of panic. I emptied the bottle but kept it between my legs as Sam tried and failed to explain himself.

"I just hope you don't—"

Three loud drums of a knock on my door had me almost jumping out of my skin. The temperature in the room suddenly shifted, and on the other side of the door I picked up two signatures: elemental magic that identifies a witch or wizard like a thumbprint. Unbidden, my pulse started racing, and I found it hard to breathe.

"Jani..." Sam's warning was too little and way too late. Nothing would save him from the shit storm I'd level at him as soon as I landed back home.

"Not another damn word, big brother."

One of the bodies out in the hallway radiated heat and a familiar spicy, rich smell that made my mouth water.

"Jani...let me explain."

Sam's voice was rushed, muddled as I left the bed and stood in front of my door, my hand hovering over the handle. I didn't need to look through the peep hole to know who stood out in the hallway.

"Whoever stole the Elam used old magic. They needed an old bloodline to make the hex work." I squinted, looking over my shoulder toward the laptop as I twisted the handle, then didn't blink or breathe at all as my gaze lifted to see Bane Iles. He stood on the other side of the open door.

"Yeah," he said, as if he had been listening to our conversation. Just as shocking as his appearance at my door was the fact that his face was bruised, and there was a cut along his bottom lip —injuries that shouldn't be there at all. "And that blood was mine."

Don't stop now. Keep reading with your copy of FORGOTTEN MAGIC available now.

And visit www.amberkbryant.com to keep up with the latest news where you can subscribe to the newsletter for contests, giveaways, new releases, and more.

Don't miss more of the Spirit Seeker series coming soon and find more from Amber K. Bryant at www.amberkbryant.com

Until then, try FORGOTTEN MAGIC by City Owl Author, Eden Butler.

Bane Illes never smiled. He never spoke.

But each day, that brooding wizard gave Janiver Benoit a glance. And when she could not take another quiet stare, or the warmth that look sent over her skin, she took from Bane something he'd never give freely—a lingering, soul knocking kiss.

Ten years later, someone has stolen the one thing that keeps magic hidden from the mortals in Crimson Cove and only Janiver can recover it. But returning to her hometown means she'll have to face the past and all the secrets she left buried there, including the one person she promised herself she'd never see again.

The dangerous wizard that might make leaving Crimson Cove the last thing she wants to do.

Please sign up for the City Owl Press newsletter for chances to win special subscriber-only contests and giveaways as well as receiving information on upcoming releases and special excerpts.

All reviews are **welcome** and **appreciated**. Please consider leaving one on your favorite social media and book buying sites.

For books in the world of romance and speculative fiction that embody Innovation, Creativity, and Affordability, check out City Owl Press at www.cityowlpress.com.

ACKNOWLEDGMENTS

A huge thank you to my editor, Tee Tate, for once again loving my story and helping me make it sparkle. I'm deeply grateful to Tina Moss, Yelena Casale, Marianne Hull, and everyone at City Owl Press. This has been a weird year, but City Owl has never stopped reaching out to their authors to check in on them. They continue to take the press in exciting directions.

I am thrilled and surprised every time I discover that someone in my family reads what I write. Thank you all for making me feel like this crazy writing dream maybe isn't so crazy after all. Thank you to the two people I see all day every day: Drew and Silas. You told me you're proud of me and did so even after months of quarantining together. Silas, thank you for putting up with my tiger mom homeschooling tendencies. Drew, thank you for teaching him math so I didn't have to.

To my writing friends, there are not enough gifs in existence to express how much your continued friendship means. To the Wattpad Stars and Paid Stories crew, thank you for the opportunities and guidance. To my readers, especially my Spirit Seeker Launch Team: you are the reason Sybille's story continues. Margot is baking up some delicious apple tartlets just for you!

And finally, to everyone in hospitals and on the streets working and marching with the courage of a thousand Sybilles, thank you for reminding me that this world is still worth fighting for.

ABOUT THE AUTHOR

Amber K. Bryant is an award-winning speculative fiction and romance writer living deep within Sasquatch territory in Washington State. Her stories have gained millions of reads on Wattpad, where she has built a world-wide fanbase. She collaborated on a short story with R. L. Stine and won several contests judged by Margaret Atwood. When she isn't writing, she works as a librarian and spends time with her husband and son enjoying the beauty of the Pacific Northwest. She has yet to spot Bigfoot but has faith it will happen one day. Spirit Seeker: Blood Fae, is her second book with City Owl Press.

| Photography by Drew Kunz

www.amberkbryant.com

facebook.com/amberkbryantauthor
twitter.com/amberkbryant
instagram.com/bryantamberk

ABOUT THE PUBLISHER

City Owl Press is a cutting edge indie publishing company, bringing the world of romance and speculative fiction to discerning readers.

www.cityowlpress.com

www.ingramcontent.com/pod-product-compliance
Lightning Source LLC
Chambersburg PA
CBHW020828260626
47169CB00003B/876